LOVE, HATE & CLICKBAIT

"Quick-paced, sharp, and thoroughly entertaining.
I couldn't put it down!"
—Helen Hoang, *New York Times* bestselling author

"One of my favorite reads this year. *Love, Hate & Clickbait* is
a steamy and satisfying romp on politics, public life, and our
private hearts."
—Jean Meltzer, author of *The Matzah Ball*

"Bowery keeps the romance light and engaging…
With political intrigue, social media virality, fake dating,
and an enemies-to-lovers romance…it's a charming, breezy
rom-com."
—*Publishers Weekly*

"Bowery's debut is a great read with a wild ride through
hate, lust, and love in the world of political social media
influencing. Highly recommended."
—*Library Journal*

"Offers all of the electric, budding sexual tension that comes
with fake dating."
—*Kirkus Reviews*

LOVE, HATE & CLICKBAIT

LIZ BOWERY

mira

mira™

Recycling programs
for this product may
not exist in your area.

ISBN-13: 978-0-7783-1189-8

Love, Hate & Clickbait

For questions and comments about the quality of this book, please contact us at
CustomerService@Harlequin.com.

Mira
22 Adelaide St. West, 41st Floor
Toronto, Ontario M5H 4E3, Canada
BookClubbish.com

Printed in U.S.A.

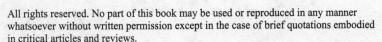

To Chris
My soul mate, best friend, and favorite person
n+1

LOVE, HATE & CLICKBAIT

★ 1 ★

When he cared enough to try, Thom Morgan was great with people. For one thing, he was very handsome, which led most people to believe that he was charming. He also had bullet-proof bullshitting skills, thanks to a lifetime in politics. And it was especially easy to win people over when they were caught up in emotional crap—like at a wedding.

So it wasn't a surprise that he was a hit at his girlfriend's sister's wedding. Her family was eager to meet the boyfriend that Ashley had told them all about, and not just because of his looks or his charm. Everyone loved politics these days, and every Californian had an opinion of his boss, their governor, Leonora Westwood. Luckily, whenever someone tried to ask him something boring about the true business of governing—*What's she doing about forest management? Don't you think taxes are too high? There's a pothole outside my house*—he could remind them what he really did for a living.

"Actually, I'm the governor's top political consultant," he said, injecting just the right amount of apology into his tone to make the boast go down seamlessly. "So I have less to do with the day-to-day and more—"

"Ahh, I got it, your eye's on the White House," said— Thad? Chad? Something bro-y, Thom hadn't been listening. They were with the rest of the wedding party in a wallpa- pered bedroom, waiting for the ceremony to begin.

"Oh, no, of course not," Thom said. "Right now we're just focused on keeping forty million Californians happy."

"Right *now,*" Chad said predictably. "But when the pri- maries roll around?"

Thom feigned a gaping mouth, as if he didn't pretend to be caught off guard by this question dozens of times a day. "I mean, by then, who can really say..."

"Sure," Brad said, looking fucking ecstatic to be in on the world's biggest open secret: that Leonora Westwood would be running for president next year, which was exactly why she'd hired Thom.

Thom winked at him and took a swig of his beer. Then he glanced at Ashley across the room and sent her a silent plea for help with his eyes. She muffled a laugh behind her hand before quickly crossing the room to them, saying to Thad, "Excuse me—I have to steal him away for a second."

Out in the elegant hallway of Ashley's parents' home, Thom slumped against the wall in relief. "Thank god," he said, phone already in hand. "Any more small talk with the yokels and I would've melted down."

"Uh, hey," Ashley said, batting his hand away before he could look at his phone. "Don't I deserve more thanks than that?"

"You're right," he said, grinning and reeling her in with his arms around her waist. "Thank you, thank you..."

He trailed off as he kissed her. After a moment, she made an unhappy noise against his lips. "What?" he asked, pulling back. "Don't like my technique?"

"I can feel your phone in the small of my back," she said.

He grinned wider. "Is it a turn-on?"

"Definitely not." She pulled away. With a sigh and a glance down the hall, she said, "I should go make sure my sister's ready. It's almost time."

"Fine," he said. "Leave me here alone."

"Don't stay on that thing the whole time," Ashley said as she backed down the hall. "Go mingle! Network. Do your thing."

"Trust me," he told her, "the only person here I care about is you."

A small, happy smile flashed across her face. Then she ducked away, down the hall.

That left Thom alone with his phone, so that he could finally—*finally*—check on news from the office. Governor Westwood—or Lennie, as her staff called her—had just wrapped up an incredibly successful trip to Singapore, and he was eager to see how it was playing in the news. International trips weren't exactly standard fare for governors, but given the size of California's economy, it made sense for Governor Westwood to travel overseas to develop the state's trade relationships. Of course, the real reason for the visit would come across plain as day but go tastefully unspoken: an international trip made Lennie look like a head of state.

Like, say, a future president.

Thom grinned as he scrolled through all the good headlines the trip was generating so far. Lennie's plane should have just touched down in Van Nuys, so she'd be back in the office soon. Itching with impatience, he slid his phone back into his pocket and strolled over to a window at the end of the hallway. He was in no mood to rejoin the other groomsmen, so he took his time scanning the crowd that was milling around in the garden among the spindly white chairs that had been set up for the ceremony. Ashley's family was vast, well-off, and very well-connected, and he'd met many of them at other pre-wedding events. Unfortunately, it seemed that some of her most notable relatives had decided not to attend. Shame.

His phone pinged in his pocket. When he checked it, he jolted in excitement: it was an email from a *Politico* reporter he'd been chasing for months. Finally, the guy had gotten back to him—he wanted to stop by the office to chat about a possible article on the Singapore trip, and he wanted to do it now.

National coverage. Thom's mouth watered, and he made a quick but easy decision.

Sliding his phone into his suit pocket, he strolled back down the hallway to the room Ashley had disappeared into. He knocked gently, and when he poked his head in, he was greeted by a cloud of perfume and tulle. "Hi, ladies," he said with a grin. "Ashley, can I grab you for a sec?"

She rolled her eyes, clearly thinking he wanted to get her into a dark corner to make out some more. "Give me a second, girls," she said, and followed him out into the hall.

Outside, she ran her hands up the sides of his suit jacket, looking put-upon but also warmed by the attention. "What now?" she asked. "More small talk you want to avoid?"

"Mmm," he said, and kissed her before pulling back. "No, sadly. Um, I hate to do this—"

She frowned. "What is it?"

"Nine-one-one at the office," he said, grimacing as if this was paining him. "I have to go."

"Go? What do you mean, go?" She blinked, confused. "Thom, you're *in the wedding.*"

"I know."

"You—you *asked* me to be in the wedding," she said in dawning outrage. "You bothered me about it constantly until I forced my sister to make you a groomsman."

He winced, saying, "I know, but—"

"No, are you kidding me?" she demanded. "You're really going to leave?"

"They need me over there!" *To fluff a reporter.* "It's an emergency."

"No," Ashley said firmly, shaking her head. "You work all the time. I'm sure they can spare you long enough not to ruin my sister's wedding."

"I'm so sorry, babe," he said, pouting. "I'll make it up to you."

"No!" Ashley shouted quietly, seemingly struggling between her anger and her desire not to cause a scene. "I'm serious, Thom. *No.*"

He said nothing. As she realized that he was really about to leave, she stared daggers at him and whispered, "If you leave this wedding, we're over."

Thom pressed his lips together, making a point of looking pained and indecisive. When he felt like it had been long enough, he sighed and said, "Okay."

Ashley was stunned. "You're…you're breaking up with me?"

"I don't want to," he said. He kind of did want to. The relationship had really reached the limits of its utility for him. "But, babe, I told you—"

"You have to go to work," Ashley said bitterly. "You always cared about your job more than me."

True, but he'd been willing to put in his time anyway—after all, her uncle was a Supreme Court justice, which made her family nothing short of DC royalty. But being a groomsman had paid off a lot less than he'd hoped in that regard, and her uncle hadn't even bothered to fly out for the wedding, which probably meant he was going to die soon anyway. So much for that connection.

Thom took Ashley's hand in his. "I'm sorry," he said, his voice low and passionate.

Ashley glared at him, tears hovering in her eyes. Thom was used to that look—he saw it a lot when his relationships ended, if he even bothered doing it face-to-face. He just couldn't understand why the women he dated got so invested in him. Most of them were in politics too, or in similar fields where winning and advancing were all that mattered. Why did they let emotions get in the way of that?

Ashley yanked her hand out of his and walked away. Thom blew out a relieved breath and jogged outside to meet his Uber.

Once he was on the way, he scanned the headlines on his phone again. Right now they were in the midst of one of the most delicate stages of campaigning: the pre-primary. The first presidential primary contests were so far-off that it was too early, and would be viewed as unseemly, to be openly campaigning. Instead, Lennie had to achieve a favorable position for the upcoming primary without seeming like she was doing anything at all. It was like trying to win a race she couldn't afford to be seen running in.

And she had her work cut out for her, because the current front-runner in both the pre- and actual primary was not Lennie but Senator Samuel Warhey. A veteran and former elementary school teacher, he'd become famous for having saved dozens of students during a dangerous flood in the eighties. That star-making moment had propelled him to the governor's mansion and then the Senate, and he maintained the glow of nonpolitical celebrity. He was on the older side, but young enough for it to come across as gravitas. He was moderate in his voting record but passionate on the stump. He was experienced, he was popular, he was good on TV, and his staff had not returned any of Thom's calls.

So, he'd ended up taking a job with Lennie. And that was to his liking, anyway: he could stay in the city that he loved. Technically, the office of the Governor of California was in Sacramento, but Lennie was smart enough to know that she wouldn't recruit any top-flight talent if she forced them to relocate to that shithole. Interns and volunteers were thick on the ground in Los Angeles, and so were many of the top political reporters on the West Coast, who were much easier to entice to cover Lennie's campaign when it was in their backyard.

Thom had grown up in the sleepy inland California suburbs, but he'd moved to LA as soon as he'd had a chance. As his ride traveled from the secluded, leafy neighborhood where the wedding had been to the dense heart of the city where Lennie's office was located, glittering high-rises surrounded them. A shadow fell on Thom's face as the sun was blotted out, and he smiled to himself.

Senator Warhey was from Indiana. DC, Thom would relocate for, but the Midwest? No fucking thank you.

Anyway, taking Lennie from the middle of the pack to the White House would be his crowning achievement. Thom had managed some mayoral and state senate campaigns in his day, ghostwritten a few speeches, done a few good media hits, but it hadn't been enough to build him a national profile, not just yet. He'd have been one more aspiring staffer to Warhey. To Lennie, he was a lifeline.

The plan was this: in three months, right after New Year's, Lennie would officially announce the launch of her campaign. She'd follow the announcement with a nationwide tour of stump speeches and town halls, highlighting her bio and her accomplishments. From there it'd be Iowa, debates, the general election, and Thom getting a sun-soaked apartment in Foggy Bottom with a nice short commute to the West Wing.

He could see it already. Propelling Lennie to the White House was a crucial part of his life plan. Since joining the campaign he'd already gained some much-deserved notoriety—he'd finally gotten that blue checkmark on Twitter, and he was racking up followers. With the Singapore trip having gone so well, it felt like all the pieces were finally falling into place.

At the office, three separate staffers congratulated him on how the trip was playing. Every TV in the bullpen was set to news coverage of the trip so that he could drink in the spoils of his plan.

And leaning against his desk, the cherry on top of his perfect day, was Felicia Morales. Felicia was Lennie's chief of staff, and had been with her roughly since birth. As usual, she held a cooling coffee in one hand and her phone in the other. Her black hair was coiled in a neat bun at the nape of her neck, and her golden skin somehow always glowed even though she saw as little sun as Thom. Her lips and eyebrows were set in a perpetual, subtle smirk that said *Don't fuck with me.*

He had definitely thought about fucking her anyway. But he and Felicia had built a good working relationship over the last year. As one of Lennie's newer hires, it had taken time and patience for him to win her trust. Sure, she was gorgeous, and there was occasionally a tension between them that hinted there could be more, but Thom was fine with things as is. He didn't want to rock the boat.

"Seems like it's going well," Felicia said mildly, not looking up from her phone.

Thom grinned and shucked his jacket, draping it carefully over his chair. "Where's the governor?"

"Her plane was scheduled to land a few minutes ago, so she should be en route."

Thom sat down. "You're not going to congratulate me?"

That finally got her to glance at him. "I said it was going well, didn't I?"

He leaned back and closed his eyes, basking in the glow of his success. "Hey, great job," another staffer said as he walked past Thom's office.

Before he could respond, another voice called out, loud and brusque, "Fuck yeah!"

Thom rolled his eyes as Clay Parker strolled into view, pointing at the guy he'd thought was talking to him. He stopped when he reached Thom's office doorway and added, loudly to make sure he'd be overheard, "Man, it's good to finally be getting some recognition around here."

Clay was one of the governor's most recent hires, brought on to helm their data analytics department, whatever that was. As a person, Clay was both thoroughly unimpressive and massively impressed with himself.

"Uh, Clay?" Felicia said. "He was congratulating Thom."

Clay scowled. "For what?"

Thom stood up and walked over to him. "The real question is, what would he have been congratulating *you* for?"

Clay crossed his arms as Thom came closer. He was a tall guy, but his frame wasn't intimidating so much as gawky. It didn't help that he wore ugly bargain-basement suits that he clearly didn't get tailored, based on the way they gaped and bunched in strange places. His sandy-brown hair was tufty and bowl shaped, like his mother cut it for him, and he had broad, blunt features that could have made him look brooding or mysterious, except that every single emotion Clay felt appeared immediately on his face.

And every single one of Clay's emotions was terrible.

Clay answered smugly, "Uh, for being the guy who's single-handedly keeping this campaign afloat?"

"Oh, god," Thom muttered.

"What do you even do around here?" Clay asked. "Oh, you sent her to another country? How is that helpful, Thom, she's running for president of *America*."

"Well, we can't all sit in our offices and tweet all day," Thom said.

"Hey, I'm generating the most valuable currency this campaign will ever have—page views and clicks, baby." Thom shuddered as Clay rubbed his fingers together. "I'm building buzz."

"Ew," Felicia said.

"Clay, what can I do to get you to leave my office?" Thom asked. "Wait, I have an idea." He reached for his door to slam it in Clay's face.

Clearly predicting this, Clay jerked to the side and quickly said, "You're just jealous about the article."

Thom narrowed his eyes. "What article?"

Clay grinned in a way he probably thought was intriguing. "You didn't hear?" he asked, and brazenly sauntered past Thom into his office. Thom stiffened, but Felicia held up a hand as if to say *Let's see where this goes*.

Clay stopped by the TV in Thom's office, which had been silently playing cable news. He tapped around on his phone until the screen flickered off, then lit up again with what must have been on his phone. "Read it and weep," he said.

Thom sighed and looked at the screen, which was showing a profile of Clay on some website he'd never heard of.

LOVE, HATE & CLICKBAIT

"Ousted Pinpoint Founder Clay Parker…" He read the start of the headline and didn't bother to read the rest.

Clay's past career, if you could call it that, had been in Silicon Valley, where he'd cofounded a database management program with his college roommate. The software had taken the tech world by storm, but right before they'd all gotten rich, Clay had been unceremoniously dumped from the company. The rumor was that his roommate had invented the whole thing and Clay had just hitched on for the ride. There was no way to tell for sure, but just weeks after the company sold, Clay's roommate had been snapped up as the head of data analytics for Senator Warhey, and they'd gotten a nice round of press coverage about their cutting-edge campaign. Lennie had hired Clay the next week.

Clay was standing by the big-screen version of the article with his arms crossed, smug satisfaction radiating from every pore. "Great," Thom said. "You got another gullible journalist to write about your sob story."

"My quest for justice," Clay corrected him. "My *noble* quest."

"And why the hell did you do this now, anyway?" Thom asked, irritated. "This whole week is supposed to be about my Singapore trip."

"The governor's Singapore trip," Felicia interjected.

"Hers, ours, the trip," Thom said, waving his hand back at her and then at the screen. "*This* was not on the message calendar this week."

Clay's cocky smile just widened. "Wow. You *are* jealous."

Thom ground his teeth. Felicia, meanwhile, seemed more concerned about the substance of the article, squinting as she quickly skimmed it from the screen. "Clay, this is all about you and Pinpoint," she said. "You don't even mention the governor. How is this supposed to help the campaign?"

"I work for the campaign," Clay said, as if this was obvious. "So an article about me brings publicity to the campaign."

"Not really."

"Uh, guys, I'm a *celebrity*," Clay said, emphasizing the word so hard it made Thom's jaw crack. "That's why you hired me."

The only way in which Clay was a celebrity was that he'd become a meme based on some footage of him having a meltdown outside the courthouse where he'd been locked in a legal battle with his former roommate. Clay had gone in close to one of the news cameras and yelled, "Lawsuit, bitch!" These days people mostly used it as a reaction GIF.

"You're not a celebrity, Clay," Thom said. "You're like a D-list Winklevoss twin."

He smirked. "At least people know who I am."

"Then I feel sorry for them."

"Oh, come on," Clay said good-naturedly, turning back to the screen and scrolling on his phone so that the article jerked downward with a pixelated blur. "You don't—"

"Clay," Felicia interrupted him, staring down at her phone with a taut expression. "Is your stupid screen mirroring thing interfering with our Wi-Fi?"

"What?" Thom bleated, feeling an instinctual jab of panic as he looked at his own phone. Shocked, he realized that he hadn't gotten any new emails in the last two minutes. Horror flooded him.

"It may have jammed the signal a little," Clay said defensively. "But only because the office's Wi-Fi already sucks, which by the way I've been *trying* to get you to—"

"Fix it," Thom hissed, grabbing Clay's tragically off-the-rack jacket in his fist. "*Now.* I cannot be offline."

"Wait," Felicia said. "It seems like it's coming—oh. *Shit.*"

Thom went cold. "What? What is it?"

Felicia's phone was buzzing intensely, dozens of backdated messages flowing in as the network came back online. Thom's phone did the same a second later.

"Uh, guys?" A staffer poked his head into Thom's office, an ominous look on his face. "I think you might want to see this."

Dread climbing up his throat, Thom followed Fe out into the bullpen, where another staffer was turning up the volume on one of the TVs. On the news, a clip was playing of the governor at the airport just a little while ago. It was a shaky handheld video of Lennie walking across the airport tarmac to her car, smiling and laughing as she bantered with reporters. She looked a bit disheveled from her long plane ride, and a lock of hair was sticking up oddly on one side of her head, like she'd slept on it funny. As she drew even with her car and someone opened the door for her, one of the reporters shouted, "Governor, what's with the hair?"

Lennie frowned and put a hand on her head. Then she rolled her eyes and said, at a volume the mics picked up distressingly well, "Well, that's what happens when you have no gays on your staff."

The clip froze, and silence fell across the office.

"Fuck," Thom said.

"Double fuck," Felicia said.

This was going to *fuck* them in the campaign. It would kill all the good press Thom had gotten from her international trip. In the invisible race, this was like falling into a sinkhole.

The comment made Lennie look homophobic. It made her look retrograde. It made her look like a senile relative everyone dreaded seeing at Thanksgiving. Their base voters were liberal—hate-has-no-home-here, we're-glad-you're-our neighbor, the-A-is-for-Ally liberal. Bigotry was basically the worst thing they could be accused of.

On the TV, the clip had ended and the cable news anchor was shaking his head, looking incredibly disappointed as he cut to a six-person panel. Felicia had a look of fixed dread on her face that Thom was sure matched his own. In his palm, his phone buzzed again, and he glanced down to see a text from that *Politico* reporter he'd promised to meet up with: Almost there. Spoiler alert: I'm writing about the gaffe now, not the Singapore trip.

"Fuck." His week of perfect news coverage was crashing and burning before his eyes. "Why?" he heard himself whine to Felicia. "Why the fuck would she say that?"

"Because I know I can always count on assholes like you to clean it up for me," a silky-smooth voice said from the doorway.

Lennie Westwood was exactly what you'd want in a political candidate: beautiful, charming, and ruthless. Most voters thought of her as a down-to-earth farmer because she mentioned her family's beloved almond farm every chance she got, despite the fact that most of her millions came from massive agribusiness and GMOs. She picked her policy positions with the help of Thom and Felicia's polling data, and she was smart enough to seem warm instead of smart on TV. She had honey-brown hair and big hazel eyes that usually seemed wide and understanding.

Right now they were staring daggers at Thom. "Uh. Madam Governor," Thom said feebly. "I—I didn't—"

"Oh, I know you didn't, Thom," she said warningly. "I know you wouldn't be so fucking disrespectful after I just worked the whole way back on a sixteen-hour flight that *you* sent me on."

"Ma'am," Thom said, swallowing, "I really—"

"Maybe we should do this in private," Felicia broke in, glancing around the office.

"Great idea," Lennie said, with a poisonous smile. "Thom, grab us some coffee, would you? Maybe that's a job more suited for your talents."

Meekly, he responded, "Happy to, ma'am." As Felicia followed the governor into her office, he grabbed her arm and said under his breath, "The blinds."

Felicia glanced at the blinds on the interior windows of the governor's office and nodded. Reporters were always drifting in and out of the office looking for quotes or consulting with someone on a story, and Thom didn't want any of them to see the campaign in crisis mode. After the door shut behind her, Felicia drew them closed.

Thom turned around to find the entire bullpen staring at him. In the background, the cable news coverage was still dissecting the gaffe, and Thom heard one commentator say, "Is this the end of the Westwood campaign?" His heart was racing, and everyone in the office seemed as on edge as he was. Everyone except one.

Clay strolled past Thom, whistling under his breath. Thom straightened the cuff on his jacket and followed him down the hallway.

When they were sufficiently out of view of the bullpen, Thom grabbed Clay by the arm and threw him against the frosted-glass wall, balling his fists in Clay's jacket and leaning in close to hiss, "*You*. How do you always manage to fuck up everything?"

"What?" Clay protested, though he didn't actually push back against Thom's arms pressing him into the wall.

"It's always you making this office look ridiculous," Thom spat. "If you ever fucking cut me off from the internet again, I will personally cut your balls off of your body, okay?"

"Let me go," Clay said, squirming against him. He was a good deal taller than Thom and should have been able to fight back, but instead he was like a child, huffing and clawing at his wrists ineffectually.

"God, you're pathetic," Thom commented.

"Shut up," Clay said. "You're just pissed because you're threatened by me."

Thom barked out a laugh. "Threatened by you?" He tightened his fist in Clay's shirt, pinning him in place. Clay's whole face was flushed, his mousy hair frizzed and sticking up in all directions. Thom lowered his voice and leaned in. "Do you not understand what a joke you are?"

Clay flinched.

"My god," Thom breathed. "You're so useless you don't even know how useless you are. I bet you think you're like me, some power player with real influence around here. But you're not. You're nothing."

As Thom spoke, Clay's face went from furrowed in anger to slack with shock and humiliation. As always, Thom could read every thought that flitted across his face. It actually made his blood run cold, imagining what it would be like to be that transparent, that *vulnerable*—to have no poker face whatsoever.

Clay's breath was coming fast, his wide shoulders taut where Thom was pinning him. But his pale green eyes were fixed on Thom, blinking sluggishly. As the seconds ticked by, it became clear that he was searching for a comeback, but couldn't quite think of one.

Thom wondered what that was like. To not always have something venomous on the tip of your tongue.

The silence had gone on too long, and Thom felt more exhausted than victorious. His heart was still pounding, though it was starting to slow. He let go of Clay's collar, shoving him away.

"Fuck you, Thom," Clay said hollowly, and lumbered off.

From around the corner, Thom heard Felicia call his name sharply. "You coming?"

He sighed, and followed her into the lion's den.

The mood in Lennie's office was grim. Her body man, Bex, had correctly deduced that Thom would forget to bring coffee and was preparing a mug for the governor. Despite being barely five feet tall and ninety pounds at the most, Bex was a formidable presence when she decided Lennie needed defending. At all other times—like right now—she was practically invisible.

Felicia was pacing in front of the governor's desk. Lennie was slumped backward in her chair, looking like her rage had run its course and left her more tired than angry.

"So, ah," Felicia began diplomatically. "Why don't we start with, um...what happened?"

"I don't know." Lennie sighed and rubbed her eyes, then looked up at them sharply. "I mean, jeez, there were like twenty policy people with me on that plane. None of them could've told me my hair looked weird?"

"I don't think that's the point," Felicia said, just a hint of gentle reproach in her voice.

"What *is* the point?" Lennie asked irritably.

"Uh, well, we need to put out an apology statement," she said. "Right away."

"We need to do more than that," Thom said, pacing. "Gaffes like this—"

"Hey," Lennie said, frowning.

"Sorry, ma'am," Thom said. "*Incidents* like this—an apology won't be enough."

"What do you want me to do, Thom? Flog myself? Wear a hair shirt?" Lennie demanded. "It was a stupid joke."

"No, I think Thom's right," Felicia said, a tiny frown between her brows. "Voters will… Ma'am, they'll worry you're bigoted and only apologizing because you got caught."

"I'm not homophobic!" Lennie shouted. "It was a compliment! I'm a Californian, you think I don't have gay friends?"

"Let's not include that in the apology," Fe said quietly.

Lennie glowered at her. After a moment of awkward silence, Felicia's phone buzzed. Looking down at it, she announced reluctantly, "Warhey just put out a statement that doesn't mention you by name but affirms his commitment to 'equal protection under the law for all citizens regardless of who they love.'"

A chilly silence fell. "Well, that's a kick in the balls," Lennie said, seething at the both of them.

"It's…not much better on Twitter," Fe said, reading off the early reactions. "Ew, gross, nope—"

"Yes, thank you, Felicia," Lennie said testily.

"'This ain't it, chief—'"

Lennie scowled in confusion. "What?"

"It's internet speak for—never mind," Thom said. "The point is, we need to address this, and quickly. We don't want voters to think you think of gay people as a punch line. Or that you really believe those kinds of stereotypes."

"It's worse than that," Felicia said, wincing when the governor shot her a dark look. "Well, it's not like we can ignore the actual substance of the quote. We don't exactly have the most diverse staff. Which—people could interpret," she rushed to soften the statement at Lennie's glare, "as our being…not as tuned-in to the diversity of the country."

"What if we promote someone?" Thom asked.

"For being gay, you mean?" Felicia drawled.

"Yes!" Thom said impatiently.

Felicia blinked. "Fair." She ticked off names as they occurred to her. "Pat? Mariella?"

"No," Lennie said morosely. "I hate them both."

"Clay?" Felicia suggested.

"No," Thom said feelingly.

Lennie seemed to agree. "I'm not drawing any more attention to that dweeb. He's not exactly media-ready."

"Definitely not," Thom said.

Felicia threw up her hands. "Maybe promoting someone is the wrong move. Maybe we just sidestep the issue of our campaign staff entirely, and, I don't know…make a big donation to an LGBT charity?"

"How big?" Lennie asked skeptically. "I don't want to piss away money over something that might just blow over."

"I…don't think it'll blow over," Felicia said. "Especially given the contrast with Warhey."

"Contrast?" Lennie asked. "What do you mean?"

Thom's phone buzzed in his pocket, but he ignored it. "Well, you know," Felicia was saying. "He's viewed as… slightly more progressive on gay rights."

"Oh, come on," Lennie said. "I have an A rating from HRC."

Thom winced. He remembered Felicia spending days on the phone with the Human Rights Campaign twisting their arms until they'd bumped it up to an A from a B-minus. Lennie's platform on gay rights was fully supportive now, but apparently she'd cast some bad votes on LGBT issues years ago when she was in Congress, to prove that she was a "family values" candidate back when that was a thing. Thom wasn't familiar with all the details since he hadn't been working for her then. "That's true," Fe said obliquely.

Lennie squinted at her. "What is it?"

"Warhey has an A-plus," she mumbled.

"Those fuckers," Lennie seethed.

Thom's phone kept buzzing insistently as Felicia said,

"We just have to think of something we can do that will help change the conversation, get us past this." She looked at Thom, her eyes wide in a *help me out, here* kind of way. "Any ideas?"

Silence fell. "Anything?" Felicia asked again, a slight edge of desperation to her voice.

Drawing a total blank, Thom decided to check his phone to stall for time. It turned out that all of that buzzing had been hundreds of notifications racking up on his social media, mostly on Twitter. Frowning, he opened the first one.

Then he nearly dropped the phone.

That journalist he'd been texting before, the one he'd been planning to talk to about the Singapore trip—it looked like he had stopped by the office after all, because he'd taken a photo of Thom and tweeted it out. The photo, just a few minutes old, was of Thom and Clay in the hallway—the very *public* hallway where Thom had reamed him out. Shit, he'd been so pissed he hadn't noticed where they were.

The picture was blurry with motion, but it was clearly the two of them. Thom was hauling Clay toward him, and their faces were almost level, bent in close. With Thom pressing Clay against the wall like that, he could concede that it did look a bit…intimate. Thom could vividly remember screaming at Clay in that moment, but in the photo, for some reason, they both looked hungry instead of pissed. Their eyes were locked on each other. They looked like they were about to fucking kiss.

And the tweet above the photo read: Maybe @GovWestwood has some gays on her staff after all…

★ 2 ★

Clay was used to people laughing at him.

Kids at his high school had laughed at him, but that hadn't stopped him from going to a kick-ass college. Then people at college had laughed at him, but that hadn't stopped him from founding a multimillion-dollar company. And yeah, the people at that company had kicked him out. But that was how he'd ended up working for Governor Westwood, who was going to be the next leader of the fucking free world. Everyone who'd ever laughed at him, he'd proven them wrong.

So he wasn't exactly surprised, when he was summoned to the governor's office, to find her and Felicia nearly doubled over with laughter. "Uh, hey," he said, grinning tentatively in case they were laughing at something else. "What's going on?"

At the sight of him, Lennie and Felicia dissolved into laughter again. He scowled.

The only other person not laughing was Thom, who was pacing in a corner of the room. At Clay's question, he glared at him. "Look at your phone, dumbass."

Clay swiped his phone open and nearly jumped in surprise. He had hundreds of notifications—email, Twitter, Insta, everything. He was going viral? He felt himself starting to smile.

The smile evaporated a second later. The notifications were all about a photo of him and Thom from a little while ago, when Thom had shoved him up against the wall and gone all psycho. In the picture, Thom had a fist in Clay's jacket and was scowling up at him, his whole body tensed and pointed toward Clay. Clay looked like an idiot—his mouth was open, and he had a heavy-lidded, dazed expression on his face as he stared down at Thom. He cringed in embarrassment.

But that wasn't even the worst part. For some reason, everyone sharing the photo seemed to think—what the fuck, that they were *sleeping together*? Horror and humiliation burned through him. *"Ew,"* Clay said, holding the phone away from himself like it was toxic.

Felicia was wiping tears from her eyes.

"You two," Lennie said, still breathless with laughter. "How long has this been going on?"

Crisply and angrily, Thom said, "Ma'am, I'm—*offended* that you think I would ever touch Clay."

God, Clay hated him. He hated what a joyless asshole Thom was, how arrogant he was, how clearly he thought he was better than Clay. Clay had come into this campaign perfectly willing to put up with a decent amount of hazing and new-guy bullshit, but Thom seemed to genuinely despise him.

And who the hell called themselves *Thom*, and not *Tom*? That was some "Topher" bullshit. Pretentious dick.

He'd clearly gotten everything he had in life off his looks. Yeah, he was stupidly hot—he had a face like a fucking Disney prince, except for the glitter of menace in his eyes. He wasn't as tall as Clay, but he had a slim, wiry build that looked obnoxiously good in a suit. He had black hair, dark-rimmed brown eyes, a smattering of freckles across his nose, and a perpetual blue-gray shadow on his jaw.

And Clay hated having to notice all that every time Thom found some creative new way to insult him. "What the—no, *I'm* offended!" he shouted back. "Madam Governor, I would like to be on the record as the offended one."

"I mean, the wedding vows write themselves," Lennie marveled.

"I—just," Felicia stammered. "How?"

"It was Thom's pathetic attempt to intimidate me," Clay snapped.

"Clay was being obnoxious and I was telling him to fuck off," Thom said as if he hadn't spoken. "This is a totally distorted picture."

Felicia, who was still glued to her phone, was barely suppressing giggles. "Yeah, they just happened to get the one angle it…looks like you're about to rip your corset open?"

"Ew," Clay said again. "I'm not interested in gonorrhea."

"You think *I'd* give *you* gonorrhea?" Thom said derisively.

"What the fuck is that supposed to mean?"

"Oh, wow," Lennie said, a hand on her stomach. "I needed this today."

"Can we please all get back to work?" Thom said tightly. "In case this…abomination has wiped everyone's memory, we still have a crisis to deal with."

Felicia went very still. "Oh my god," she said quietly. She looked down at her phone with wide eyes, and then back up at the rest of them, holding it out to display the picture. "You're right. And *this* is how we deal with it."

"What?" Clay asked. Thom asked the same thing, though he sounded more amused.

"We have to change the conversation," Felicia said, looking like she was surprised at her own words. "This definitely changes the conversation."

"The what?" Clay asked again.

"You're joking, right?" Thom said.

Ignoring Clay, Felicia shrugged and answered Thom. "You're the one who suggested promoting someone. To make sure the press knows how *diverse* our staff is."

Lennie had taken Felicia's phone and was peering at it through thick glasses. "Huh."

"No. No!" Thom said with escalating alarm. "We're not—I'm not—I *will* not—"

Finally at the end of his rope, Clay exploded, "Will someone please explain what the fuck is going on?"

"The whole internet thinks you and Thom are dating," Felicia said, "and that kinda...works for us."

Clay sputtered for a moment. *"What?"*

"This picture of you two, it's all over Twitter. It's picking up on Reddit, and when Tumblr sees it—" She laughed. "I've already got requests for comment from *HuffPo*, *Mic*, and *BuzzFeed*. The people who were yelling at us about the hair gaffe—well, they're talking about this now. The internet loves it."

Clay stood up straighter. "Really?" he asked, looking down at his phone again.

Not having previously worked in politics, Clay had been surprised to learn that there were people who made celebrities out of the staff of high-profile politicians. Like, just because Lennie *might* be the president someday, people cared who Clay made out with apparently.

Okay, maybe they cared who Thom made out with. Either way, it was weird. Clay's family followed sports religiously, and tech was its own strange jungle of public perception and quasi celebrity, but he'd never get over the fact that there were *politics* groupies.

Still, his notifications were racking up dizzyingly fast, and he'd just scrolled through a dozen comment threads about himself. And they were good comments too—people talking about wanting to *climb him like a tree* and *slap his doofy face*. And everyone knew that a slap was the internet's highest form of crush.

That photo of him and Thom made him queasy with anger and embarrassment, but he also couldn't help feeling kind of light-headed with glee.

"Excuse me," Thom said disbelievingly, though there was an undercurrent of panic to his voice. "I mean, what are we even talking about here? You want us to…?"

"Date," Lennie said simply. "You and Clay are dating now. As far as the campaign's concerned."

Everything in Clay revolted at the thought. *"No,"* they both said at once.

"Let me be clear, I will one hundred percent be gay for the campaign's sake," Thom said quickly. "But, ma'am, let me date a—a—celebrity chef, a cable news anchor, Christ, even some other Silicon Valley bro. Believe me, I could line up some very willing candidates—but I, and, we, as a campaign, can do much better than *Clay.*"

Clay scoffed in hurt disbelief. "Hey," he said. "Maybe I don't want people to think I'm dating someone who's so fucking creepy that people think a picture of you *beating me up* is how you'd look during sex."

"But…" Lennie pouted, showing them the phone. "They're already drawing little hearts around you two."

Clay flinched away from the picture. Looking at it gave him a hot flush of shame, because he could kind of see why people were getting the wrong idea. Thom *was* pushing him up against a wall in the photo, and his angry expression, out of context, did look kind of sexy and intent. Clay was even worse—in the photo, he was just staring down at Thom, looking almost enthralled.

"I mean, they love it," Lennie said, rattling off tweets. "'I feel so woke being more surprised that Clay Parker is getting any than that he's gay.'" Thom laughed. "Huh. This one is just Thom's screen name and a picture of Kermit the Frog drinking tea."

Clay barked with laughter. Thom scowled, but Lennie just smiled at them, then at Felicia. "I like it."

"Madam Governor, I would happily debase myself in a million different ways to put you in the West Wing," Thom said. "But this—"

"Senior advisor," Lennie said.

Thom frowned. "Ma'am?"

"Senior advisor for campaign strategy," Lennie mused. "That sounds even better."

"*Is* it better?" Thom asked.

"It can be whatever you want it to be, Thom," she replied smoothly. She was speaking in a low, dangerous voice Clay had never heard her use before.

"Uh," Clay said. "What are we—"

Lennie turned to him without missing a beat. "And you… you could be, ah—" she waved a hand vaguely "—senior consultant on technology. I don't know, Felicia will come up with some impressive-sounding title. And I can throw in a raise for each of you."

Thom scoffed, but Lennie didn't miss a step. "C'mon, Thom," she said. "I'll arrange for some *Politico* puff piece about how invaluable you are. If we get your face out there enough, after the campaign K Street'll be fighting over themselves to suck you off. Or..."

Thom seemed intrigued despite himself. "Or what?" he asked.

"Prominent role on the campaign, sympathetic narrative?" Lennie said, shrugging suggestively. "You could even run yourself, someday."

Thom went quiet, his gaze turned inward.

Clay shook his head. "This is crazy," he said. "I'm not— pretending to date Thom."

"No?" Lennie asked, unfazed. She tossed the phone back to Felicia, sat down, and put her elegant shoes on her desk. "You're the *one* person who didn't get into politics to get famous?"

The word *famous* snagged his attention. Of course he'd taken this job because he wanted the attention—look at how the whole world had fawned over Derek when he'd gone to work for Senator Warhey. If he helped Lennie get elected president, he'd get mountains more publicity than he'd ever gotten at Pinpoint, more than enough to launch another company. And this one would be all his.

On the other hand, Thom was a giant fucking douche, and the idea that anyone would think Clay would want to date him was unacceptable. "I... I already am famous," he said feebly.

"You can never be too famous, Clay," Lennie said indulgently. She stared at him, the weight of her gaze heavier than he had ever felt. "This is your moment to shine."

To shine. Lennie was offering him publicity, status, and power—everything he'd ever wanted, especially since his ignominious departure from Silicon Valley. If he did this—if he agreed to this crazy scheme—he could be responsible for saving the campaign.

They *needed* him.

"I don't know," Clay said eventually. "I mean, even *I* might not be able to convince people that this is real."

Thom made a noise that sounded like a strangled growl. "They're already convinced, Clay," Felicia said.

"Well, I don't know if people would buy that I'd date someone so much older than me," he added.

"Oh, fuck you," Thom snapped. Clay grinned. He was twenty-five, and based on how sensitive Thom was about it, he was guessing he'd just turned thirty. *Dick.*

"Do we have a deal?" Lennie asked.

Clay wavered and glanced at Thom. For as much as Clay hated him, he did feel that they were cut from the same cloth. Thom was ruthlessly ambitious, and Clay had that same all-consuming drive. They were both cool and confident, the kind of guy others envied. Sure, Thom was an unabashed dick and a scheming manipulator, but he always seemed to come out on top. Clay could respect that.

At the moment, Thom was glaring at him with seething rage. It was enough to make his heart race with the instinct to back down. But taking this deal was exactly what Thom would do.

Technically, Thom was vehemently opposed to the idea. But it *felt* like what Thom would do. That was enough for Clay.

Eventually, the silence stretching after Lennie's question served as the answer from each of them. Thom looked back down at his phone. "Jesus Christ," he said hollowly. "My life is over."

Lennie beamed at them. "That's the spirit."

★ ★ ★

After the governor dismissed them, Clay found himself in Thom's office, his head spinning. He was internet famous (again)! He wanted to call his mom and tell her. Well, first he'd have to explain what "internet famous" meant (again). Also, he'd have to pretend he was dating the guy he'd been complaining to her about for months. *Fuck.*

For as much as he was reeling, though, Thom seemed to be taking it way worse. He was pacing back and forth, mumbling to himself worryingly. "Can't be. Can't be," he chanted over and over again, a pen stuck between his teeth. "There's gotta be a way..."

Clay was torn between vicious satisfaction at seeing Thom brought so low and irritation at the knowledge that it was because he'd be forced to pretend-date Clay. He was just about to ask Thom what he was muttering about when he jerked to a stop and pointed at him. "Oh! Are you dating anyone?"

It was the first time Thom had ever asked Clay anything about himself. It was weird. Thom showing interest in him—in anybody else—felt like doing something backward, like wearing a coat inside out. "Uh," he said, "no."

"Of fucking course not," Thom said, slumping and chewing on a fingernail.

"Why?"

"I'm trying to think of a way to get us out of this!" he shouted.

"There's no way out of it," Felicia said, coming into the room and shutting the door behind her with a decisive *snick.* "You were in there, Thom. It's done."

"But—c'mon, this'll never work," Thom pleaded. "Me and Clay? No one will buy it."

"Everyone already buys it," Felicia said.

"Yeah, based on one picture, maybe," Thom scoffed. "But an extended charade? We're talking about Clay here."

"Hey!" he shouted.

"How's he gonna appear in public and seem, y'know. Normal enough to date?"

"Joke's on you, Thom, I took *two* improv classes in college," Clay said.

Thom buried his face in his hands.

"Okay, so," Felicia said delicately. "We need an announcement strategy."

Right. Some way to announce to the *world* that he and Thom were—ugh, dating. Suddenly Thom's pen-chewing and pacing didn't seem so out there. "Like what?" Clay asked. "Do we do, like, a press conference?"

Felicia and Thom's eyes met in a look Clay had started to recognize. All at once, their dissonant moods harmonized into a unified front of mockery. "No, Clay," Thom said. "We're not doing a press conference."

Clay felt himself blush when Felicia smirked. "Then how is that stupid photo of us going to help the governor?" he demanded.

To his satisfaction, they both seemed stumped for a second. "Instagram?" Felicia suggested.

Thom shook his head and waved, and Felicia nodded in agreement. It was as if they'd had an entire wordless conversation about why her idea wouldn't work in the span of a second. "Interview?" Thom said.

Felicia cocked her head skeptically, and Thom tilted his as if to say *good point*. Clay ground his teeth.

"I could tweet about it," he offered.

"*No,*" Thom and Felicia shouted at him in unison. He threw up his hands.

Felicia shook her head. "We're overthinking this," she

said. "The internet already likes you two. We don't want to spoon-feed them anything more, we want the opposite."

Thom frowned. "Keep it secret? I'd be fine with that."

Felicia rolled her eyes. "Think about it," she said. "How do celebrity couples announce they're couples? They don't. They get caught on a date."

"But we already got caught—" Thom started, and then cut off, looking uncomfortable. It made Clay's face heat again.

Felicia, though, was grinning. "So let's get you caught again."

⋆ 3 ⋆

The next day, Lennie held an event at a farmers market. She toured the stalls and greeted constituents, talking about sustainable farming, small businesses, climate change, and any other hot topics Thom and Felicia could shoehorn into the conversation. It was the perfect event for the pre-primary: issue-y without being overtly political, and set at a picturesque park on a gorgeous Southern California day that would make for great pictures.

Normally Thom would be soaking in the attention of his candidate, the voters, and, most importantly, the scrum of journalists following Lennie around, but today he sulked in the distance, in the shade of several towering, deep-green trees.

"Stalling?" Fe asked him.

"Just—" Thom snapped. "Give me a minute."

Across the field, far from both the event and Thom, Clay

wandered aimlessly, occasionally squinting up at the sun. He'd ditched his jacket, leaving him in just a wrinkled white button-down and dark slacks, swinging his long arms back and forth like a restless teenager. The heat had made his normally frizzy light brown hair stick to the shape of his skull. The sight of him out there, a sore thumb amid the otherwise perfect day, made Thom almost itchy with irritation.

"It's not going to get any easier if you put it off," Fe told him.

It was true. He was already getting glances—*both* he and Clay were—and not even just from the reporters huddled around Lennie. At least they had the dignity to try to mask their curiosity; that viral photo of him and Clay wasn't news, it was just trashy internet gossip, so none of the reporters were supposed to be interested in it. But Christ, even regular people at the farmers market seemed to be glancing at them. Fucking hippies who spent all day reading about politics online, that's who went to farmers markets.

"Come on," Fe said.

He turned to her, pleading. "We don't have to do this today."

"We do," she said firmly.

"It—I'm still not convinced this is a good idea," he said.

"It's an incredible idea," Fe said, looking at him like he was a moron. "And the fact that you're overriding your own political judgment—"

"Would *you* pretend to date Clay?" he demanded.

"Fair point," she said. "Still. We put out the apology—now we need to change the conversation."

Thom groaned. They had put out Lennie's apology statement yesterday—*I apologize unreservedly, stupid and insensitive remark, remain wholly committed to LGBTQ rights*, blah-blah-blah. Thom had even quote tweeted her statement with a carefully phrased *I believe Governor Westwood*. And the whole thing had gone over about as well as he'd expected: like a lead fucking balloon. The gaffe had been bad, and Felicia was right. The best way to handle it was to get people talking about something else.

Like a stupid political 'ship. "If it makes you feel any better," Fe said, "everyone already thinks you're sleeping together."

He was hit with a wave of despair as he realized that she was right. But she was also right about what needed to be done. If he was going to live in a world where people thought he was fucking Clay Parker, it was time to turn that to his advantage.

Clay turned and frowned at him as he approached. Before he could say anything, Thom took a deep breath and grabbed Clay's hand. It only took a few moments for the reporters to notice, and soon they were all snapping pictures, along with some of the people attending the farmers market.

That was it, then—the photos would be all over the internet in seconds. Thom and Clay, holding hands like a pair of high school sweethearts. They had officially confirmed that they were a couple. Thom was dying inside.

"What are you doing," Clay asked, scowling down at him.

"What the fuck does it look like?" Thom hissed, keeping a smile pasted on for the pictures' sake.

"Why are you holding my hand like that?" Clay said, his own hand squirming and twisting against Thom's.

"What do you mean? Stop," Thom said, trying to force him to be still.

"That isn't how people hold hands," Clay said, using his other hand to pry at Thom's. "C'mon, you've gotta—like this," he explained, lacing their fingers together.

"Oh my god," Thom muttered. At least Clay had calmed

down, and his hand wasn't clammy like Thom had been expecting—it was warm and dry. "Fine, are you happy?"

"I'm just trying to get it right," Clay said mulishly. They started walking toward the main activity of the farmers market. "This is how people hold hands when they're, y'know. Dating."

"Like you know anything about dating," Thom replied.

"More than you."

A few folks who were browsing the stalls smiled at them tentatively, and Thom smiled and nodded back. "I'm not going to dignify that with a response," he whispered through his teeth.

"It's true."

"Okay."

"You only date people for their political connections," Clay said. Thom glanced around at the other customers, but thankfully no one seemed to be able to hear them. "Or status. Or power," Clay continued. "Or if you think there's something else you can get from them."

"That's what dating *is*."

Before Clay could reply, they were interrupted by a woman approaching them. "Hi," she said, beaming. "I just wanted to say, you two are adorable."

"Thanks," Thom said. He decided to dial up the romance by pulling Clay against him with their joined hands and leaning his head against Clay's shoulder.

The woman ate it up, actually blushing a little. "Aw," she gushed. "You're just both so handsome!"

Thom chafed a little at *both*, but he made himself smile and say, "Thank you. I hope you'll take a minute to chat with the governor while you're here."

"Sure!" the woman said, and wandered past them.

"Ugh, get off me," Clay said, nudging Thom away from him. "It's too hot for this. Can we stop holding hands yet?"

"Be quiet, people might hear," Thom hissed. "And no, not unless you can figure out something else couple-y for us to do."

Clay frowned, then grabbed a bite-size brownie from a nearby table, holding it up as if he were offering to feed it to Thom. "Over my dead body," Thom gritted out through a cutesy smile.

"Ooh, someone might overhear," Clay singsonged at him. Thom yanked him by his hand over to the next stall, and Clay winced and yelped, rubbing his shoulder.

More than a few of the reporters around Lennie were still discreetly watching them. That was both horrifying and, Thom supposed, technically a good sign. When Clay saw where Thom was looking, he glanced in the same direction, then grinned and started to wave. Thom had to lunge for his other hand. "Don't wave!"

"I thought the point was to be seen."

"Yes, *seen*," Thom said. "Not *look like you're trying to be seen*."

"I don't understand the difference," Clay said.

"Because you're a moron."

"I'm not the one who got us into this mess."

"You absolutely are," Thom said. They'd reached a stall selling organic scarves and other knitwear. He grabbed one and held it up against Clay, as if he were thinking about buying it for him.

Clay frowned, looking uncomfortable. "No, that stupid picture looked like we were—whatever," he whispered, "because *you* threw me up against the wall."

"Because you took down our network just to show us a fucking article about yourself."

"Like you're such a humble public servant," Clay muttered.

Thom tossed the scarf back on the stall and they moved on. "You're in this for yourself and your career, just like me and everyone else."

"Except that, unlike you," Thom said, "I'm good at my job."

"Well, right now your job is to date me, and you suck at it."

"Homemade candles?" interjected a cheerful salesman at the next booth.

Thom and Clay both startled, but Thom recovered first. "Wow, these are…great," he said, as sincerely as he could manage. Most of the candles were lumpy and looked like several colors had run together to make something that resembled dark earwax.

"They're very romantic," the salesman said coyly, smiling at them.

"Sure," Thom said uneasily. The heat was sweltering even in the shade of the salesman's tent, and with Clay pressed against his side, it was even worse.

The salesman might as well have had hearts in his eyes as he gazed at them. Leaning closer, he whispered, "I saw you two on the internet."

The longer they stood there, there more it felt like it was Clay's long form plastered to his side that was swelteringly hot, not the sun beating down on them from above. It was a different kind of heat—soft and slightly humid; tactile in the way only another person's body heat could be. It was strangely personal, and Thom didn't like it.

"That's great," he said to the salesman limply, trying to shuffle away from Clay without looking like he was doing it.

"You know," the salesman said conspiratorially, "some of my customers use my candles for lovemaking."

"Okay," Thom said, walking away and pulling Clay briskly behind him. They stopped at a cheese stall, where hundreds of delicate little cheese balls were stacked on top of each other in a towering wall.

Shaking his head, Thom lifted his face to take advantage of a cool breeze, and muttered, "I can't believe this is working."

Clay frowned. "What?"

"That people think we're actually dating," Thom spelled out.

"Wow," Clay said, taking offense. "FYI, I could do a hell of a lot better than you."

"Please," Thom scoffed.

"It's true," Clay said, and he started ticking things off on his fingers. "I'm successful, I'm a tech genius, I'm a celebrity, I'm a solid eight—"

Thom snorted. "Clay. I'm handsome and charming and accomplished. Your Wikipedia entry is a subcategory of someone else's."

Genuine hurt spread over Clay's face. "You're such a dick," he said.

"Maybe that's why the internet loves us," Thom mused. "They're amazed that *anyone* would date you."

Clay was starting to get really agitated now. "Fuck you, Thom."

Thom glanced at some of the people around them, who had started to notice Clay's voice rising. "Calm down," Thom said, trying to sound soothing. "Look at me like a loving boyfriend."

Clay grimaced down at him in the world's worst imitation of a smile, gritting through his teeth, "Then stop insulting me."

Thom snorted out a laugh before he could help it. It was just Clay's face whenever Thom insulted him—it twisted in an excellently satisfying way, and made it impossible for him to stop. "No."

Clay fumed and yanked his hand away from Thom's as if he wanted to make some big, dumb gesture with it. Thom clamped his fingers down on Clay's, trying to salvage their lovey-dovey pose, but Clay just wrung his hand away from Thom's faster and harder until finally he freed it, sending his arm flying backward and smacking into the wall of tiny cheese balls.

The cheeses started tumbling, and Clay whirled around in distress. Panicking, he tried to catch some as they fell, then twisted, stumbled, and lost his footing. In the next second all six-foot-three of Clay went crashing backward into the table, sending cheese balls flying everywhere.

People gasped and ran over to help. Thom hastily smothered his impulse to laugh and helped Clay to his feet. Clay mumbled an apology to the slack-jawed proprietor of the cheese stall, and Thom jumped in as well. "We're so, so sorry, ma'am, my—uh—boyfriend wasn't looking where he was going," he said. She seemed dazed, and simply nodded in response.

As his amusement receded, Thom inwardly cursed himself. This whole farmers market thing had turned into a disaster. They'd have to pay the cheese lady back out of the campaign account. More importantly, they had just ruined their stupid "coming out" event with this fiasco. Clay looked like an idiot, which meant the campaign would look idiotic.

There were tiny squished cheese balls all over one side of his cheap suit. Very aware that people would be taking pictures, Thom brushed Clay's shirt off as best he could, working quickly and efficiently, then reached up to pluck a cheese ball out of Clay's hair, all while Clay stared at him dumbly. "Fucking moron," Thom muttered. Everything was ruined.

Felicia came running up to them. "Um, oh my god," she said quietly.

"I know," Thom said darkly. "It was Clay's fault."

"Fault?" Fe said, sounding puzzled. "What are you talking about? This was perfect."

Thom and Clay both gaped at her. "What?!"

★ 4 ★

It was a nightmare. Clay scowled down at his phone, looking through the photos from the farmers market the day before that were circulating online.

In every single one of the stupid pictures, Thom looked like a gallant hero tenderly caring for his oaf of a boyfriend. There were pictures of Thom helping Clay up from the ruined cheese stall. Pictures of him brushing the debris off Clay's clothes. The most popular picture by far was the one where Thom reached up to pick a cheese ball out of Clay's hair with what looked like a soft smile on his face.

OMG so adorbs!!!! wrote one commenter, followed by a string of fire, alarm, and sparkle heart emojis. Clay seethed. He distinctly remembered that moment—Thom had been smirking at him, not smiling sweetly, and he had definitely been trying not to laugh. It was his fault Clay had even crashed into the stupid cheese pyramid in the first place. How had the pictures come out so differently?

He scanned the reactions online, not even sure what he was hoping to find. Swipe, cute comment. Swipe, I love them!! Swipe, fan art of him and Thom. Yikes.

It was infuriating. How was it that no one could see the truth?

Disgusted, he pocketed his phone. He was waiting in a conference room at the office, where he'd been summoned for some kind of farmers market postmortem meeting with Thom and Felicia. He took a deep breath and looked out the window, trying to let the view of the LA skyline and dusty green-and-brown mountains in the distance soothe him. But instead, it only made him wonder whether it had been a mistake to take this job with Lennie—to stay in California, after everything that had happened with Pinpoint. He closed his eyes, remembering the first time he had ever set foot in this state—that moment he'd stepped off the airplane Jetway to feel that warm West Coast sun on his face, the mountains in the distance stained purple and pink just like on a postcard.

That's where it had all gone wrong.

Clay had arrived at college bursting with energy and eager to make his mark on the world. He'd always been good with computers, and he'd known early on that coding would be his path to mega-success, and the wealth, fame, and respect that came with it. He'd been psyched to learn that his freshman year roommate, Derek, was a coder too. That year, Clay had come up with dozens of incredible start-up ideas. But everything had changed the day Derek had confided in him that he'd gotten an idea for a new database program he was calling Pinpoint. Clay had known instantly that it would be massive, a game changer, and he'd offered to help Derek in any way he could. Derek said yes.

Things had moved quickly after that. By their senior year, they'd pulled in a half dozen more coders. Derek called the shots, but Clay was his right-hand man, always there when they needed pizza or beer or to organize a night out to let off steam. He did his fair share of coding too, following Derek's exact instructions to help make Pinpoint the best it could be. And he never complained when Derek shot down his ideas for the product, because he was a team player. The most important thing was that Pinpoint became a success.

When they'd launched, it had become much more than that—it was a *smash* success. Pinpoint was a huge leap forward for interoffice data storage and organization, and it'd been a particular hit with political campaigns. Buzz started swirling that Derek was going to be the Steve Jobs of politics, bringing campaigns and data analytics into the twenty-first century. Once Pinpoint got big enough, they'd moved out to California and hired hundreds of people. Clay had never been prouder.

It was only slowly that he'd started to realize that something was wrong. Derek was the one getting the glowing magazine profiles and going to fancy parties, while Clay had been relegated to a tiny office on the first floor without so much as a window. Derek started showing up to the Pinpoint campus in one of those fancy robot cars that drove itself, while Clay was barely earning enough to make rent in San Jose. Derek got all the glory, while Clay didn't seem to be in charge of anything.

Eventually it all came to a head. It was his parents' fault, really—his mom had been sure that Clay was entitled to stock options and glitzy photo shoots and a robot car of his own. They'd goaded him into confronting Derek, into standing up for himself. So he'd gone up to Derek's shiny, glass-walled office one night and laid out everything he'd done for Pinpoint—

LIZ BOWERY

all the code he'd written at Derek's direction, the hours he'd toiled away, the sacrifices he'd made. He'd asked for his fair share of the company, as Pinpoint's cofounder.

Derek had laughed in his face.

The memory still gave him a stomach-dropping flush of shame. Derek had said that Clay had just "been there" when *he* had invented Pinpoint. That he'd never contributed anything original. That he'd only let Clay hang out with him and the others out of pity. That none of Pinpoint was his.

And when Clay had started arguing back, Derek had had him escorted out of the office.

After he was fired, Derek and the rest of the staff had put out all these bullshit rumors about him, making him sound like a loser and a hanger-on who was trying to profit off Derek's genius. Worst of all, once he'd been fired, he'd realized that most people in the industry didn't know anything about him at all. It was like he'd never even been a part of Pinpoint.

His parents had forced him to hire a lawyer. Then one thing led to another, that clip of him outside the courthouse went viral, and eventually Clay did become famous. Not the kind of famous he should have been, though—as a tech entrepreneur and genius. No, he'd become famous as the butt of jokes, framed through Derek's story, not his.

He slipped his phone out of his pocket and pulled up the photos from the farmers market again. At least this time he was going viral for something marginally less embarrassing than the fallout from Pinpoint. He winced as he saw a photo where one of the cheese balls was mushed against his eye. *Marginally* less embarrassing.

Thom, of course, looked perfect in every photo. Thom always looked good; he glided through life with effortless confidence and a bottomless appetite for crushing his enemies. It

52

was as if nothing could ever hurt him. Clay could have used some of that while he was still at Pinpoint.

He lingered on one of the most popular photos, the one of Thom as the internet's dream boyfriend, an affectionate smile on his face as he helped Clay to his feet. Then he lowered his phone to look at the real Thom, who was currently bent forward in a chair over the conference room table, glaring down at his own phone with a grim set to his jaw. His dark hair looked a little more uneven than usual, like maybe he hadn't slept well, and his pale skin looked sallow out of the sunlight. Felicia hadn't shown up yet, and they'd been sitting alone in the conference room for at least ten minutes waiting for her. Thom hadn't said a word to him since he'd arrived.

"This is your fault," Clay said.

Thom slammed his phone down on the table. "Oh, I made you go barreling into a wall of cheese?"

"Uh, I was selling it, okay, Thom?" Clay said. "I was making it work, and you were being an unprofessional dick."

Thom opened his mouth to say something probably vulgar, but he was cut off when Felicia arrived, along with Bex. Without breaking stride, Felicia walked past them and snatched Thom's phone out of his hand. "Hey, I need that!" he yelled at her.

"No you don't," she said shortly.

"What's your problem?" Thom asked, slouching back in his chair. "The plan fucking worked. The pictures are everywhere, everyone's talking about us, and no one's talking about Lennie's gaffe." He drummed his fingers impatiently as Bex took a seat across from them. Felicia stayed standing, looming over him with all of her five feet and change. "So why are we here?"

"Are you kidding?" Felicia demanded. "It was pure *luck* that made it a success. You two idiots were sniping at each other the whole time. If anyone had overheard, we'd be screwed."

"It was Clay's fault," Thom said.

"It was *not*," Clay said hotly. "You—"

"I don't care!" Felicia shouted. "This fake relationship could save this campaign or it could sink it. You two need to figure out how you're going to pull it off without killing each other, or, more importantly, all of our careers."

"Whatever," Thom said, sitting back in his chair. "I can swallow my pride and pretend to date Clay if he can do the same."

"You couldn't yesterday," Fe said.

"Yesterday worked out great," Thom said. "You said it was perfect."

"The part you two fucked up was perfect," she said coolly. "The rest of it was garbage."

"Well, the internet loves us, so I'm not seeing the problem."

"Are you really this fucking dense?" Felicia hissed. "You almost revealed to the entire world that you're faking being gay and in a relationship with another campaign staffer to distract from a homophobic gaffe. The press would have a field day. It's like fucking Watergate on acid. This campaign would be over."

Thom tried to interject, but Felicia just kept going, her voice slashing across the room as she picked up steam. "Now, Thom, I know you think you're god's gift to political consulting. I know you're only here to build your résumé and get on TV, and that if this campaign does implode you will somehow fail upwards into whatever campaign, greenroom, or bloodsucking corporate lobbying firm will have you next, because you have no soul," she spat. "But some of us are in this for more than that. Some of us actually want Lennie to win."

"Jesus, calm down, Pollyanna," Thom sighed. "Message

received—we'll be more convincing next time." Standing up, he asked, "Is that it? Because I have—"

Quietly, Bex said, "Sit. Down."

The silence that followed was loud as a thunderclap. Thom shakily folded back down into his chair. Clay felt glued to his.

Bex rarely spoke. Her whole thing was fading into the background—that was what a good body man did. She had to be unobtrusive enough to blend in with campaign staff, political heavy-hitters, and even Lennie's family. She witnessed all of the campaign's most high-pressure, high-stakes moments. She had to be there when Lennie wanted her and invisible when she wanted space.

But when Bex decided that she needed to be seen, she was *seen*. Clay swallowed nervously.

Felicia waited a beat before taking the metaphorical mic back, saying in a much calmer tone, "We can't leave this to chance." She sat in the chair next to Bex, facing Clay and Thom over the conference table. "We're not leaving this room until you two can pretend to be a couple without bickering out the sides of your mouths the entire time. So," she said, shaking her head and summoning a vaguely threatening smile, "convince me that you're in love."

They sat there in stubborn silence for a few moments. "What are we supposed to do?" Thom eventually snapped.

Felicia took a deep breath. "Thom," she asked. "How long have you and Clay been together?"

"Two wee—" Thom started, but at a glare from Felicia, he changed course. "...months. It's early, but. It's..." Twisting his mouth, he finished, "Like no other relationship I've had before!"

"Do you see that?" Clay said. "He's doing that thing, where he says something that sounds nice but he means the opposite."

"It's called politics," Thom said cattily.

Felicia cleared her throat in a menacing way.

"Thank you, Thom," Clay said dully. "You're…really special to me."

"Aww," Thom said mockingly.

"Where did you meet?" Bex asked.

Clay said, "The office," and Thom said, "At work," their voices overlapping messily.

Felicia shrugged and gave them that one. "Who asked who out?"

"Clay asked me out," Thom said quickly.

"No, no I did not," Clay insisted. "Thom asked *me* out."

"Why would I do that?" Thom asked. "*I'm* having a sexuality crisis. Apparently."

"You can't just use a sexuality crisis to get out of being the ask-er!" Clay said.

"Fine," Thom said flatly. "I asked Clay out when it became clear that he was desperately in love with me and never going to get over it."

"Well, clearly it worked," Clay said smugly. "So."

"How did you know Clay was the one?" Bex asked.

"Whoa," Thom said, scowling. "I said I'd pretend to date him. I'm not declaring that he's my fucking soulmate."

"See?" Clay said. "He is *not* cooperating."

"Clay, how did you know Thom was the one?" Felicia asked.

"I'm not gonna say it if he won't say it!"

"Jesus Christ," Thom said. "Our eyes met over polling data late one night under the office's glowing fluorescent lights, and that's when I knew he was the one."

Clay shook his head, and almost despite himself he grumbled, "He's kind of funny, I guess."

He regretted it as soon as Felicia and Bex's faces lit up in approval. "See?" Felicia said. "There, was that so hard? Thom, let's try your answer again."

Thom sighed. Under Felicia's unrelenting glare, he cleared his throat and sat forward, locking eyes with her. Slipping into an instantaneous, charismatic intensity, he said, "This man is incredibly important to me. And I don't want to turn our relationship into something political, but here's the thing—the personal *is* political. I need to know that the man I've chosen to be with won't be stopped from sharing in my life the way straight couples are allowed to do. That's why I'm with Governor Westwood. She supports LGBT rights."

For a final flourish, Thom grabbed Clay's hand. Clay jolted in surprise at the hot, rough feel of Thom's palm on his.

Thom finished his epic speech by turning on the puppy dog eyes and saying somberly, "It's personal for me."

Clay blinked at him, taken aback.

Felicia was unimpressed. "That's a slogan, not a relationship."

Thom threw Clay's hand away from his like it had scalded him. "What do you want from me?"

"You know what I want!" Felicia said. "I want you to put your considerable political skills to use, and convince me of something completely bullshit. Can you do that, Thom? Can you do your fucking job?"

Looking murderous, Thom sucked in a frustrated breath through his teeth, tilting his head back. Then he slumped, as if letting go of it all. When he sat up in his chair again and looked at Clay, he'd gone quiet and appraising. His sharp features, normally taut with anger or impatience, were softened, his brown eyes deep and searching. Clay felt almost uncomfortable under his scrutiny.

Then he spoke, his voice low and unguarded. "I really like Clay's persistence," he said. "He's been through a lot, but he never gives in. No matter how many times he gets knocked down, he always gets back up. He always fights."

He smiled slightly, and it wasn't his usual cynical, mocking grin—it was a warm, real smile, and it was almost unbearably handsome. Holding Clay's eyes, he said, "That's what made me fall for him."

Clay wasn't sure what to say. Thom looked at Felicia, then at Bex.

Then he glanced back at Clay, and the affectionate mask fell away between one blink and the next. "How was that?" he asked briskly.

Felicia's lips were pursed in consideration. "It was okay."

"See? We can fake it," Thom said. "Are we done now?"

Bex and Felicia narrowed their eyes at each other, then stood and retreated to a corner of the room to confer.

Clay was left to sit in awkward silence with Thom. At least, it was awkward on his end. Thom already had his phone open and was scrolling through it, his face wiped clean of any emotion. He could've been a corpse if it wasn't for the flicking of his thumb.

Clay had always known that Thom was a charming sociopath, but it was downright unnerving to have that directed at him.

Weirdly, it made him think of Pinpoint again. The whole time he'd worked there, he'd thought that those people were his friends, but it had turned out they'd all been pretending. At least this time he *knew* Thom was only pretending to like him.

It should have been comforting, and it was, in a way. But it also felt like walking on a high wire, where he could see the fall laid out in front of him on both sides.

Bex and Felicia walked back over to them. "Okay," Felicia said. "You did better today."

"Thanks," Thom said drily.

"*But,*" Felicia said. "I'm still not convinced you can pull this off. I want to test you somewhere. See if you can do this whole couple-y thing without a meltdown."

"Oh my god, not again," Thom said, sinking into his chair.

"I'm sorry, Thom," Felicia said sternly, "did you not think that *publicly* dating someone might involve occasionally going out in public?"

"Fine, what," Thom said. "Where are you going to 'test' us?"

"The state legislature brunch," Felicia said. "Tomorrow morning."

Clay had never heard of the brunch, but Thom seemed familiar with it. "Really?" he asked, raising his eyebrows. "There won't be a lot of people there swooning with romance."

"Exactly," Felicia said. "You'll be surrounded by jaded political insiders who'll be watching your every move. They're not sappy, they're cynical. To fool them, you'll have to be completely convincing as—"

"Yeah, yeah, I get it," Thom interrupted her, pushing to his feet. "We'll be lovesick idiots."

He glanced back at Clay, scorn etched in every line of his face. "No one will know the truth."

★ 5 ★

The last Sunday of every month, the Los Angeles–based members of the California state legislature hosted a breakfast for themselves, their donors, journalists, and any other power player who could prove their stature. Lennie and her staff always attended—it was an excellent opportunity to maintain relationships, get stories out, and twist arms for her various legislative priorities.

Normally Thom loved the breakfast. It was his time to shine. But today, the ripple that went through the room as he walked in had a distinctly different tenor. It felt like everyone there was staring at him and whispering behind their hands. Thom was used to being the center of attention at these events, or close to it, but usually that meant that he was the focus of admiration, envy, or fear. He honestly didn't really care which of those feelings he inspired; they were all a form of power.

Today, it felt like he was caught in a maelstrom of gossip, helpless to its whipsaw currents. He wasn't in control anymore.

Irritated, he straightened one of the cuffs of his jacket and tried to ignore the intangible spotlight of attention on him. Technically, Operation Gaffe was a smash success. The farmers market photos had spread even farther and wider than the original, furtive photo of Clay and Thom, and had generated such a froth of online interest in their relationship that it had sufficiently quelled outrage over Lennie's stupid comment. In fact, people seemed way *more* interested in Thom and Clay than they had been in the original scandal. Speculation about them was rampant. There were think pieces and Twitter threads being written about them as a couple. The internet seemed to love them.

But here at the breakfast, the people staring at them didn't have gooey eyes and lovesick expressions. Instead, he could hear giggles, harsh whispers, and snorting laughter. In the distance, he was pretty sure someone was doing a *lawsuit, bitch!* impression. Humiliatingly, he felt his face go hot.

"Deep breaths," Fe muttered next to him, grabbing a mimosa off a passing tray.

"I'm fine," Thom said.

"Yeah, you look fine."

"God," he said under his breath, pressing his fingers to the bridge of his nose. "Why did I ever agree to this?"

"I don't know what you're talking about," Fe said obliquely.

"This is a bad idea," Thom whispered harshly. "Look at them. They're all gonna know."

Felicia turned to face him, a condescending frown pinching her brows together. "Yeah, Thom—look at them," she said slowly. "They're laughing and staring at you. They're making fun of you."

Thom glared at her, half furious and half confused.

"They're mocking you *because they buy it*," Fe said, as if he was an idiot. "They think you're with Clay. It's working."

Thom blinked, simultaneously growing calmer and more unsettled as he realized that she was right.

Ever since they'd embarked on this wild scheme, Thom had been, on some level, stunned that it was working at all—not just that it had deflected attention away from Lennie's gaffe, but that people had bought into the idea of him and *Clay*.

He glanced at his fake boyfriend, who'd arrived with them and was somehow already bickering with one of the waiters about how many hors d'oeuvres he was allowed to take from a single plate. There was a barely noticeable stain on the sleeve of his jacket, a spike of hair was sticking up at the back of his head, and he seemed as blithely unaware of all the attention on them as Thom was keyed into it.

Who in their right mind would think that someone like Thom would be with someone like Clay?

He took a deep breath and tried to remind himself that this would all be worth it once Lennie was in the White House, and he was holding the world's biggest IOU from the commander in chief. Until then, all he had to do was lie back and think of Washington.

Clay immediately tried his patience by loudly sighing and asking in what he probably thought was a whisper, "Why do I have to be here again?"

Felicia just smiled at Thom. "Enjoy," she said, and took Lennie's arm to steer her into a conversation with some important donors. Thom and Clay were left in stilted silence.

Clay filled it in the strangest possible way. "So I told my parents about us. Or, y'know. *Us*." He made air quotes, and Thom suppressed a shudder.

"Okay," Thom said, unsure why Clay was talking to him about his personal life.

"They were kinda mad they didn't know we were 'dating' before the whole thing went viral. My mom kept me on the phone for over an hour making me apologize for keeping my *new beau* a secret." He grinned. "My mom's a dork."

Thom said nothing. "Anyway, it wasn't that bad," Clay continued. "What about you? How'd your family react? 'Cause just FYI, if they want to meet me or something, I want some notice."

Thom snorted harshly. "They're not going to want to meet you, Clay."

"Why not?" Clay asked, indignant. "I'm awesome."

Thom needed a drink. Where were those waiters with the booze?

Clay was staring at him, obviously waiting for an answer.

"They don't bother asking about my private life," Thom told him. "They know I'm not exactly gushy about the people I date."

"Well, sure," Clay said. Then he frowned. "But. They didn't even ask?"

Thom honestly couldn't remember the last time he'd spoken to his parents. He was sure it hadn't been more than six months. Maybe a year.

He wasn't some sob story with a broken home or a bad childhood or anything. His parents were normal. His hometown was normal. He'd grown up in a boring-as-shit house in a boring-as-shit suburb, dreaming about big cities and screaming crowds and lights so bright they made your eyes water. Now he had that life, the one he'd always dreamed of—he was a power player on the national stage, someone of significance. And his parents were happy as clams back in the burbs.

And they weren't really interested in Thom's dream life, or why he'd wanted it.

He cleared his throat. "Please tell me you're not trying to deflect from the fact that you've already scheduled some sort of event with your extended family."

Clay grinned ear to ear. "Nah, they're in Waltham, Massachusetts, and they're terrible at Zoom," he said cheerfully. "Also, you should be so lucky as to win Leslie Parker's stamp of approval, she is a badass."

"Jesus Christ," Thom sighed.

Clay was making a face like he was thinking something he wasn't saying, which would of course be a first for him. "So a fake relationship isn't going to change your life at all?" he pressed.

"Are you serious?" Thom said. "My mentions are full of this crap. It's ruining my reputation."

"You really are a psychopath," Clay said. "You don't have a girlfriend or anything?"

Thom clapped him on the shoulder. "I do now."

"Problematic," Clay said, pointing. "You see, Thom? You need me. Let me show you the gay ropes. They take a *very* long time to learn."

Thom was distracted when he spotted Kerry Pham across the room. He grabbed Clay by the elbow and said, "Get Lennie—Kerry's here."

"Who?"

"Kerry Pham, idiot," Thom said, shoving him. Clay looked wounded and dense, but stumbled off obediently in search of Lennie.

Kerry Pham was a rising star in local activism. She was the first person in her working-class family who'd gone to college, and she'd become a physical therapist to support them. But it turned out that the student loans she'd taken out to go to school were administered by some shady corporations, and she'd nearly lost her family's home when an error calculating her interest almost forced her into bankruptcy. A local lawyer had undone the damage in the nick of time, and since then Kerry had become a passionate advocate for reforming the student loan system to prevent abuse. Pretty and softly sympathetic but strong as iron, she made for a *very* media-friendly advocate—the perfect bait for an image-conscious governor.

She looked especially good today, in a bright but sophisticated cocktail dress. She caught Thom's eye and smiled. "Kerry," he said, pushing forward to shake her hand.

"Thom," she replied. "Thanks for inviting me."

"Glad you could make it," he said. Kerry and the governor had just wrapped up a series of local media hits urging Congress to pass a student loan reform bill that would help young people get some of their money back and rein in the most abusive programs. Thom and Felicia had decided a while back that Lennie's "brand" as a candidate would be appealing to young people, mostly because she was younger than Warhey. Once Thom had learned about Kerry, it had been easy to reach out to the California delegation and some of Lennie's other allies in Congress to put the student loan reform bill together. The plan was for the bill to pass about a month before Lennie's big campaign announcement to give her momentum going into the primary.

Inviting Kerry to the breakfast had been Thom's idea, to give her the sense that she'd formed a genuine working relationship with the governor, and to test the waters of introducing her to the national stage as they drew closer to the launch of the campaign. If it worked, she could become a very valuable ally—the pretty young face of Lennie's youth vote focus. He glanced around the room, taking note of where a few journalists were milling nearby. If they could come out of this breakfast with some pictures of Lennie and Kerry to-gether, that would be ideal. "The governor is very excited to talk to you."

Kerry looked faintly surprised. "Really? That's wonderful."

Clay had in fact navigated the party's currents to bring Lennie over to them, cocktail in hand. "Ma'am," Thom said. "You remember Kerry Pham."

"Of course!" Lennie said, exuding a lacquer-thick veneer of warmth. "We're so glad you could join us."

"Oh, uh—sure!" Kerry said, looking a bit overwhelmed. Thom waved over a photographer to get a picture of them shaking hands. Kerry blinked in confusion as the picture was taken, but refocused on the governor quickly. "Thank you so much for your work on the bill."

Lennie beamed. "That's what this is all about, right?" she said. "Helping the kids."

"… Right," Kerry said.

"Well, thank you again for coming," Lennie said, wrap-ping up. "And, listen, if there's anything at all we can do—"

"No, no, you've already done so much," Kerry gushed, still clinging to Lennie's hand. "The latest draft of the bill—it's incredible. Those aggressive anti-fraud provisions are really going to make a difference for people."

Lennie frowned, which Thom could tell was confusion—she never had been particularly detail oriented when it came to policy. He jumped in as they finally dropped hands. "Yes, we're very pleased with the latest draft. The governor's been taking meetings all week on those fraud provisions. Speak-ing of which, Kerry, there's someone else I want to intro-duce you to here," Thom said. "Clay, can you take Kerry to Delegate Gordon?"

Clay sighed and tugged on Kerry's elbow. "Uh, okay," she

said, looking uncertain. "But thank you so much, Thom! And it was lovely to see you again, Madam Governor."

Thom sighed. *Believers.*

Lennie downed her cocktail as soon as she was gone. "What was that about?"

"The bill?" he reminded her. "Student loan reform? Kids like her will get thousands of dollars back in reined-in interest and fees."

"I remember that much, Thomas," Lennie said. "What was she saying about the latest draft?"

"Don't worry about it," Thom said. "There's enough money on both sides of the aisle for it to get out of committee." Thom had ensured that the bill, in addition to adding tough anti-fraud language for Kerry's coalition, also included a quiet little provision that would jack up so-called swipe fees, the fees charged every time a credit card was used in retail. Credit card companies were poised to make huge profits if the bill passed. Coincidentally, Lennie's portfolio contained significant investments in credit card companies and their corporate backers. So did most of her donors, and her colleagues up and down the ticket.

Essentially, the bill would endear him to Lennie, grease the donors, *and* thrill the base. Wheeling and dealing this effectively before noon made Thom hard.

Then he glanced across the room and saw Clay, who was standing by the punch bowl and making finger guns at someone across the room who probably didn't exist. Thom ground his teeth. Clay was obvious and eager and so basic it made him want to weep. It was infuriating how out of step he was with every other aspect of Thom's perfect life.

"If you say so," Lennie said. Clay spotted Thom looking and waved.

Then Lennie grabbed Thom's sleeve. "Crap, it's Wayne. Get me out of here."

Wayne Stentich was Speaker of the California State Assembly and a perennial pain in Lennie's ass. They battled over legislation constantly, and traded off leaking menacing rumors about each other to their respective friendly political blogs of choice. Wayne had all the charm of a used car salesman, and the looks to match.

He approached Thom with an enthusiastic, greasy grin. "Hey, Tommy, how's tricks?" Thom forced himself to smile at the nickname and shook Wayne's damp hand. Lennie had melted back into the crowd with Thom's help. "I see we've missed our lovely governor."

"A lot on her plate today, sir," Thom said. "I'll give her your regards."

"Oh, please do. Speaking of which," Wayne said, "I hear felicitations are in order. The whole town's talking about your news." He smirked. "Such great timing, for your…secret love to blossom."

Thom went cold. This was exactly what he'd been worried about—people suspecting that his and Clay's "relationship" had been faked to distract from Lennie's gaffe. The timing was too much of a coincidence.

But there was no way Wayne had proof. "I'm not sure what you mean," Thom said, maintaining a relaxed grin.

"Come now, Tommy boy," Wayne said, coughing out a laugh. "We're men of the world, aren't we? Even if men in my day weren't, quite, ah…"

He trailed off, looking distracted by something. Thom turned, and realized that he'd been caught by the same thing Thom had—the sight of Clay by the punch bowl, looking juvenile and embarrassing. Humiliation burned under his skin.

A second later, however, he realized something. "Yes," he said tentatively. "My Clay is very special."

Wayne looked uncomfortable. "I didn't know you were so tenderhearted, Tommy."

But he was too uncertain to be threatening. Uncertain, Thom realized, whether to trust the instinct that Thom was playing him, and the relationship was a hoax, or to trust the instinct that *no one* would associate themselves with Clay unless they had to.

Clay was so completely obnoxious that it actually made people *less* convinced that Thom was conning them. The uncertainty meant that Wayne couldn't be sure which strategy to take. He wouldn't want to railroad Thom if he were genuine or underestimate him if he were scheming.

Somehow, Thom had found himself in Schrödinger's Relationship. It was perfect.

"What can I say?" he told Wayne with a smile. "I'm a softie."

Before he could respond, Thom gave Wayne a short nod and strolled across the room to Clay. He took the glass he'd been holding from his hand and put it on the bar without a word. "Thom—uh, what?" Clay asked, as Thom crowded in close.

"Look like we're having a moment," Thom murmured to him, straightening Clay's tie.

Clay glanced down at Thom's hands working his collar, then back at Thom. "What? Why?"

"Too complicated to explain," he said. Leaning up as if to whisper in Clay's ear, he glanced at Wayne and saw him frowning in their direction.

"Just trust me," Thom whispered, "it'll help Lennie." He lowered back down, and took one of Clay's hands and brought it up between them.

"Uh," Clay said, "okay."

Thom was surprised—Clay didn't offer a single argument or snotty reply. Though he was obviously uncomfortable, he tried to play along with Thom's efforts to unbalance Wayne—gazing at Thom dopily as he played with Clay's long fingers. "Good," Thom murmured.

In the corner of his eye, Thom saw Wayne shake his head and walk away. Thom smiled, and experienced the odd sensation of being grateful to his fake relationship—and to Clay—for having netted him a win.

"Did it work?" Clay asked, eyes still locked on his. Though he clearly had no idea what was going on, he seemed intensely invested already.

Thom didn't know why he was so surprised. Clay may have been bratty and obnoxious, but he'd always been a team player. Still, for some reason this moment felt like the first time that he and Clay had really been on the same team.

Thom shrugged. "Maybe. You're not bad at this, Clay. I think you might actually be useful to me."

Clay rolled his eyes, but he was blushing a little as he smiled.

★ 6 ★

Clay scowled at Felicia from across the locker room, arms deep in a musty cardboard box full of jerseys. "Why do I even have to wear a uniform?"

"It's part of the event, Clay," Felicia said, exasperated. "You're playing on the school's team."

"They're not going to have anything in my size," he muttered.

"These kids get recruited straight to the NBA," Thom said, not looking up from his phone. "They definitely have something in your size."

As the weekend drew to a close, it had become clear that Clay and Thom's fake relationship had gone from a convenient way to draw attention away from Lennie's gaffe to a full-on campaign asset in its own right. They were officially a hit—the internet was full of political junkies and other Very Online folks speculating and gossiping about them. So, as bizarre as it seemed to Clay, they were doubling down on it—Felicia had gone into a flurry of scheduling events and media appearances for them, because every post about Clay and Thom was a little more attention for Lennie and little less for Warhey. Apparently, until Lennie's big kickoff campaign announcement, *this* was how they planned to keep her in the news.

That was how Clay had gotten roped into playing in a charity basketball match at a local high school. The idea was for "ringers" to play with the kids and gin up a little publicity, with all the ticket sales going to new books and chemistry kits and junk like that. Thom was there to…watch Clay play, or something. So far he'd mostly just been annoying him.

"It's offensive," Clay said, ignoring Thom. "Basketball? Because I'm tall? That's so lazy."

"Clay, if you're one of those tall guys who sucks at sports, *please* tell us now," Felicia said.

Clay scowled into the cardboard box, pulling out a jersey and shorts that he hoped would fit. "I have an actual job, y'know," he said. "One that's not pretending to be Thom's boyfriend."

"No you don't," Thom said. "I, on the other hand, have way more important things I could be doing."

"Yeah, speaking of which, Thom," Felicia said, "we need to talk about your wardrobe."

Thom finally dropped his phone, making a comically dismayed face. "Excuse me?"

Felicia produced a garment bag as if from nowhere and removed a dark gray sweater, still in the dry cleaner cling-wrap. "I was thinking something softer," she said, eyeing the stark lines of Thom's suit. "Y'know, more…approachable."

"I don't do soft," Thom said. Though his voice dripped

with disdain, he got up and examined the sweater with a curator's eye.

"I have a brown belt to go with it," Felicia said, rummaging around in the bag.

"No," Thom said. "If I have to wear the stupid sweater, at least let me keep my belt."

She draped the brown one over his shoulder, evaluating it. "My press hit. My wardrobe."

Thom rolled his eyes and pulled the belt off his shoulder, taking the garment bag too. "Fine. It is *your* event."

Clay watched them as Thom walked into the showers to change. He and Felicia had that sparkling kind of energy that made you wonder if they'd slept together, or were about to, or just got off on acting like they might. It was the stuff sitcoms and period pieces were made of—or maybe Clay was just getting a little too in character as Thom's fake boyfriend. Annoyed with himself, he stalked into the opposite shower to change.

Before he was done, he heard Fe whistle. Clay stuck his head around the tile half-wall and saw Thom doing a little twirl for her. He did look good in the slim-fitting sweater—the gray complemented his dark hair and eyes, and just like Felicia had said, the touchable fabric made him look softer. Like the kind of guy who might actually have a personal life.

Clay scowled and emerged in his own uniform. The shorts were a little too short, the jersey a little too big, and he knew the bright purple of the school's colors made his skin look washed-out and his limbs gawky. Striking a confident pose anyway, he asked, "What about me?"

Thom and Felicia burst into laughter. "Oh, fuck you guys," Clay said.

The school was in a relatively poor neighborhood Clay had never been to before. Though the building itself seemed older and neglected, the basketball court was bright and cheery, and the stands were packed with the kids' family and friends. As they walked onto the court, Clay was surprised to see a few people who looked like journalists wedged into a corner—apparently Felicia had done her job.

Even more surprisingly, a half dozen people streamed out of the stands once Clay emerged from the locker room, surrounding him and Thom. They shouted questions and shoved their phones in Clay's face, almost like a low-key version of a celebrity-obsessed mob. He glanced at Thom, who seemed just as surprised as he was.

"Can I get a selfie?" one student asked, arm already cocked to the requisite angle. Across the court, Felicia looked like she might burst with joy.

"Sure," Thom answered, though he sounded queasy.

They arranged themselves behind the girl, but she only scowled at them. "Get closer," she chided, and glanced pointedly at the screen showing her face, Thom's torso, and Clay's legs.

"Right," Thom said, and stepped closer, tucking his chin over her neck. The girl giggled and blushed, and Clay gritted his teeth and crowded in on her other side.

She pasted on a brilliant smile and hit the button, and instantly dozens of other phones came out as the rest demanded their picture. There were a few awkward ones at first as they struggled to nail the pose, but then Thom took initiative. He snaked his arm around Clay's waist, taking advantage of being shorter to tuck himself against Clay with Clay's arm over his shoulders, so there was a perfect space for a student to dart between them to take a picture. It just meant they had to stay glued together as person after person ducked in.

Clay tried to focus on the students, who were smiling and chatty and seemed nice enough. Thom's fingers shifted impatiently on Clay's hip, and his shoulder felt hot under Clay's palm.

He was relieved when an older guy with an air of authority waded into the crowd, dispersing the students with a few stern reprimands. He offered Clay a hand and said, "Jonas Harold, nice to meet you."

This must've been the principal—a nerdy-looking guy brimming with do-gooder energy. Clay and Thom introduced themselves. "Glad to see you're suited up," Jonas said, nodding at his uniform. "I'll introduce you to the others."

"The others?" Clay asked.

"The other 'ringers,'" Jonas said.

"Oh," Clay said, finally noticing that Jonas was also wearing one of the school's jerseys. "There are other charity players?"

"Of…course," Jonas said, now squinting at Clay. "You thought you were going to be the only adult? Playing on one student team…against another?"

"Uh," Clay said. Two more people, also in jerseys, had come to stand by the principal. "No, of course not."

"Uh-huh," Jonas said doubtfully. "At any rate, this is Councilman Chang, and Mia Reynolds." Clay recognized the woman from the local news, and Thom already seemed to know the councilman. "Clay, I'll play with you, and they'll be with the other team."

"Awesome," Clay said, grinning. "Get ready to eat some pavement."

The others' smiles wavered. "For the kids," Jonas said uncertainly.

Clay glanced at Thom, only to find that he'd already weaved his way across the auditorium, sitting in the stands with Felicia.

Clay followed along as Jonas directed him where to stand

on the court, and then the principal strode up on a little platform and officially started the event, thanking everyone for coming and talking about how the money would be spent. The speech went on for a good long while, and eventually Clay noticed a basketball lying just a few feet away, and picked it up to give it an experimental dribble. It was a little louder than he'd expected, and Jonas turned back to look at him midspeech, startled, but continued on without saying anything. From the stands, Felicia glared at him. He rolled his eyes and kicked the ball away.

After the speech, the game got going. Clay had expected it to be a chore—being a tall kid meant getting prodded into all kinds of athletic activity whether you wanted to or not, and his teen years had left him with an aversion to sports. Still, once the stupid high school kids stole the ball from him twice in the first ten minutes, his competitive edge won out over his apathy, and he started playing more seriously. Eventually his muscles loosened up, he leaned into the game, and the kids cheered when he caught a quick pass and scored. He grinned and traded high fives with two of them. By halftime, his team was ahead.

Felicia, in the locker room, was unimpressed. "What the fuck was with that dribble during the principal's speech? Are you twelve?"

"How about *Thank you, Clay, for being awesome at basketball*?" he demanded.

"The kids are awesome," she said. "*You're* here to make good press, not win a game."

"Listen to Fe, Clay," Thom said dully, looking at his phone.

"And you," Felicia snapped, snatching the phone out of his hands. "Put this goddamn thing away! You're supposed to be rooting for your boyfriend, not checking Twitter."

Clay felt a bizarre stab of wounded pride at the thought

that Thom hadn't been watching him. "Hey, c'mon!" Thom protested. "Okay, I'll check it less, but I need my phone!"

"I'm running this event. You're *cast* today," she taunted him. "I'm crew. Do what you're told. Be pretty for the newsmen."

Thom pouted dramatically, and Clay twitched with irritation once again. Here he was, sweating his ass off doing actual work, and Thom was being a whiny baby because he couldn't ignore Clay to fuck around online. He whipped off his jersey and emptied a water bottle over his head, scrubbing his hair and chest dry with a hand towel. Without his phone to look at, Thom stared at Clay as he looked around for a fresh jersey.

"Ready?" Felicia asked.

Once he was on the court again, Clay couldn't help glancing at Thom. Even without his phone, he didn't exactly seem like he was paying attention to the game. As Clay watched, he leaned close to Felicia to whisper something.

He let his eyes linger on Thom a second too long and nearly plowed into a student, who promptly stole the ball and ran it up the court to score.

Clay barely held in an explosive curse—his turnover had knocked them out of the lead. Of course, *now* Thom was watching. Clay shook his head and took the ball again, determined to school these teens.

There were less than five minutes left on the clock. For the first four, they traded points back and forth. Clay tried to keep his focus on the game, but he was startled at one point to hear Thom chant, "C'mon, Clay!" from the sidelines, clapping loudly. *Just doing his job*, Clay reminded himself. *He's supposed to be cheering for me.*

He still couldn't keep himself from glancing at the stands as he made his way across the court. Thom was definitely watching him now—he was sitting forward, his elbows on his knees. But oddly, there was a small frown on his face, as if he was still distracted by something. His focus was wholly on Clay, his eyes intent, but he still seemed distant, as if something he saw surprised him.

Either way, Thom was watching, so Clay forced himself to concentrate on the game. The score was even. For a moment it seemed like it might end on a tie, but then the stupid local news reporter drove through Clay's team and scored.

This time he didn't hold back a loud *"Fuck!"* A few of the kids giggled, and on the sidelines, Felicia glared at him thunderously. Thom had his head down, a hand over his mouth, and his shoulders were shaking.

"Mr. Parker," the principal said sternly.

"Yeah, sorry, whatever," Clay muttered, still fuming. His team was down two, with only seconds left.

When the game started again, one of the students on Clay's team had the ball, but he was being mobbed by other players. Clay jogged across the court and yelled for the kid to pass to him. Looking desperate, the student passed him the ball, and Clay took a wide shot from just past the three-point line.

It sank in right before the buzzer.

The crowd erupted in cheers. Clay felt himself grinning from ear to ear. His team mobbed him, and the principal shook his hand. Clay laughed as the crowd carried him off the court and over to the stands, to the klatch of eager journalists and adoring students, and to Thom.

Thom seemed just as swept up in it as everyone else, grinning widely, clapping and cheering. He'd gotten to his feet, and when Clay reached them Thom laughed and wrapped him in a quick, jubilant hug. When he pulled back, though, Thom's smile had faded. They'd both realized at the same time what came next.

It was what the moment called for, what a real couple would do. Still, it had never really occurred to Clay that this fake-relationship crap would involve actually *kissing* Thom Morgan.

The crowd was still roaring its approval of the win. Clay glanced at Thom's lips, and felt nearly unbalanced by the sharp sensation of being *seen*—the pressure of a hundred eyes all focused on them. Luckily, Thom seemed more resigned to the inevitable than Clay, and with a determined look, he drew close again.

And it was…just a kiss. Thom's lips were soft and warm, but he himself was stiff, which Clay supposed was to be expected of a fake kiss. He took a deep breath and forced himself not to break away too soon. He felt keenly aware of his eyes being closed, and wondered what they looked like. The crowd was *woo*ing them. Thom's stubble scraped his chin. He smelled nice. *Of course he smelled nice.*

Then Thom shifted against him. It was just a small change, bringing them slightly closer together, their lips meeting at a slightly different angle—but it made heat steal over Clay's skin in uneven bursts, matching his thudding heart. Thom sucked in a breath and grabbed a fistful of Clay's jersey, dragging him closer to kiss him again, openmouthed and deep. There was something dark in the way Thom was kissing him, like thunderclouds stealing over his thoughts, slow and hot and electric. He put his hands on Thom's waist for balance, and found that he couldn't stop his fingers from twitching, digging into the soft flesh there. Thom's hands slid across his face and into his hair, and everything else shuddered to a stop.

Until Thom abruptly pulled back. All at once, Clay heard a lot of giggling around them from the kids.

He stood there dumbly until Felicia steered them toward all the people Clay still had to thank and glad-hand before they left the event. Thom was by his side through all of it, and was still standing close to Clay when he casually wiped at his lip. No one else would have likely noticed the gesture, but to Clay, it was unmistakable—he wanted to erase the kiss. Clay understood; his thoughts were a jumble, and he would have gladly erased the last few minutes if he could. He was sure he looked ridiculous, red-faced from the game and hair mussed from Thom's hands.

But when Clay met Thom's eyes, he didn't look annoyed or dismissive. He looked satisfied—like how he'd looked at the breakfast, when he'd leaned up toward Clay, telling him to play along with his romantic nonsense. When he'd whispered in that low, secret voice, *Trust me.*

★ 7 ★

Thom went back to the office as soon as the basketball game was over. The lights were off and the place was deathly still, but there was always more work to do. Lennie's student loans bill would be going into markup soon, and if he didn't keep track of every development, every horse trade, every amendment that could potentially be offered and its implications for the constellation of interest groups the campaign relied on, he'd get totally blindsided.

And honestly, it gave him that same sore-but-satisfied feeling as a good workout, staying at the office past midnight every night, reading tip sheets and scanning Twitter and spitballing phrases to use in the stump speech or the next social media push. He needed his eyes and ears and influence on every part of Lennie's operation and as much of the broader political world as he could manage. It was exhausting. It was what he lived for.

Plus, it helped keep his mind off the slow-motion car wreck that was his "relationship" with Clay.

That, and the kiss.

"Y'know, staying late every night like this makes you look like an asshole," Felicia said, leaning against the door frame of his office. Felicia was one of those rare creatures who looked *better* under sallow fluorescent office lights at—he glanced at the clock—12:14 a.m. There were no dark circles under her eyes, and her skin still glowed. Maybe it was how she did her makeup. Or maybe it was because she was made of the same stuff as Thom—she thrived under pressure too.

She did, however, have her bag on her shoulder. Ah, so she was leaving and felt guilty. He swiveled in his chair to face her and shrugged. "Probably fair."

There was a smile lingering on her lips. That wasn't good for his guilt theory. "Wanna know what I've been working on?"

"Do I?"

She crossed the room and handed him her phone. He opened it easily—too easily. "No password?" he asked.

"Nothing bad on there."

Thom snorted. "Everyone's got something bad on their phone."

Then he saw what was on her screen, and grimaced. It was news coverage of their day at the basketball game, disseminated far more widely than he'd been expecting. "You did this?" he asked tightly.

"Mmm-hmm," she said, leaning against his desk. "Wasn't as hard as I thought it'd be either, getting reporters to bite."

Thom scrolled through the stories, trying not to listen. Admittedly, his fake relationship with Clay was doing exactly what it was supposed to do: each article was another positive media point for Lennie. Lifestyle shit like this—people interested in the narrative, instead of the policy—it was price-less for a campaign. That's what went viral, what got people invested. Detailed white papers were fine and all, but if they could become a cultural touchstone? That was the goose that would shit gold for the rest of Thom's career.

And the relationship was doing all that because, well—it had been a good event today. Community charity, bit of a sports angle, and everyone's brand-new politics 'ship. The pictures had come out surprisingly well. Something about his being in that stupid sweater and Clay in his basketball gear, the bright sunny day, the kids all grinning behind them—Christ, it could've been a campaign ad, it was so wholesome-yet-woke.

"Yup, you really did me a favor," Felicia said, twisting the knife. "I mean, if *I'd* had to kiss Clay, I don't know that you would've had such a good picture to work with."

And there it was. He tossed her phone onto the desk, as if he couldn't care less about the pictures. In fact, they were already seared onto his brain: Clay looking almost stunned, his eyes closed and his expression soft as Thom had leaned up against him, holding Clay's face in his hands.

He decided to go on the offensive. "What are you, twelve? Were we playing seven minutes in heaven?"

"So kissing Clay was heaven?"

"Wow. Never took you for a romantic, Fe."

"So you're saying this—" she held the phone facing him "—was one hundred percent fake."

He paused for just a fraction of a second too long.

Felicia collapsed into laughter.

"How did you know?" Thom demanded.

She sniffed and caught her breath, saying solemnly, "I didn't, until right now."

"Oh, fuck you."

She laughed again. "Okay, I could tell at the time. You blushed!"

"No, I didn't!" He could feel his face heating even as he said it, but Thom Morgan didn't blush, so it must have been a rugged, masculine flush of rage.

She nodded, pressing her phone to her lips to keep more giggles in. "Yes you did! Just for a second. Just a *tiny* bit."

"You're so full of shit."

"And I thought, anything that would make the great Thom Morgan blush—"

"Shut up."

"Must've been some kiss—"

"Shut *up*."

"Who would've thought, Clay Parker, a good kisser—"

"He was *not*," Thom said emphatically. That was the one thing he could say for certain—Clay wasn't a particularly good kisser.

Granted, he'd been expecting much worse. It was Clay, after all, and when they'd found themselves staring at each other after the game, Clay all sweaty and dumbfounded, Thom had been mildly horrified at the prospect of kissing him. But he was a professional, so he'd sucked it up and did what needed to be done.

And it hadn't been that bad. To Thom's surprise, there'd been no stabbing tongue or Hoover-like suction. There hadn't been any aggression on Clay's part; he'd let Thom take the lead. His lips were warm and dry. He'd smelled sweaty from the game, but in a fresh, inoffensive way. He'd still been breathing a little heavily.

It'd taken Thom a moment to realize that they were just... standing there. Kissing hesitantly, stilted, when they needed to convince the world that they were boyfriends celebrating after a game-winning shot. So he'd grabbed Clay and kissed him like he meant it. Clay's skin had still been hot from the game, and his frame was less gangly than Thom had been expecting—when he pressed himself closer, he found firm, flat muscle. Clay's arms had gone around him, clumsy but warm. The crowd had loved it.

So no, it hadn't been awful. But Clay definitely wasn't an amazing kisser.

That's what was so strange. It had just been a regular, run-of-the-mill kiss—an awkward, fake kiss, even. But when Clay's mouth had opened under Thom's, it had set off a flicker of heat at the base of his skull, like a spark catching in the dry grass on a blistering summer day.

He scratched the back of his neck uncomfortably. Felicia's laughter had subsided into what was, for her, a kind smile. "Seriously, Thom," she said. "Uh—if you need to, like… talk about anything…"

He frowned at her. "Talk?"

"Um," she said. "I mean, you…kissed a guy today? And, apparently liked it? So…not to go all Katy Perry on you, but—"

"Oh, Jesus." He pressed his fingers into his shut eyes, mortified. "You don't need to read me the whole *It Gets Better* script, Fe."

"Excuse me for trying to be decent for once," she said drily. "By all means, be a dick."

"You think I'm having some sexuality crisis?" he demanded. "Apparently I'm bi-curious or whatever. Who cares?"

And honestly, Thom did not. He'd never cared whether someone was gay or straight, just ally or enemy. He lived in one of the most liberal cities on the planet, and he had no unenlightened family to worry about disappointing. It didn't change anything about his sex life to add a new source of attraction to the mix—it was less a terrifying new reality than something to explore, like a type of food he'd never tried. Of note, but not a game changer. Thom knew this was supposed to be the sort of thing one agonized over, but he genuinely didn't have the time or interest.

Felicia looked surprised, but also calculating. "Okay," she said, drawing out the word. "So, it's not being attracted to men that's bothering you. It was...kissing Clay?"

"Would *you* want to kiss Clay?"

Felicia didn't answer. She stared at him, running odds behind her eyes.

"What," he said flatly.

She chewed her lip for a minute, uncharacteristically hesitant, before saying, "Just be careful, Thom. Clay's not like us. Well, he's not like you."

"What does that mean?" he asked.

"Clay's ugly on the outside," Felicia said. "Not his looks, I mean, his personality—he's braggy and childish and bro-y. It's annoying as shit, but ultimately harmless. You and me, we wear our ugly on the inside. I try to use mine to help people. But you..."

Thom sighed. This was exactly why nothing had ever happened between him and Felicia, and why nothing ever would. He was grateful for the reminder—Felicia was beautiful and smart and devious, and every once in a while he needed to remember why it would never work.

Thom didn't want a girl who wanted to save him. Maybe, at most, a girl who dimly fantasized about it. Not one who'd actually say it to his face.

"I think you've been watching too many of those Netflix rom-coms," he told her.

She ignored him. "Just make sure Clay knows."

"Knows what?"

"That if someone ends up hurt," she said, "it's going to be him."

Thom scoffed. "Wow, Felicia. Profound."

"Okay, Thom," Felicia said, sliding her phone into her bag and turning her back on him.

He didn't look away from his screen as she left.

★ 8 ★

Clay wished he didn't know what Thom's tongue felt like. That was not something he had ever wanted or needed to know.

Yeah, obviously Thom was hot, but Clay had never really been into him. He was an asshole. He was full of himself. And he was one of those effortlessly hot guys Clay usually scorned anyway. His looks were too neatly packaged, and he was too smarmy about it.

But the stupid kiss had ruined everything. It was bad enough just having to pretend to be Thom's boyfriend. Now that he'd kissed him, even boring work meetings carried an extra layer of irritation: having to focus to avoid drifting off looking at the flat shape of his lower lip, his freckles and the soft black waves of his hair, thinking about how good he'd smelled that day, and the feel of the pads of his fingers on Clay's face.

"Clay," Thom snapped.

"What?" he said, throwing a pen at him from across the room. Angry was better than distracted and horny, he figured.

"What the—?" Thom glanced incredulously at the pen on the floor. "I said, what do you think?"

"Of what?" Clay asked. At least two people sighed.

"Felicia's idea," Thom bit out. "To put us on a podcast."

Clay's heart leaped. Ever since their "relationship" had become a thing, he and Thom had ascended to the level of at least midtier local celebrity, but even he was surprised they were ready to make the jump to podcasts so soon. "Are you serious? What—which one? *Pod Save America? The Daily?*" He sucked in a nervous breath. *"FiveThirtyEight?"*

"Uh—"

"None of them, you idiot," Felicia answered, leaning back in her chair. "A local show."

"Oh," Clay said. Definitely midtier local celebrity, then. "That still sounds cool."

"So glad you approve," Thom said witheringly. He waved at the press interns. "Get us briefing materials for this show."

They jumped at the chance to get out of the meeting, taking the rest of the press staff with them. "Good," Felicia said as she gathered her things. "This will be a good next step for your, ah, public profile."

Clay grimaced. Podcasts were cool; having to pretend to be with Thom was not. "So, I guess this is working? Y'know— *us*?" he asked, using air quotes.

"Gross," Thom said. "And, yeah, it's fucking working. Didn't you see the *Vulture* thing?"

"The what?"

Felicia handed him her phone, which opened to a *Vulture* article titled "Ten Clay/Thom Fanfics You Need to Read Right Now."

Clay blushed and handed it back to her. The only fanfic

he'd ever read had involved tentacles and had scarred him for life. Also he might've downloaded a copy of it, whatever. "People are wild about us, for some reason," Thom said, sounding bored. "This should keep it going."

"By all means, sound like a martyr," Felicia said with a sigh. "I do both your jobs whenever you run off to play house."

An intern stuck her head back into the room. "We're all set for tomorrow, nine a.m."

"Wait, we're doing this tomorrow?" Thom demanded.

"It's a local show," Felicia said, shrugging. "They have city councilmen they could interview every week. We had to jump at the slot."

"*We* had to pitch *them*?" Thom asked.

"Don't worry, you two are still trending," Felicia said. "But podcasts are hot right now."

Clay nodded vigorously. Thom rolled his eyes.

"So I'd get cracking," Felicia added.

"On prep?" Thom said. "Felicia, I do media hits all the time." To Clay, he said, "Let me do all the talking."

Before Clay could yell at him, Felicia said, "Not 'Press Hits 101,' jackass. You have to prep for your first interview as a couple."

"We did the farmers market as a couple," Thom said. "The breakfast, the basketball game…"

"Those weren't interviews. You barely spoke to anyone, you just had to look all couple-y in public," Felicia said. "This time, you'll get some policy questions, sure, but they'll also expect more banter. Can you answer basic questions about this thing? How you got together? What you do for fun?" She glanced between them dubiously. "Do you know…anything? About each other?"

90

Thom glanced at Clay uncertainly. Clay gave him the same look in return.

Felicia checked the time on her phone. "I'd get started."

They agreed to meet at the office at eight the next morning, right before the taping of the show. It was basically still dark outside, so Clay did what any proper Massachusetts boy would do and stopped by the Dunkin' by his apartment to get the biggest iced coffee they had.

Thom scoffed at it when Clay showed up at the office, a Starbucks cup in his own hand. "Dunkin'? Really?"

"Starbucks is only cool to back-half millennials," Clay said.

"Back-half what?" Thom asked.

"Y'know," Clay said, putting his stuff down at his desk. "Older millennials. The ones born in…" He paused for dramatic effect, and then said, "The eighties."

Thom's face darkened, and Clay grinned to see that his shot had hit. As Thom sat in the chair across from Clay's desk, he heard him mutter something that sounded like *'89, dipshit.* "What was that?" he asked.

"So. This podcast," Thom said, putting his shiny black shoes up on Clay's desk in a blatant sign of disrespect.

Amiably choosing to move past it, Clay said, "Yeah, I had some ideas."

"No need," Thom replied, fishing something out of his briefcase and handing it to Clay. "I've got it all figured out, you just need to memorize this before they get here."

Thom handed him an honest-to-god paper notepad, white with neat blue lines and much messier black handwriting all over it. "What?" Clay asked. "What is this?"

"I wrote it all out," Thom said, smoothing down his tie smugly. "Our first date, our anniversary, cute dumb stories we can tell. The works."

"On paper?" Clay asked dubiously.

"Are you kidding? We can't risk people figuring out that this is fake," Thom said. "We've gotta be leak-proof. That means paper."

Clay couldn't even bother responding to how stupid that was. Instead, glancing at everything Thom had already scrawled down about their fake relationship, he said, "I thought we were supposed to figure this stuff out together."

"I know what plays well, and this will play well."

Clay stared at him. Eventually, Thom asked, "What?"

"Nothing," Clay said, looking back down at the notepad. "You just forgot to doodle *Mr. Thomas Parker* in the corner surrounded by hearts."

"Shut up," Thom said. It looked like he might have been blushing a little, but that was probably just the shit lighting in the office so early in the morning.

"Fine," Clay said, sighing as he tried to decipher Thom's chicken scratch. "Our first date was…drinks at… Pot Karen?"

"Apotekeren," Thom corrected. "It's a bar, a nice one. Anderson Cooper was there last month."

"I don't go drinking at places I can't pronounce," Clay said.

"And where do you take guys on a first date?" Thom asked. "Bitcoin convention? Video game tournament?"

Clay could feel his own face light up.

"No, you did not take me to a video game tournament," Thom said sternly. "Jesus, Clay."

"Dave & Busters?" he asked hopefully.

"Ew," Thom said with emphasis. After a moment he waved his hand and said, "Let's just say a bar. We don't need to specify one that's too low-rent for me to be seen at or too nice for you to understand the drink menu."

Clay rolled his eyes and scanned the notepad again. Frowning, he pointed to something. "What does this say?"

Thom leaned over to squint at it in the low light, bringing his face so close to Clay's thumb on the edge of the paper that he could feel the warmth of his breath. It made his pulse pick up slightly. He scowled and shook himself a little, willing it away.

"Whose place do we stay at," Thom recited.

And Clay was going to march right past *those* mental images.

"Mine, obviously," Thom added.

"Why obviously?" Clay asked with a scowl.

"My place is nicer."

"You've never seen my place!"

"I make more money," Thom said. "And I have better taste."

"Oh yeah," Clay said. "Because that's what we're doing when we're there—admiring your *taste*."

Thom raised an eyebrow, and Clay cursed himself internally. What did he care who stayed where in the course of their fake relationship? And why had his objection sounded more like flirting than arguing?

"Fine," Thom said. "They're not gonna ask us that anyway." He snatched the notepad away from Clay, scribbling corrections onto it.

Clay shifted uncomfortably. "What about the other stuff? Like…personal stuff?"

"What do you mean?" Thom asked, his voice muffled with his pen poking out the side of his mouth.

"Like, I don't know," Clay said. "How'd you get into politics?"

"I was a press intern on a mayoral race. And *you*," he said, pointing with his pen, "were purchased by Lennie so we could plant a piece in *Politico* about how tech-savvy her yet-unannounced campaign will be." He grinned. "I told 'em no comment."

"I meant *why*," Clay said, "asshole."

"Oh." Thom shrugged. "I dunno."

Clay ground his teeth. No douchey rehearsed speech about how *I'm in this for the right reasons*? Apparently Clay didn't even merit Thom's full bullshit charm offensive. It was like he was trapped in a bubble around Thom, forced to watch him dazzle and distract the rest of the world, while Clay saw his true self—a hollow, manufactured jerk. Who he had to kiss.

"Bullshit you don't know," Clay muttered. "You were probably a narcissistic sociopath at age eight."

Thom blinked at him, but rather than snapping back with some witty retort, he just sat there with sort of a shuttered look on his face.

Clay shook his head as a new question occurred to him. "What about like—when did we say *I love you*?"

"Please," Thom scoffed, looking unimpressed. "I don't even say that in my real relationships."

"What real relationships," Clay said under his breath.

"Good point," Thom said brightly. "You'd obviously be jealous about the many, many girls I dated before you, so if they ask, we can use that to show like, look, we have fights, we're a normal couple."

"We're a—*what*?" Clay said, sitting up in his chair. "They're not gonna ask us stuff like that!"

"What then?"

"I don't know." Clay shrugged helplessly. "Have I met your family?"

That shuttered look returned to Thom's face. "No."

Clay opened his mouth, but before he could ask a follow-up, Thom abruptly stood from the desk. "They're almost here, and I need more coffee," he said, staring down into his empty Starbucks cup before tossing it in the trash.

Clay hurried after him as he strode into the kitchen. Thom fiddled with the Keurig while Clay leaned against the countertop, thinking about something Thom had said to him at the state legislature breakfast. "Do you really not talk to your parents a lot?"

Thom didn't look up from his perusal of the office's K-Cup selection. "Sure."

"Huh. Are they not really into politics?"

"Clay—" Thom started, sounding annoyed.

"I need to know for the podcast," he shouted, throwing his hands in the air. "You can't kneecap me on something as basic as *family*."

Thom sighed, a cutoff, frustrated noise. "My family is... normal. Boring. They live in the suburbs—cul-de-sacs, white picket fence, that whole thing. They have cookouts and love baseball. And my brother literally has two-point-five kids. One on the way."

"You have a brother?" Clay asked. It was hard enough to picture Thom doing regular human things, much less two of them.

Thom made a dismissive noise. "Theo. He lives back home, just down the block from my parents."

"So why don't you talk to them?"

"Do I look like a suburbs and cookouts kind of guy?" Clay shrugged, conceding the point. "I couldn't wait to get out of there. But Theo, he loves it. He actually runs the local Little League. I mean—Jesus." Thom shook his head like he was mystified by it, then returned his careful focus to the coffee machine. "They're happy with him. They don't need me."

Clay didn't say anything. Thom slid his K-Cup of choice into the Keurig and hit the start button, but the familiar whirring and whooshing didn't start. The screen was blinking insistently, and Thom sighed again, harsher this time, and gave the machine a shove. It made an unhappy noise, and the screen blinked more rapidly. Thom hissed through his teeth, "You've gotta be kidding me."

He seemed more irritated than an uncooperative coffee machine would merit. "Thom—"

"Just—" He made a choppy *stop* motion at him. "I just need some more fucking caffeine if this day is going to be bearable."

Clay watched as the machine spiraled further and further downhill the more Thom wrestled with it. "But if you just—"

"I got it." He shoved at the water tank, jabbed at the screen, and then reached for the tank again.

"Oh my god," Clay snapped, and grabbed his hand to stop him before he made it worse.

His skin was startlingly warm, jolting him to a halt. He'd only meant to stop Thom's flailing, but now he could feel his palm under his fingertips, the fine articulation of his knuckles and tendons. Thom's eyes shot to Clay's, and a tense, silent moment passed as neither of them moved.

Then Clay yanked his hand away and cleared his throat. "Uh," he said, "you just have to—here."

Gingerly, he stepped behind Thom to reach the other side of the machine, stretching his arm out to tap at it. But rather than sidle away from Clay as he was expecting, Thom stayed right where he was. Clay ended up with his arms on each side of Thom as he fixed the machine, prickling awareness creeping over him as the heat from Thom's body sank into his chest and his arms. He was careful not to touch him, but the sleeve of his shirt brushed the inside of Clay's elbow as he worked on the machine, and a few strands of his hair tickled his chin. In his peripheral vision, he could see the nape of Thom's neck.

Finally, the machine started spitting out coffee. Clay dropped his arms and backed up, acutely aware of how cold he felt as he stepped away.

"Great. Thanks," Thom said gruffly.

"No problem," Clay said.

They fell silent again. Over the rim of Thom's coffee cup, steam started rising.

★ 9 ★

When Thom arrived at work on Tuesday, Kerry Pham was waiting in his office. People showing up at his office without an appointment was always a bad thing.

He gave her a wide smile. "Kerry! So great to see you. How are you doing?"

"I'm well, Thom," she said, smiling uncomfortably. Civilians always had such terrible poker faces. "And you?"

"I'm great," he said, sitting down. "What can I do for you?"

"Well," she said, "I saw the article in the *LA Times*."

Thom frowned. "The food blog thing?" Some tipster had claimed to have seen Thom and Clay having a romantic dinner at one of LA's newest restaurants. They'd done no such thing, but Felicia had still clipped the item out of the actual, physical newspaper, she was so proud of how their little project was going. They were apparently so popular now that struggling restaurateurs were faking their presence to create buzz. It was like *Inception* or something—fake sightings of a fake relationship.

Obviously Thom wasn't so committed to this relationship nonsense that he'd take Clay out to a meal just on the off chance that they might be spotted by a reporter. What if no one spotted them, and he ended up just...having dinner with Clay?

He wasn't outright avoiding Clay, but he wasn't not-avoiding him either.

Things had just gotten a little weird between them lately. Thom's mind kept drifting back to that kiss at the basketball game, to the feel of Clay's body against his and Clay's hands sliding onto the small of his back. And it wasn't just the kiss. The podcast interview had gone well—great, even—but he'd been jumpy the whole time, distracted by the sense memory of Clay stepping up behind him to fix the coffee machine, his arms caging Thom in on both sides. He'd tried to focus on Clay's answers so that they'd be consistent, but he kept finding himself staring at Clay's hands instead, recalling the feeling of being caught in the cradle of his arms, and distracted by the inconvenient suggestion of all the ways they might fit together.

He snapped back into focus at the confused look on Kerry's face. "No," she was saying, "the column on the governor's student loans bill."

Oh. "Right," Thom said, clearing his throat. "I thought it was great, mostly positive—"

"It was really positive," Kerry said, shuffling through her bag and bringing out a jumbled collection of papers, including a newspaper.

"Oh, you've—got it with—" Thom began halfheartedly, but Kerry cut him off.

"The bill gets rave reviews from some teachers and advocates," Kerry said, scanning the article. "And…this guy here, who the writer calls a philanthropist, but who actually runs a hedge fund."

"Wow," Thom said. "We're really winning people over."

"Why does a hedge fund manager like our student loans bill?" Kerry asked him. Her controlled, even tone was giving him the sinking suspicion that she already knew why. "Banks won't like the debt forgiveness provisions. It's bad for business."

"Sure," Thom said, "but—"

Before he could finish, Kerry slapped another sheet of paper onto his desk. "What is this?" she asked, pointing to a highlighted paragraph.

Thom cursed internally. "It's a subsection of the bill."

"Repealing another law," she said, starting to look impatient.

"So it would seem."

"Thom," Kerry said. "C'mon. This section repeals a law limiting credit card swipe fees."

Thom nodded. "Yes, it does."

She threw her hands out to the side. "So—what is it doing in a bill about student loan reform?"

He blinked at her. "Kerry. I know you know what pork is."

"Pork is supposed to be some bridge that gets built where they don't need it," Kerry said, starting to get worked up. "But— we're going to let credit card companies jack up swipe fees?"

"Sure," Thom said, shrugging. "What's wrong with that? You're a fan of big-box stores?"

"I'm a fan of milk! And gas! And clothing!" she shouted. "Every time they raise swipe fees it's not Walmart that takes the hit, it's customers—the fee gets passed on. Basic stuff that families need gets more expensive."

"That…can happen," he allowed.

Kerry seemed to have difficulty putting words to her rage. "So this bill is going to hurt the very people it's supposed to help!"

He sighed. "Look, we crunched the numbers, Kerry. This provision only allows the swipe fees to go up by a tiny amount per transaction. Yes, that'll hit people, but it's a drop in the bucket compared to what they'll get from the debt relief. They'll still come out ahead."

"A drop in the bucket for people who already can't put food on the table?" she demanded. "They need *all the drops*, Thom!"

"This bill gives the average California community college grad 982 dollars a year back, even after accounting for the *slight* increase in cost of living due to the swipe fees," he rattled off from the private study they'd had done. "I don't feel bad about that."

"The average person?" Kerry challenged. "What about the unaverage person? The unusual case? Can you promise me no one will be worse off under this bill? That no one will go bankrupt, or lose their house?"

"I can't promise you that about any bill," Thom countered. "It's a big country. We don't pass a law for each grad who got screwed over by their for-profit school."

"But you don't have to put an unrelated corporate give-away into a bill that's supposed to help people," Kerry said. "You could *just* help people."

Thom sighed and dropped his head into his hands. Kerry's speech would have won the day in an Aaron Sorkin show, but in the real world, there was far too much money at stake to touch the swipe-fee provision. Money not just for the legislators who were about to vote the bill forward, but for Lennie's donors and for Lennie herself. It wasn't coming out.

It was unfortunate that Kerry had noticed it, but her righteous outrage wasn't as important as the bigger picture. Aside from the profits it would bring Lennie, the student loans bill was going to be the signature plank of her campaign—a sign that she could deliver for her voters, compromise and get things done. Plus, Lennie's campaign announcement was coming up quickly—even if there was political will to remove the provision, they'd never be able to do it in time to tee up the bill passing before her announcement. It couldn't be done.

So Kerry would likely be disappointed, but that didn't mean Thom had to alienate her completely. He took a deep breath and looked at her. It was a look he used often but hadn't quite perfected yet, unlike his *come hither* or *I'll kill you* looks. This one was *please understand*—it was meant to broker compromise; a compassionate, firm, gentle letdown that wouldn't create blowback. It worked about two-thirds of the time.

Kerry was determinedly in the remaining third. "Do any of these credit card companies donate to Governor Westwood?" she asked.

Thom dropped his compromise face. "A lot of people support the governor," he said coldly.

That got her to step back from his desk. She pressed a few fingers to the bridge of her nose and took a deep, rattling breath.

"Just fix it, Thom," she said. "Please?"

There were dark circles under her eyes, and her shoulders slumped as if weighted down. She looked exhausted. In a world where it made no difference to Thom's career, he would have helped her.

But there was no world where Thom's career didn't come first.

"Thanks for coming in, Kerry," he said quietly.

★ 10 ★

Clay got to the office early on Monday. He'd picked his suit that morning with care, brushed and gelled his hair into submission, and used his most formidable body spray.

He was facing his archnemesis today.

Finally, it was time for the depositions in his lawsuit against Pinpoint. The lawsuit had been going on for years now and by this point had sprawled into dozens of separate, interlocking lawsuits that his lawyer had tried to explain to him once before giving up. Clay had sued Derek first, for kicking him out of the company he'd helped found (or at least, helped Derek found). But then Pinpoint had sued him back, and these days it felt like Clay was on the being-sued side a lot more often. After the cost of all the legal fees, he wasn't sure he'd even get anything from it.

But it wasn't about the money for Clay. Derek had stolen

his company, his reputation, and what he'd thought were the best years of his life. He couldn't get those things back, but he could tell his side of the story. Set the record straight.

And depositions meant that they were finally making progress. Derek and his lawyers were scheduled to depose Clay at the office that morning. He got in so early that the only person who'd beaten him there was Felicia. After dropping his bag in his office, he paced the lobby all morning, planning the perfect cutting thing to say to Derek when he walked in.

He'd narrowed his list of devastating burns down to the top three when the elevator doors opened, and a well-dressed group stepped out, led by—*Emmy?*

"Clay," she said, pasting on a fake-friendly smile. "How are you?"

Emmy Stropko was basically Derek's secretary. She'd been a high school intern at Pinpoint when they'd founded it, and couldn't be more than twenty-one or twenty-two now, but she swanned around as if being close to Derek meant she was a senior VP or something. She had no coding experience, but her TikTok had a billion followers.

He glanced at her, the suits behind her who were clearly the lawyers, and behind them—the empty elevator. "I— where's Derek?"

Emmy laughed awkwardly, as if Clay was making a scene. "He's not coming."

"He—" Clay sputtered. *"What?"*

"Why would Derek come to this?" Emmy asked. "You're the one being deposed."

Clay felt sick. "Yeah, in my lawsuit against Derek!" he shouted.

"Actually, this is part of our lawsuit against you," Emmy said. "Hey, do you have coffee?"

"What," Clay floundered. "I mean—yes, we have a…a kitchen—"

"Great!" Emmy said, and without a word she and the lawyers brushed past him.

Clay was still gaping after them when Thom arrived. The second he stepped past the door, his gaze shot to one of Emmy's lawyers setting up a camera in the conference room. He really was a born political operative—he could probably sniff out recording devices a mile away.

Before Thom could chew out the receptionist for letting a camera be set up in his kingdom without his say-so, Clay jumped in. "It's for me."

Thom frowned at him. "For you?"

"Deposition," Clay said glumly. He couldn't believe he'd been so excited for it just minutes ago, and that Thom was witnessing it right as it crashed and burned.

Thom, however, just looked mildly confused. "Oh. Right," he said slowly. "Well. Don't answer any questions about the campaign."

Clay glared at him witheringly. "Thanks, Thom."

Thom wrinkled his nose. "Oh, god. What are you wearing?"

Before he could reply, Emmy and her cohort returned with coffee cups from the kitchen. She peered into the conference room, seemed satisfied, and asked Clay, "Are we ready to go here?"

Clay threw up his hands. "I don't see how we can be, but whatever!"

Now everyone was looking at him as if he was making a scene. Clay fumed and glared at the wall.

Then it got a million times worse. Emmy turned to Thom, pasted on a much more believable smile, and offered a hand. "This must be the famous Thom Morgan!" she said. "I've read so much about you."

If Thom were one-half of a real power couple, it might

look something like him and Emmy: the two of them equally beautiful, polished, and the picture of success. He took her offered hand with his reflexive, perfect Thom Morgan grin, and her own flirtatious smile widened in response, her cheeks dimpled and her lips full and red and perfect. Next to them, Clay felt like the office's shitty beige carpet—bland, worn, and unimpressive.

Thom glanced at him briefly before he replied, "At least some of it good, I hope. And you are?"

"Emmy Stropko. I'm with Pinpoint," she said. "These are some of our counsel."

Clay watched, nauseated, as Thom gave her a once-over. Emmy had always been pretty, but money had given her that shiny influencer prettiness that seemed impossibly chic. Her outfit screamed Silicon Valley: a black wool skirt suit, knee-high leather boots, striking matte lipstick, and a series of earrings in each ear. It was a look that said *I usually wear fraying T-shirts to work, but I'll dress up when the old economy requires it.*

Judging by the look on Thom's face, he appreciated the statement. Thom, a creature of politics, looked right at home in his crisp, formal business suits. It was only Clay who never really looked right in anything, and whose transition from Silicon Valley to LA politics had left him unsure of his footing, caught between both worlds and looking right in neither. He was acutely aware of the scuffs on his shoes.

"Well, welcome," Thom was saying. "Just don't keep Clay too long, alright?"

Emmy *snorted.*

Thom stared at her.

"Yeah, Emmy," Clay said hotly. "I have an actual *job.* But for some reason, Derek's too busy—"

"Derek has a job too, Clay. Remember?" The last word came out so smarmy that it made her real meaning perfectly clear—that Derek's job was infinitely more impressive than Clay's, because everyone expected Derek's new boss to crush Lennie in the primary. Even now, Clay apparently couldn't hold a candle to Derek. "Plus, he's still a board member for Pinpoint."

"For now," Clay challenged, but it came out hollow. Behind Emmy, the lawyers smirked at each other.

"Okay," she said, with a tone that was placating on the surface and exasperated underneath. "Why don't we get started? I don't want to deprive Governor Westwood's campaign of their *tech genius*."

Now it was unmistakable that she was mocking him, and for a moment Clay could only gape at her in disbelief. This girl used to get his coffee, and now she was who Derek sent to occupy him when he couldn't be bothered? He searched for something, anything that would serve as a good comeback, but as her lips tilted in a satisfied smirk, he felt the burn of humiliation flood through him.

Maybe he was as useless as everyone seemed to think.

"Y'know what I love about you Silicon Valley types?" Thom asked. Clay startled a little—he'd almost forgotten Thom was there.

"What's that?" Emmy asked.

"How bad you are at PR," Thom said casually. "I mean, other industries that are poisonous and deadly have at least figured out how to stay out of the spotlight. But you guys keep putting out statements about how you value everyone's privacy and you're definitely not evil, and then the next day there'll be a story about how you're vacuuming up everyone's data or fomenting violence all over the world. And for what? Oil companies are literally destroying the planet, but at least oil *does* something. No wonder everyone hates you."

Now Emmy was the one gaping. "Excuse me?"

"I'm sure you've already figured this out, but we campaign people only keep you guys around because we like it when our Wi-Fi works," Thom said, his voice never straying from the same polite tone he'd greeted her in. "You might be a big deal in Palo Alto, but you're nothing in politics. Because politics involves actual work, not going to Burning Man and billing it as a business expense. We work twenty-four seven, three sixty-five, in shitty cubicles, for government pay, because we've figured out the difference between what's trendy and what matters. You're a bunch of kids burning billionaires' money, making useless toys, thinking it means something. I do more in a day than they'll fit into your entire obituary."

Emmy stared at him, mouth open. One of the lawyers had put a hand over his heart.

"Your start-up sounds cute. Clay works for the next leader of the free world," Thom said. "Have a nice day."

Clay could only stare at him. Thom gave him a brief nod, then glanced at the conference room. "Oh, and we're gonna need that room in half an hour," he said to Emmy. "Make it quick."

"I—" Emmy protested, but Thom had already walked away.

"I need one minute," Clay said, and sprinted off after Thom. Behind him, he could hear the lawyers frantically murmuring.

Clay skidded to a stop outside Thom's office. "What was that?" he asked breathlessly.

Thom raised an eyebrow at him, already bent over a desk full of cluttered papers. "You're my boyfriend, remember?" he said lowly. "Would've looked weird if I hadn't defended you."

"Right," Clay said, his heart pounding. "Right."

He didn't even care if Thom had meant it. Thom's insults were always works of art, beautiful to behold in their own right, but this had been something even more special. That had been a classic Thom Morgan takedown, one for the ages, and it had been for *him*. He felt giddy.

He was Thom's *ally*. That turned him on way more than he cared to admit.

Thom was popping a button on his collar and loosening his tie, his fingers moving deftly. "Clay," he said. "Your deposition?"

"Right," Clay said, and left to do battle with the lawyers.

★ 11 ★

Most campaigns gave their senior staff one day off a month. Those days would disappear once Lennie's announcement kicked the campaign into high gear, but in the early days of the pre-campaign, Thom got a whole two days off each month. He didn't exactly enjoy not being in the office, but he knew that the time off was important—he could jog during the day, getting that crucial tanning/leg day synergy; he could really focus on his social media presence (always be posting, as he liked to remind Felicia); and of course, he could take meetings with other politicos and campaign types, getting the dirt on his rivals, the gossip on his friends, and fielding job offers that he was always at least half-considering.

He'd just finished a very productive day off and was waiting for his dinner to be delivered when he got a text from Felicia. Sure enough, he saw that the news was starting to hit Twitter as well—there'd been a terror attack in Europe, and his day off was over. He put a note on the door for the delivery guy to keep the food, and headed in to the office.

He ended up instead at Mahmood's, a diner across the street from the office that was a perpetual staff hangout. He found Felicia and Clay in a booth at the back. "What are we doing here?" he asked, putting a hand on one of the vinyl seat backs. Thom had been to Mahmood's before, though the last time he'd actually eaten here had been the day Lennie had chewed him out so badly for issuing the wrong draft of a press release that he'd decided to temporarily break his ban on carbs and trans fats.

Felicia and Clay had a sizable pile of each in front of them already. "Couldn't stand to be in that fucking office another minute. Plus we were hungry," Felicia said dazedly, not looking up from her computer. Clay looked equally dead eyed. His suit jacket was crumpled up beside him and his shirt-sleeves were rolled up, revealing surprisingly well-articulated forearms.

Thom cleared his throat. "Bad day?"

At the question, Clay finally looked up at him and then blinked, dumbfounded.

Thom knew he was hot. He'd been blessed with good bone structure, and he worked hard to make sure his body was just as appealing. He also knew, from having worked in suit-and-tie offices his whole life, the contrast it made to see someone for the first time in casual clothes instead. And Thom picked his casual clothes very carefully: tonight, he wore slim-fitting dark jeans, a vivid blue T-shirt that pulled over his breastbone, and a dark gray hoodie that hugged his shoulders so tight there wasn't a wrinkle to be seen.

Clay looked like he'd forgotten how to speak English.

Thom suppressed a smile as he slid into the booth next to Felicia. Clay struggled to get a sentence out, and eventually coughed and buried his head back in his work. Thom relished his own smug satisfaction, almost humming under the positive attention. He didn't even feel sorry for Clay; though he wasn't really in Thom's league, the publicity from their fake relationship had actually scared up a few Clay groupies online. More than a few, if he was being honest; some corners of the internet seemed to find Clay downright hot.

There was a time when that fact alone would have made Thom's stomach turn, but not anymore. He'd been so irritated by Clay's personality ever since meeting him that he'd let that irritation flow over onto his looks, but that wasn't really fair, he was discovering. Clay may not have been classically handsome, but when he wasn't bragging about something or grinning that terrible, shit-eating grin, he was… decent looking. Appealing. There was something plain yet engaging about him, somewhere between the bluntness of his features, his bright, focused eyes, his wide-shouldered build, and the sharpness of his smile.

As he let his gaze linger, Clay glanced up again like he could feel him looking. Their eyes locked.

Thom blinked and tried to focus on Felicia, who was finishing an explanation of what had pissed off Lennie that day, culminating in an already exhausted staff when the terror news broke. "And now we're waist-deep in Soviet bloc shit," Felicia said.

Thom frowned. "Wait, I thought it was a terror attack."

"It might have been sponsored or condoned by some separatist group," Felicia said. "And of course the president's chief foreign minister's cousin or something is a member, and—"

"Elections are coming up soon," Thom said, starting to remember.

"So we can't put out a statement until we're one hundred

percent sure we're not going to piss off someone Lennie's going to need once she's in the Sit Room," Felicia concluded.

"Shit," Thom said, pulling out his own laptop. He turned to Clay. "Why are you here?"

Clay jumped, like he hadn't actually been sure Thom could see him. "Pulling polling numbers on international relations stuff," he said. His tone was oddly tentative.

"And he's been helping me trawl Wikipedia on the eight hundred members of this guy's cabinet," Felicia said dully.

Thom shrugged and said, "Okay." His question to Clay hadn't been meant as hostile. He and Felicia may have given Clay a lot of shit, but he was still part of the team. When they were all in the foxhole—or an Iranian diner at 9:52 p.m. on a Saturday—he'd be there. Thom opened his laptop and started working.

After half an hour or so, Felicia left to take a call with some foreign policy expert. A few minutes later, Clay tapped on Thom's computer. "Look who it is," he murmured.

Thom glanced where he was nodding, and spotted an Axios blogger a few booths down from theirs nursing a coffee over his own work. For convenience, Lennie's campaign headquarters were in an office building just around the corner from city hall, which meant Mahmood's wasn't just popular with the staff, but political junkies and journalists generally.

Thom nodded. "Everyone's working late tonight."

Then a new thought occurred to him. He flipped his laptop around and got up from the booth to slide in next to Clay. "What are you doing?" Clay asked.

"Nothing, *babe*," Thom said with a wink. He glanced over at the blogger, and sure enough, the slight commotion had gotten his attention. He waved at them, and Thom waved back, then gave Clay a quick kiss on the cheek.

When he looked back at the blogger, he noted with triumph that he had his phone up, tilted to landscape for a better photo. *Always be posting.*

Clay was focused determinedly on his laptop screen, though it looked like he may have been blushing. Thom's lips tingled from the scratch of his stubble. Felicia raised an eyebrow at them when she came back, but took Thom's old seat without complaint.

Thom startled a little when Clay burst out with a loud sigh a few minutes later, hanging his head back against the vinyl seat. "This is the worst."

"Get more coffee, Clay," Felicia said.

"Ugh," Clay said, but all he did was take out his phone and slouch back in his seat, haphazardly kicking his legs out in such a way that his foot bumped up against Thom's under the table.

Thom frowned and waited a minute, but Clay's foot didn't move from its position against his. He snuck a glance at him, and found Clay staring down at his phone with a distracted, slightly stupefied expression on his face. He clearly hadn't done this on purpose. He looked like he hadn't even noticed they were touching.

Thom shook himself a little and returned to his work. He wasn't sure what the big deal was, anyway; if someone did glance under the table and saw that their feet were touching, they'd probably think nothing of it.

Or they'd think that they were dating, which was the point.

But it was weirdly distracting, having Clay's foot pressing against his, this...random point of connection between them. There was no warmth coming through Clay's shoe, but Thom's foot felt warm anyway. He was wearing relatively thin sneakers, so he could feel the firmer edge of Clay's leather oxfords digging against him.

He was not going to move his own foot. That would be like a kind of admission that this was—getting to him, somehow, when he couldn't have cared less. Clay could press his foot against Thom's, accidentally or not. It didn't matter to him at all.

His foot was tingling. He kept visualizing Clay's legs under the table, long and splayed, and recalling the sensation of Clay's stubble scraping against his lips. He wondered what Clay's knee would feel like pressed to his, what his thigh would feel like under Thom's palm.

Goddamn it, this was turning him on. What was he, fourteen? He took a deep breath and made himself read the paragraph of text on his screen, reciting the words in his head but absorbing none of the content.

After another moment, Clay readjusted his position and tucked his legs backward, still seeming completely oblivious to Thom's inner turmoil. He sighed. It was over.

His leg jiggled impatiently. His ability to concentrate on work was long gone. He was still feeling the phantom warmth where they'd touched.

He had a stupid idea.

Keeping his eyes firmly planted on his computer, he casually kicked his right foot back so that it touched Clay's. He felt him jolt a little—not a lot, but enough that he knew he'd noticed this time. He could see Clay looking at him in his peripheral vision, and kept his face totally impassive—as if he was absorbed in his work and had done this wholly by accident. He held his leg still, cocked at a strange angle to keep up the connection.

He heard Clay swallow. He shifted in his seat and looked away. And then his legs fell open, his left knee hitting Thom's.

Thom's vision blurred. Their legs were pressed together ankle to knee, denim scraping against wool. Now he could clearly feel the heat from Clay's body. He fought the urge to close his eyes.

He was fully aware of how stupid this was. He was playing footsie, for Christ's sake. He'd indulged his ridiculous, libido-soaked impulse; now it was time to shut this thing down.

Clay nudged against him slightly, creating a barely there rustle of fabric. Thom bit his lip and contemplated turning his ankle to wrap his foot around Clay's. He could see Clay's knuckles turning white on the countertop next to him.

Then Felicia's phone rang. They both jumped, but thankfully Fe didn't seem to notice, frowning at the screen as she got out of the booth to answer.

"I'm, uh, gonna get some air," Thom choked out. Clay nodded quickly, not meeting his eye.

It was refreshingly cool outside, a welcome balm to the way Thom's heart was beating uncomfortably hard in his chest. He didn't let himself glance back inside the diner at where Clay was waiting in the booth alone.

What the hell had he been doing just now? And why had Clay played along? He didn't like how much he enjoyed that particular quality of Clay's—his willingness to go along with the dumb shit Thom pulled. A cooperative Clay was certainly better than an argumentative one, but it also presented a new question for Thom, one that had been growing in size and detail in the hectic landscape of his mind, and one he'd been trying to ignore.

What would Clay be like in bed?

Would he surprise Thom as much as their kiss had? Would that spark of heat he'd felt fan into something more? What else would Clay agree to?

His newfound pliability suggested that Thom could discover the answers to those questions.

He cursed himself. A one-night stand with Clay was a

ridiculously bad idea. Even kissing him had been a terrible idea, as was their absurd faux relationship. He hated himself and mostly his libido. And he hated Clay.

The problem was, Thom had always been a fan of hate-fucking.

He shook his head and headed back into the diner. Soon after that, the Russian prime minister made a speech, and it sent their work careening in a different direction. Before long, soothing professional obligations had quieted the tumult in Thom's mind.

It was two in the morning by the time they finished their work. By that late at night, it had gone from cool to cold, even in downtown LA, and the three of them huddled on the corner outside as they waited for their Ubers. The diner's neon lights seemed to light up the air around them, bouncing off the sheen on Fe's blouse and the errant, untidy strands of Clay's hair.

Thom tried to ignore the familiarity of the setting: the crisp late-night air, the grip of sidewalk concrete beneath his shoes, the potency of waiting for rides home to arrive. The delicious uncertainty of wondering if you're about to get laid.

Thom usually loved this moment. He'd perfected his smile for it over the years, and he was an expert at deploying it, and waiting for the answering look in a woman's eyes that told him he had the green light to lean in.

It was all too easy to picture: Clay would get caught in that smile, Thom knew he would. Those bright eyes of his would grow hazy, and he'd lean closer probably without even realizing he was doing it. Thom would lean up, brush his hand against the back of Clay's neck, and kiss him more smoothly than he'd done at the game. It wouldn't be awkward or stilted this time; Thom would kiss him like he always kissed dates this time of night, a kiss designed to make sure that two rides home became one.

Instead, Clay was pacing and fidgeting in the cold, and Thom felt like an idiot.

They all took separate cars, of course. Felicia told some stupid joke just as they arrived, and Clay laughed so hard his head snapped back, a huge, dumb smile on his face.

Thom rested his head against the car seat as his Uber pulled away, and tried to quiet the *what if, what if, what if* chasing around his mind.

★ 12 ★

Clay was not what you would call a *hard worker*. He preferred working efficiently: tiny bursts of pure genius, interspersed with crucial hours of loping around the office, getting up-to-date on the office gossip, reading really important tweets, and just generally making sure he was feeling and performing at his best. Thom called this goofing off and yelled at him about it, but the system had worked out pretty well for him so far.

Occasionally, though, he changed things up. He'd had this idea a few weeks ago while working on some data sets—an idea for a new coding project. Usually his ideas for coding projects came and went, like his ideas for screenplays, or recipes he was never going to actually try. But this particular idea stuck with him, and over time it had become one of those things you pick at, like an unraveling sweater or a weird skin thing. Eventually it had led to tonight, when Clay was still in the office well past sundown, a crick in his back and dry, twinging eyes from staring at his screen for so long. But the pains of genuine hard work were worth it, because he thought he might—just might—have something.

He jumped when someone knocked on his door, and was startled when he looked up to realize just how empty and dark the office was. Thom was in the doorway, coat over his arm and an insultingly shocked look on his face. "What are *you* still doing here?"

"Uh, I work here, dick," Clay said.

"C'mon," Thom said, putting his stuff down and coming around the desk. "What are you really doing?"

"Jesus, Thom. Do you have to be an asshole all the time?"

Thom quirked an eyebrow. "Are you actually working? Your insults are even more underwhelming than usual, as if you're...tired from some sort of...work-related activity."

Clay scrubbed his face in his hands. He really *was* tired; looking away from the screen had broken the trance he'd been in, and now he could feel the day weighing on him. He hadn't zoned out while coding like that in years. "Yes," he said into his hands, "I'm really tired, because I've actually been working. You dick."

"On what?"

Clay felt a wave of nerves, but tried to sound like they were still just messing around when he said, "I'm not gonna tell you *now*."

"Oh, c'mon," Thom said, laughing and leaning down to see Clay's screen.

"Stop!" Clay said, warding him off. He was careful as he did it, though, not to touch Thom or even get close. Just having him there, leaning over his shoulder, was bad enough—with the waves of heat coming off him and settling into Clay's back and the sensitive arch of his neck. It reminded him of how touchy-feely they'd been lately, in big ways like the kiss, and in all the tiny ways that were somehow worse—footsies at Mahmood's, holding hands in public, the pervasive sense that he was expected to be around Thom, get close to Thom, be intimate and familiar with Thom. It was distracting.

And, of course, even though it was late and Thom had also been working all day, he still smelled amazing.

Clay pushed away from his desk. The thought of showing his work to Thom made him unaccountably jittery, but giving in would be worth it if it'd make him go away. "I just had this idea, okay?"

Thom was still smiling, his eyes bright with mischief. "Yeah?"

"It's—" Clay sighed. He closed some of the windows on his screen so Thom could see the main architecture of his idea. "I'm still working on it. It's probably dumb."

He glanced off into the dark corners of his office for a few moments, giving Thom a chance to look at it, but mostly just waiting for the inevitable crushing insult. Eventually, he peeked back at him, and was surprised to see him staring at Clay's screen with a sober expression. "Is that a map?" he asked.

"It's not Pinpoint-level stuff or anything," Clay said hesitantly. "I just—"

Thom waited, eyebrows raised, and the prospect that he might actually be interested prodded Clay enough to say, "It's—it's this algorithm. It predicts, based on where someone used to live, where they'll live next when they move. So I thought—if we have a file on a good voter, and they've moved and we don't have follow-up, we can predict what neighborhood they might be in. If a neighborhood ends up having a high index of potentially resettled voters, I dunno. Prioritize canvassing there."

Thom stared at Clay with a considering expression.

"I know!" Clay said, irritated. "It's not brilliant or anything. It'll give us, maybe, like, a tiny edge in voter turnout and—"

"It's smart," Thom said, looking at the screen. "If it works. Can you tell what the error rate is?"

Clay was slow to answer—he hadn't expected that Thom would have follow-up questions. "Uh, not completely," he said, "but I've been working with this professor who studies urban resettlement—I'm pretty sure it won't send us in the wrong direction."

Thom nodded. "And it could help. On the margins." He had a small smile on his face. "This is smart."

Clay was confused. To him, *smart* had always meant game changer—standing out from the crowd, disrupting the conventional wisdom, coming up with some once-in-a-generation insight. Pinpoint was one of those, and it had been Clay's crowning achievement, even if in his heart he'd always known how little it was really *his*.

But Thom was smiling like none of that was true. This new idea of Clay's was small—*marginal*, Thom had called it. But he still looked excited. And Clay knew how rarely Thom got excited about anything.

Thom also had an odd look in his eye as he kept staring at him—like there was something very specific he wasn't saying. "What?" Clay asked warily.

He shook his head, looking away. "Nothing."

"What?"

Thom glanced back at him with an amused, puzzled frown. "You're just all—coy with your idea. Usually if you came up with anything even remotely this good you'd have been in my office at six a.m. making air horn noises."

Clay shrugged a little bashfully. Thom wasn't wrong, but

right now he was still glowing from the praise. Who needed air horn noises?

Of course, the moment was already over—Thom was back to looking at his phone. "You should try this *work* thing more often."

Clay laughed in response, as if he wasn't still stuck on *This is smart*. Thom was tapping on his phone and turning away, picking his stuff back up to head home. Before he could think better of it, Clay said, "Hey, wait."

Thom turned around, one eyebrow raised in lazy inquiry. "Uh, about the other day," Clay said. "When the Pinpoint people were here?"

Thom rolled his eyes. "Like I said. It was the least a fake boyfriend could do."

"Still," Clay said, coming to lean against his door frame opposite Thom. "Emmy got this constipated look on her face, and it stuck the whole time. It was awesome."

Thom grinned. "Yeah, well." He looked at the ground, then back up at Clay. "They were clearly in the tank for Warhey, and then they think they're gonna come here and trash one of our people?" He shook his head. "Nah."

"Oh, so now I'm one of the team?" Clay said, teasing.

Thom shook his head, but he was smiling. "No, no. Only when the other guys are here."

"Well," Clay said. "Thanks."

Thom said nothing. He was leaning back against the door frame. Clay ran his fingers restlessly over the doorjamb behind him. If he straightened up, he would be leaning over Thom in the small space, the two of them only inches apart. That close, Clay would be able to feel the heat radiating off Thom's body again, like he had when they'd been sitting so close at Mahmood's, like when they'd been pressed up against each other at the basketball game. As the seconds dragged on and they kept looking at each other in silence, that space between them seemed smaller and smaller.

Until Thom shook himself and looked down at his phone again, wandering a few feet away. He did that a lot—used his phone like a shield, a way of saying *This is more important than you; leave me alone.* His voice had gone flat and closed off again when he said, "Don't stay too late. People might start expecting you to actually work hard around here."

Clay cleared his throat. "I'll probably just leave now." He really did feel wiped. "Besides, shouldn't we be leaving together all the time? Y'know, if we were a real couple?"

Thom gave him an unimpressed look over his shoulder. "If you worked as hard as I do on a regular basis I'm pretty sure you'd die."

And I'm pretty sure if you were actually dating anyone they'd never see you at all, Clay thought, and then banished it. He didn't need the mental image of Thom loosening his tie at home, falling into bed exhausted, needing someone to run a hand through his hair and take off his shoes.

Thom Morgan would be an absolute disaster for anyone stupid enough to care about him.

"Probably!" Clay said. "I'll leave that to you."

Thom was already looking at his phone again. "My Uber's here," he said brusquely. "See you."

So stupid, Clay thought, shaking his head as he watched him go.

Thom and Clay's fake relationship was one month old when Lennie held her first formal fundraiser of the campaign. Of course, they left unspoken *which* race she was fundraising for, just as they'd had the PAC renamed *Leonora for Us* specifically for its fuzzy vagueness.

Thom had been looking forward to the fundraiser for weeks. Events like this were his favorite—they married the stealth and shadowboxing of the pre-campaign to the big-money adrenaline of the main event.

Tickets were ten thousand dollars a plate—Thom had wanted to start at twenty-five thousand, but Felicia had convinced him to be realistic. Their host was a prolific TV producer who'd lent them his San Marino mansion for the affair. San Marino was a wealthy suburban enclave of greater LA that took in a healthy chunk of the city's profits and kept out its culture with a chair and a whip. Lawns were trimmed with military precision, and the town smelled of orange groves and Chanel No. 5.

The property lots were big, but it was still LA, so they could only get so big. The residents therefore crammed their miniature would-be Versailles up to the very edge of their properties. The site of the fundraiser had a little dollop of a front yard behind a guard house and a mechanized gate. Twenty-foot hedges hemmed in the estate, but paparazzi were still waiting by the entrance, and at least three or four were probably dangling from branches somewhere in the recesses of the rolling backyard.

The ballroom that would host the event was extravagant— gilded columns, marble floors, massive chandeliers, and huge windows along the wall that looked out onto an expansive balcony. At twilight, the room seemed to glow. A small study on the second floor looked out onto the ballroom from above, and Thom paced there, watching his underlings greet the first few arrivals with flutes of champagne, as the staff prepared.

Lennie was in hair and makeup, looking at index cards with biographical information on the biggest donors. She wore a black-and-gold gown with an oversize silk cowl that encircled her neck and shoulders, making her look like a lioness. Bex looked dapper AF in a slim-fitting tux that left an inch of ankle showing above her black loafers. Thom had chosen a Tom Ford tux with a skinny lapel that accentuated every gym-toned angle of his body. He wandered over to a mirror and made an infinitesimal adjustment to his bow tie that was really just an excuse to admire his jawline. God, he looked good.

He could only hope that Clay would show up looking even remotely on his level. It didn't really matter, as they weren't there in their capacity as a faux couple. There wasn't even really a reason for Clay to be there at all, aside from how much he'd whined about not being included for the last few weeks. The only pictures from the event would be grainy paparazzi shots from afar.

But to be honest, Thom had been curious just how much he could put his own stamp on Clay Parker. He hadn't even made it that difficult. He'd only given him three instructions: buy a tuxedo ("an actual tux, Clay, not a suit like you'd wear to the office"), take it to Thom's tailor, and get a haircut.

He sighed, trying and failing to picture Clay standing still long enough to complete any of those tasks.

Felicia arrived next, wearing a slinky gray evening gown that just barely shimmered in the low light. Her hair was sleek and held back from her face, and her eyes were dark and smoky. She looked like the first drag on a cigarette after a good long stretch of having quit. Thom whistled. "Well done, Morales."

"Thanks." She said it like she didn't care, but he could tell she did a little.

"Hey, where was my whistle?" Lennie asked, not looking up from her cards.

"Respect you far too much to whistle at you, Madam Governor," Thom said.

"But I look nicer than Felicia, right?"

"Of course, ma'am," he said, shaking his head silently at Felicia as she pursed her lips against a smile.

The ballroom downstairs was filling quickly. "She almost ready?" Felicia asked, coming to stand by Thom.

"I think so," Thom said, glancing at his watch. "It's more I want to find the perfect time to let her loose in there. Too soon before the donors get drunk and she could end up having to talk policy."

"I heard that too, Thom," Lennie said sourly.

"I'm sorry, ma'am," Thom said, laughing. "It's just that—"

His words died in his throat as Clay arrived.

He'd followed Thom's instructions. The tux was crisp and simple—a revelation on Clay, whose fashion sense was usually careless and cluttered. It fit well, making his height and build seem imposing, not gawky. And his hair—it couldn't have been more than an inch shorter, but it wasn't frizzed and fluffy anymore; it had been combed into neat, thick waves.

And somehow, his bluster was gone. There was no smirk, no hyena grin, no petulant scowl. He put his hands in his pockets and looked at Thom from across the room, two parts hesitant and one part—calm, maybe? Self-assured?

He was still Clay. He'd never draw the eye. But once Thom was looking at him, he found it difficult to stop.

It was Felicia who broke the spell. "Clay!" she said, not masking her surprise. "You...clean up well?"

The smirk was back. "You know it," he said, sauntering over.

Felicia rolled her eyes and went to prep Lennie. Clay stopped in front of Thom. Quietly, he said, "Uh...do I look okay?"

Thom cleared his throat. "Yeah, I'd say you—you look good."

Clay's eyes flicked up to his. "The bow tie's okay?"

Thom laughed breathlessly. "Yeah, Clay, the bow tie's good."

He smiled hesitantly. "Okay."

He smelled like soap and sandalwood. Part of Thom urged him to find an exit and not look back.

"Ma'am," he called instead to the governor. "It's time."

Lennie sparkled when money was on the line. She cut through the fundraiser like a shark, always moving and ever hungry. She flitted from group to group, shaking hands, asking after grandchildren, posing for selfies and discussing matters of state. Thom stayed with her for the first few conversations and then broke off, heading straight for the bar.

He sidled up next to Felicia, who was already there. "It's looking good," she said, though she directed the sentiment mostly at her phone.

He nodded at her, waving over the bartender. The event *was* going well. The donors seemed happy, and the few who'd flagged him down with questions or requests had been easy to handle. Tonight was important: many of the people here would also donate to Warhey, because they donated to everyone purely to get their calls returned. They wanted to have options, and tonight was about convincing them that Lennie was a serious option. The vibe of the room told him that it was working.

As the waiter brought him his drink, he noticed Clay at the other end of the bar, talking to some of the constituent services staff—the people who did Lennie's actual job as governor. Trust Clay to end up talking to the least important people here. At least he wasn't chatting up the waiters.

Clay scanned the room for a moment, then stopped when he spotted Thom. As if he'd been looking for him.

He smiled, then refocused on his conversation. It was another one of those real, unassuming smiles from Clay that Thom wasn't sure what to do with. He knocked back the rest of his drink.

"Trouble in paradise?" Felicia asked, still not looking up from her phone.

"*Fuck* you," Thom said, hailing the bartender again.

It was ridiculous. Clay looked good—better—but not *that* good. And yet, even as Thom returned to the party, working the room with his usual polish, he couldn't help but be aware of Clay the whole time. Of where he was standing, what he was doing, the way his lips moved as he spoke. How he was just *there*, all night, tugging gently at Thom's attention. He tried to focus on the donor he was talking to, who was droning on about his ski lodge, but Clay loomed in his peripheral vision. He was one of the few people at the party who seemed visibly excited to be there—not just entertained, but buoyantly happy. His laugh was a little louder than other people's, his smile so wide that his eyes crinkled at the edges. It was tacky.

He really filled out that tux.

"Am I distracting you?" asked the donor he was talking to.

"Uh," Thom said, panic jolting through him. Swiftly he tried to refocus on their conversation. Shit—what had they been talking about? "No—I, uh—apologies, I—"

"Don't worry about it, son," the man said. Surprisingly, he didn't seem angry—he had a small smile on his face instead, one that almost looked coy. He put a paternal hand on Thom's elbow and said, "We've all been there, eh? Go have fun."

Thom felt dizzy on his feet at the near miss as he watched the donor wander away. He was pretty sure that guy was worth nine figures—it would have been a disaster if he'd pissed him off. Instead, apparently his inattention and unprofessionalism had charmed him. All because he assumed it was due to—

He glanced at Clay again. Unease and a sparking, unsettling warmth warred in his gut.

Thom forcefully shoved all of those thoughts out of his head and made himself focus on work. Aside from his potentially career-ending preoccupation with Clay, the rest of the fundraiser went well. Lennie did well with the brief, funny-but-not-too-funny remarks Felicia had written for her, and dinner seemed like a hit. As the party stretched into its waning hours and tiny dessert hors d'oeuvres were passed around, he realized he hadn't yet thanked their host. He asked Felicia if she could spot him.

"Mmm, no," she said, cracking into a crème brûlée the size of a thimble. "But I saw him a little while ago."

"Where?" Thom asked.

Sighing, Felicia put her half-eaten dessert on a passing waiter's tray and set off along the edge of the ballroom. Thom followed behind her. Through the windows, stars glowed in the inky night.

"Clay," Felicia said, and Thom stopped short as he realized where she'd brought him. Clay was looking at him too, instead of Felicia, who was asking, "Weren't you talking to Steve before?"

"Who?" he asked, finally looking at her.

"The homeowner?" she demanded.

"Oh, yeah," Clay said, glancing at Thom again, then around the room. "I think he was, uh—"

That was when Bex burst into their conversation, panting and gripping Felicia's arm for support. "We have a problem."

Thom's stomach dropped. "What is it?"

"It's Bash."

Sebastian "Bash" Westwood, Lennie's twentysomething son, was your classic rich-kid train wreck: entitled, slutty, and just wild about anything he could put up his nose. Felicia in particular had spent countless hours cleaning up after Bash to keep Lennie's reputation secure. At the very mention of his name, one of her eyes twitched.

If it'd been up to Thom, Bash wouldn't have been allowed within fifty miles of the fundraiser, but one of his ironclad rules of working in politics was Don't Mess with the Family. "What did he do?"

A particularly well-timed clatter came from the direction of the kitchens, and everyone except Clay winced. Clay hadn't met Bash.

Luckily, none of the guests seemed to have noticed yet. "Okay, we have to get him out of here," Felicia said.

"Without photos," Thom added.

"There has to be a side entrance for the caterers—"

"Yeah, but there's paparazzi everywhere tonight," Thom said. "They'll notice if it's Bash coming out instead of the staff. Especially if he's spackled with blow."

"Can we hole him up here?" Felicia asked. "Keep him quiet, and try to wait it out until everyone's gone?"

"I, uh, don't think so," Bex said, glancing in the direction of the kitchens.

"We'll just have to take him out the side entrance, then," Felicia said grimly. "Maybe if I throw my coat over his head the paparazzi photos won't be as good."

Thom cursed and scanned the room. She was right, it was the only play.

He glanced at Clay, who was staring back at him with a trusting, steady gaze. Everyone else was freaking out, but Clay looked calm, like he *knew* that Thom would get them out of this.

Thom thought of a better play, and tried to ignore the way it made his heart thump.

"You're right," he told Felicia. "Take him out the side entrance. Cover him up with whatever you can. But wait five minutes."

"For what?" Felicia asked.

Thom grabbed Clay's hand. "We're going to distract them."

A few of the partygoers glanced their way as Clay stumbled along behind Thom, the two of them cutting through the crowd. That was a good sign.

They dodged a waiter, shimmied through a few more

guests, and then found themselves at one of the French doors that led to the balcony. *Just to distract them*, Thom thought. *That's all this is.*

He yanked the door open, shoved Clay outside and followed him.

There was some rustling in the bushes as they strode outside. Another good sign. Thom led them to a corner of the balcony where they couldn't be seen from the party, but were still within view of almost the entire lawn. He couldn't actually see any reporters hiding anywhere, but he felt a heaviness on his skin, as if they were being watched.

The moonlight washed everything out in a two-tone of pale silver and darkest blue. Crickets buzzed, emphasizing how abruptly the din of the party had fallen away. "Thom," Clay said lowly, and turned to face him.

Thom had been trying to deny it, but with Clay right there in front of him, ripe and ready; looking gorgeous in a way Thom himself had designed; when it was a good career move to do it—all of sudden there were no more excuses Thom could throw in front of it. With Clay looking at him with that dumb, handsome, trusting face, he couldn't wave it away.

He *wanted* Clay. And the stark truth of that, the low edge of shame to it, had his hands trembling as he reached up to pull Clay's face down to his.

Their lips touched, but he immediately wanted more—he needed to quiet the tumult in his mind. He slid a hand behind Clay's neck, fisted the other in his lapel and kissed him hard, harder than he should have, no time for awkwardness or hesitation. Clay's arms came around him loosely and he kissed back, but Thom needed more. So he took Clay's jaw in his palms and kissed him softer, deeper, using his tongue and sucking Clay's lower lip into his mouth and playing with the nape of his neck until Thom was panting with it, and finally Clay snapped too.

He shoved Thom until his back hit the wall of the house behind them, pinning him against the prickly stucco to kiss him desperately. The ease with which Clay manhandled him made him flush, but it was okay, because Clay was finally kissing him like he'd wanted—like he was drunk on it, like he wanted to drag his mouth over every inch of Thom's skin that he could find. Thom moaned into Clay's mouth, and Clay's hands went roaming all over Thom's body, warm and possessive. Thom burrowed his fingers into Clay's hair, then snaked an arm around his back, under his jacket, to feel the heat of Clay's skin under his shirt.

Clay broke off to trail kisses down Thom's neck, the scrape of his stubble and soft press of his lips making him shiver. Without his mouth covered, Thom could hear how harshly he was breathing. He tried to rein himself in, only to gasp again when Clay nipped him, hard, right where his neck met his suit collar. He dragged Clay's mouth back to his, and then Clay's hands found Thom's ass, hauling him unceremoniously closer, hitching their hips together. The perfect, grinding friction broke what was left of his patience—it was time to take this somewhere private.

When the word *private* crossed his mind, he broke away from Clay in shock.

"What," Clay panted. He braced his hands on the wall, letting Thom slump backward.

"That's enough," Thom said gutturally.

He couldn't believe he'd let it get that far. He was uncomfortably hard, and he'd felt how hard Clay was too. He wished he didn't know that. He wished his hands didn't ache to touch Clay again, to press between his legs and finish this for at least one of them. He wished he couldn't still feel the heat radiating off Clay's body, even with a few inches of cold night air between them.

He glanced up at Clay, whose lips were still parted and shiny wet. A curl of almost painful desire shot through him, and he thunked his head back against the wall once, firmly, to dispel it.

"Do you—" Clay swallowed, and tried again. He took his palms off the wall so he wasn't leaning over Thom anymore, but once he wasn't, it looked like he wasn't sure what to do with himself. "Do you think it worked?"

Thom licked his lips. "I think so," he said quietly. "But—wait, we can't just go back inside."

"What?" Clay said dazedly.

Thom huffed a sigh and smiled a little, because it was dark and Clay probably couldn't see, and because the night and his life had become too absurd not to laugh at. He took Clay's hand carefully and led him to the marble balustrade at the balcony's edge.

"Boyfriends, right?" he murmured to him. "This is supposed to be a romantic interlude, not a distraction."

"Right," Clay breathed.

Thom laughed again when he saw the sorry state of Clay's bow tie. "Here," he said, and Clay stood very still while Thom straightened it, trying not to think of the moment he must have knocked it out of place.

Once it was fixed, they lapsed back into silence. Clay played with his hand as they stood there, fiddling with his fingers affectionately, like he really was curious about the shape of Thom's knuckles, the state of his fingernails, the scar on the ball of his thumb. Thom tilted his head occasionally, as if they were talking. At this distance, the paparazzi wouldn't be able to tell.

A few minutes later, his phone buzzed with a text—Felicia, confirming that they'd gotten Bash out without a fuss.

"We're good?" Clay asked.

"Mmm-hmm," Thom said, pocketing his phone again quickly so that their audience wouldn't be suspicious. Clay took his hand again when it was free, weaving their fingers together loosely. The tender skin on the sides of his fingers was sensitive, and he inhaled shakily. The silence between them was actually kind of nice—full of the droning of insects and the distant snap of camera lenses.

"Should we go back in?" Clay asked, after a moment.

Thom wasn't sure he was ready—to face everyone back at the party, or to let go of the peace and warmth out here.

He cleared his throat. "A little longer," he said. "Just to be safe."

Clay nodded. The party roared dimly along behind them, and Thom let the sound drown out the drumming of his pulse in his ears.

★ 14 ★

Thom woke up the next morning determined not to think about the fundraiser. He was choosing to focus only on the fact that their ploy had worked—there was nothing online about Bash. No photos of him leaving the party, or rumors about him causing a scene; just a few more millions in the campaign bank account and some good write-ups of the event in the political press.

He didn't want to think about the rest of it—about him and Clay alone on that dark balcony. He didn't want to think about Clay's unsteady breathing, or the wet heat of his mouth, or his dazed expression when they'd broken apart. He didn't want to think about how far he'd unraveled, or the blinding need he'd gotten lost in for those few hazy moments.

Every fevered memory made it clear just how out of control this was getting. Thom's whole world revolved around control: control over his clients, over the news cycle, and over the entire political ecosystem. Having control over himself was the absolute baseline.

With the fundraiser behind them, he was ready to turn the page. He needed to focus on his job, and not stupid distractions like Clay.

So of course when he arrived at work, someone had thoughtfully taped a torn-out page from a local tabloid to the door of his office. Gov's Guys Get Grabby! screamed the headline, below which were blown-up grainy pap shots of him and Clay from the night before.

He sighed even as his pulse kicked up. "Very funny, guys," he said. He tore it down and shouldered into his office.

"I dunno," Felicia said, following him in. "I thought it was kinda weak as headlines go. Two guys caught kissing outside a fundraiser? *Megaboners* was right there."

Thom husked out a laugh and glanced down at the newsprint in his hand. Seeing last night rendered in ink and paper made it unavoidable in a way that was almost surreal. Even at a distance and in the low light, the paparazzi had gotten a clear image of Clay crushing Thom against the mansion's pale stone wall. Their faces were a barely discernible blur that nonetheless captured the breathless urgency of the moment. He could even make out the shape of his own hands fisted in Clay's jacket. In the pictures, his entire body seemed to be straining to get closer to Clay.

He crumpled the cheap paper in his fist and tossed it at the garbage can, but it bounced off the rim.

"Thanks for taking that bullet," Felicia said.

He shrugged tensely. "It worked."

"Sure," Felicia said. She sat in the chair in front of his desk, took a sip of her coffee, and looked casually off to the side. "You could have distracted them with something else."

Thom frowned. "Like what?"

She shrugged. "A big public fight."

Thom said nothing. "Photos of everyone's favorite new political power couple in a screaming match?" she elaborated. "Would've worked just as well."

His phone buzzed shrilly. "Wouldn't have been as good for the campaign," he said. "People like us together."

"They sure do," Felicia said. He glared at her.

Before she could needle him again, her phone started buzzing too. A worried murmur had picked up in the bullpen. Felicia looked down at her phone, then up at Thom in dismay.

"Christ," he said. "What now?"

No one had gotten any pictures of Bash fleeing the party. It was worse: they'd gotten audio of Lennie laying into him in the limousine on the way home. The tape was about four minutes long, but the quote most outlets were running with was Lennie spitting at him to *grow the fuck up and stop fucking embarrassing me*.

Post-gaffe staff meetings were the worst—no one ever wanted to look the candidate in the eye. Luckily, at that moment Lennie was bent over the iPad Felicia had given her, skimming the stories in stony silence.

"Great," Lennie said when she was done, shoving the iPad back at Felicia. She stared down the rest of the staff, who seemed to be shrinking back into their seats. "So? What do we do?"

A junior staffer piped up first. Thom thought her name might be Sarah, but he was never really listening when the staff told him anything about themselves. "Well, uh, ma'am," she said uncomfortably, "as you know, we want voters to see you as sort of, um—tough, but, ah, matronly—"

"Matronly?" Lennie demanded.

Another junior staffer—Dave, maybe?—took a shot. "You know—strong, but likable."

"Oh, I just have to be *likable*? Is that it?" Lennie snarled, and Dave went white. "Listen, shit-for-brains, I'll do your fucking memes and stick to the fucking script when I'm in public, but it's *your* job to make sure no one bugs my goddamn limousine!"

"You're right," Thom said, jumping in once he was sure the junior staff had finished shooting their own dicks off. "This isn't about what happened, it's about how to fix it."

"You mean how to make me *likable* again?" Lennie said, with an evil glare at Dave. He flinched.

"Well, we can't lean right at it," Thom said. "If we put you and Bash out there doing some event together it's gonna reek of—well, this meeting."

"So, what?" Lennie said tiredly. "You want me to go out there and bake some cookies? Do a little fashion show? Should I fucking knit something?"

"Ma'am—" Fe started.

They were interrupted by Bex sticking her head into the room. "Excuse me," she said quietly. "Felicia? He's here."

That had to mean Bash was here for the inevitable post-gaffe confrontation with his mother. Thom just hoped the screaming wouldn't be so loud through the walls that it would distract the staff.

Felicia sighed and steeled herself, looking at Lennie. "Ma'am, do you want to...?"

"Ugh," Lennie said darkly. "No, but I will." She stood and gestured to everyone else still sitting at the table. "Just—do something. Put out a shiny distraction, I don't care. Keep me out of it. And kill this fucking story." She left through the door that led from the conference room to her office, and

Felicia followed. Thom caught a distinct wave of pot as the door wafted shut behind them. Yup, Bash was in the building.

Tomb-like silence descended once the governor was gone. "Ideas," Thom ordered.

"Um," Maybe-Sarah piped up. "We were thinking—tomorrow, in Echo Park, there's an adoptathon."

"A what?"

"It's like, the SPCA comes out with a bunch of dogs—"

"And cats, and stuff. Maybe gerbils," Dave chimed in.

"—right, and they're cute, and they get some blogs and local media to come and promote it, and the goal is that they all get adopted," Sarah finished. "Or something."

Silence fell again. Thom could feel a headache stirring between his temples. "So?"

"So—" Dave piped up. "If they don't get adopted, sometimes, they—"

"Jesus Christ," Thom shouted. "I know about kill shelters, Dave."

"My—my name's Dan," Dave said.

"My *point* is," Thom spat, "how does this help us? You're gonna send Lennie in there to adopt a pet? That's even more cliché than knitting or cookies."

"Oh, no, not the governor," Sarah said earnestly. "We thought—we thought maybe you and Clay could go."

Now the headache was joined by a bolt of nausea. "I don't think that's a good idea."

"Why not?" she asked. "People love dogs!"

Thom opened his mouth to tell her exactly what was wrong with the dog park idea, only to realize that there was nothing wrong with the dog park idea. People did fucking love dogs, and they also apparently loved his big gay Insta-perfect relationship with Clay. He could see the content now.

A Twitter-friendly gay couple playing with puppies? They'd go wild.

The problem was, he wasn't sure he could stand it either.

"Oh," Sarah said, now sounding worried. "Is it—does Mr. Parker not like animals?"

As they gazed at him in preemptively wounded anxiety, a chill went down his spine. Did the office plebes think that his and Clay's relationship was *real*? For a moment, Thom couldn't remember if they'd told the staff, or just trusted that word about the ruse would get out. To be fair, they rarely bothered to tell the staff anything, but he felt a mild panic at the soulful look in their eyes that plainly said they thought he and Clay were the real thing.

"No, it—fine. That sounds fine," he said. "Send me the details. Then get back to work."

They sat and stared at him.

"Now," he barked, and they scurried to obey.

He rubbed his temples when they were gone, trying to massage away his headache. Another public, shippy event with Clay was the last thing he needed. It would be awkward as fuck, and an annoying drain on his time and energy.

Or it wouldn't be awkward, and that had the potential to be much, much worse.

He thought about going over to Clay's office to give him the assignment. He'd been avoiding him all day, but seeing him in his office under the sickly fluorescent lights, back in the sad, dusty Jos. A. Bank clothes he called a wardrobe—that might actually help.

Then he pictured how Clay might smile when hearing that their assignment tomorrow was to go play with a bunch of shelter dogs.

He sent him an email instead.

★ ★ ★

When Thom joined Lennie and Felicia in Lennie's office, things weren't quite as bad as he'd anticipated. Bash was sprawled on Lennie's couch, playing with his phone, as Lennie bent over him, growling, "Sebastian, I swear to god, you cannot have your fucking magic mushrooms delivered to the office."

Thom blinked, glancing at Felicia. She shrugged helplessly.

"I'm not," Bash said. He was wearing what looked like raggedy designer sweats, and he smelled like smoke and stale beer. There was a few days' worth of patchy stubble on his jaw. "They're magic *truffles*. Much more expensive."

"Listen to me, you little shit—" Lennie started.

Felicia jumped in. "Maybe it would be more productive if we got down to talking about why we're all here."

"Okay," Bash said, putting his phone down so he could fish a cigarette out of his pocket and put it in his mouth. "Why am I here?"

Lennie snatched the cigarette away. "Seriously?" she demanded. "Is ordering drugs all you do on the internet, or do you occasionally read the news?"

Bash laughed incredulously. "No."

Lennie glared at him. "Someone recorded us in the limo last night."

Bash squinted. "The...limo?"

"After the fundraiser," she added testily.

Sounding even more confused, he asked, "What fundraiser?"

"The fundraiser last night," Lennie bit out. "You were your usual sloppy self, and we had to get you home. But someone bugged the car, and now audio of us is all over the internet."

"Someone *bugged* us?" Bash grinned. "That's so...sexy."

Lennie turned away with a banked snarl, her hands in fists. Felicia sighed and said, "Bash, can I see your phone?"

"My phone?" he asked. "Why?"

"The most likely way this happened is that someone hacked it to make it remotely pick up audio," she explained. "We've already checked the governor's phone, and it was clean. So…?"

Bash shrugged and handed it over, telling her his passcode. Thom was frankly surprised he was cooperating—as he'd told Felicia, everyone had something bad on their phone. Apparently, Bash had no shame about what was on his.

After flicking through it for a few minutes, Felicia declared the phone clean and handed it back to him. "But we should still have IT retrofit it to make sure it's secure," she said.

"I dunno," Bash said airily. "I do a lot of private stuff on here."

Lennie snatched the phone from him and threw it against the wall.

Glass was still scattering across the floor when she leaned in close to Bash. "Listen to me, you spoiled little degenerate," she hissed. "I am sick of your shit. I am not going to let you ruin this campaign the way you've ruined the rest of my life. You do whatever the fuck Felicia tells you to do, and the rest of the time you stay fucking quiet. I don't care how much booze or pussy you drown yourself in, as long as you do it *discreetly*."

Bash tilted his head. "Thanks, Mom," he said, in a quiet, mock-affectionate tone.

Thom and Felicia did their best not to make eye contact with anyone. Lennie settled in behind her desk and took a deep breath, then asked, "So. What did the brain trust come up with? How are we going to handle this?"

"We're going to put together some events to try to…draw

focus away," Thom said, praying they wouldn't ask for any more details.

Felicia nodded. "I think it'll be fine," she added. "The whole thing will probably blow over."

"Really?" Lennie asked.

"The press doesn't want to cover this story," Felicia said. "It's tawdry, and personal. We'll give them other stuff to write about, refuse to engage, and eventually they'll move on."

From the couch, Bash said, "Like it never even happened?"

Felicia glanced at him, looking surprised. "Right."

"Perfect," Lennie said. Without another word, she turned to her computer and started working.

The awkward silence stretched until Lennie finally glanced at Bash and said, "What are you still doing here? I have work to do."

Bash wavered to his feet. "Always a pleasure, Mom," he said, and slouched out the door.

★ 15 ★

It was bright and sunny in Los Angeles the next day, the picture-perfect backdrop for Thom and Clay's romantic dog park plans. Thom overslept after a restless night, took an Uber to the park, and threatened to give his driver four stars if he tried to make conversation.

He shouldn't have been this nervous. It was a fucking dog adoption event—the content creation was basically on auto-pilot. There wasn't anything to stress over.

Nothing except it was his first time seeing Clay since the fundraiser.

When he first arrived, he couldn't find him. The event was bustling—booths were set up along both sides of the park, with play areas for the dogs in the center and paths winding around them where families and couples strolled with their own pets. He was distracted for a little while—more than a few people there recognized him and wanted to chat, and the campaign had sent a few volunteers who needed his attention.

But eventually he spotted Clay standing by a clump of trees on the very edge of the park. As soon as he saw him, his anxiety lessened—far from the polished, elegant look he'd attained for the fundraiser, in the light of day Clay was back to his usual gawky self. He was wearing a bulky Red Sox sweatshirt and loose gym shorts that looked straight out of a midnineties catalogue. His hair was tousled and messy, and he was fidgeting awkwardly as he stood there.

Thom walked over to him. "What are you doing here?"

"I dunno," Clay said moodily, glancing at the rioting mess of dogs behind Thom.

He sighed impatiently. "Clay."

"I'm—" he sighed. "I'm not great with dogs."

"Jesus, they were on to something," Thom said to himself.

Clay scowled. "What?"

"You have to come play with the dogs, Clay. That's kinda the point."

"I *tried*," he said. He wound back and forth on his feet, chewing a fingernail, looking fluttery and apprehensive. "Before you got here. But they all—*barked* at me."

"You'll be fine," Thom said gruffly. "Come on."

"But I—"

"Come *on*," Thom said, and grabbed Clay's hand.

As soon as he did, he caught his breath at the drag of Clay's skin against his. He looked slowly from where their hands were clasped, up the length of Clay's arm, outstretched where Thom had tugged on it, to the stunned look on Clay's face that probably mirrored his own. The shape of Clay's palm was familiar to him by now. He had felt these hands all over his body.

And this was why he'd been nervous.

Clearing his throat, he tightened his hand on Clay's, muscling the feeling away. "Let's do this," he said. Clay followed behind him silently.

He focused on the event to quiet his nerves. They met a few different dogs, always giving noncommittal answers when pressed about whether they were ready to take one home. Thom saw plenty of people taking pictures, and got asked to take a few with Clay. He posted a few pictures of the cuter puppies, and his followers responded enthusiastically. Clay did his level best to ruin the event by squirming away from any dog that got too close, but one particular orange cat followed him everywhere he went.

By around ten, Thom figured they'd done everything they could. Most of the crates and booths were being disassembled and packed, and he was trapped in conversation with a particularly zesty volunteer who wanted to know what the governor was going to do about puppy mills. Thom's hand was already on his phone in his pocket, ready to call a ride.

"Mr. Morgan?" the volunteer was saying. "What do you think—is there anything the governor can do?"

Thom gave a thoughtful-sounding sigh, and the volunteer's shaggy salt-and-pepper terrier cocked his head at Thom judgmentally.

Before he could answer, he heard a clatter and a few dozen howling barks, and he was pelted from the side by a very enthusiastic Saint Bernard.

The shelter staff pulled the dog back and apologized profusely, but the damage was done—there were huge ropes of slobber all over Thom's shirt and a good amount on his shorts. He grimaced, and waved off the apologies and offers of help.

Only one person was enough of a dick to laugh—and he was laughing hard.

"I thought dogs scared you," he said to Clay.

Clay grinned. "Not when they're slobbering all over your designer athletic wear."

The Saint Bernard barked, and Clay flinched. Thom grimaced and pushed himself up.

After glancing around to make sure he wouldn't be overheard, Clay said, "So...we done for the day?"

"Yes," Thom said bitterly. He stank of dog. "Shit. This is gonna dent my Uber rating."

"Uh," Clay said. After a moment of looking stupefied or maybe conflicted, he said, "I mean, my apartment's a few blocks from here—I walked."

Thom blinked at him. "So?"

"So...you could change."

Thom's mouth went dry. Going over to Clay's apartment was definitely a bad idea. Going over to Clay's apartment to take his clothes off was *definitely* a bad idea. And plus, Clay's clothes wouldn't even fit him.

But the dog drool was starting to seep through his clothes to his skin, and the thought of having to sit like this the whole ride home was enough to override his better judgment.

"Yeah," he said. "Okay." Clay smiled.

As they walked, Clay complimented Thom's posts about their morning. "They're gonna be so pissed we didn't leave with a dog," he said of the commenters.

"Yeah, well, they can suck my balls."

"Thom," Clay laughed. "That's not very inventive. You're losing it."

He had a point. Thom's mood darkened further.

Clay took them a few blocks south of the park, onto the edges of Westlake. "You live around here?" Thom asked dubiously.

Clay nodded. Thom took in their surroundings with a sniff. He lived downtown, a few blocks from the office, so he'd lose as little time to the commute as possible. That meant his neighborhood was a little soulless as LA went—more corporate landscape than art or nightlife—but it was a clean, safe area, and the fact that he'd pried enough out of Lennie's war chest in salary to afford to live there was a testament to his political value. His apartment was small, but it was sleek and trendy, all glass and pale wood textures, and he had an app that sent him art for the walls that he could trade out every few months.

Westlake was, well, cheaper. For every hipster restaurant there was a faded storefront, strip mall, or overgrown, empty lot. The sun seemed to beat down harder here without skyscrapers to box it out, and it felt like it had aged these blocks more than downtown's chrome curves. "Didn't want to pay too much in rent, huh?"

Clay gave him a scathing look. "Jesus Christ, you elitist, LA's *all* expensive."

Thom shrugged.

Clay's apartment turned out to be the basement of a narrow two-story row house on a relatively quiet street. The house had bleached white stucco walls with riotous hot pink flowers growing along cracks in the plaster. Clay led him through a creaky, shoulder-height wood fence that separated the lawn from the alley that led to his unit. Chips of peeling, emerald green paint hung from his front door. Thom listened to the cicadas buzz in the distance as Clay fumbled with his keys.

The inside was pretty much what Thom had expected—one long rectangle of a living room, with an open kitchen in the right corner off to the side of the front door. On the left were several doors that presumably led to a bathroom, maybe some closets, and Clay's bedroom. Thom coughed and focused determinedly on the rest of the apartment.

The walls and floors were concrete, cinderblock, and brick,

but there were enough rugs, wall hangings, and other soft textures that it didn't feel cold. A giant TV sat on a midcentury TV stand, and magazines and clothing were strewn over a long, low gray couch. There were also a surprising number of plants in various states of decline. The apartment reminded Thom of weeds springing up from cracked concrete until they had overtaken the sidewalk.

"So, uh," Clay said. "Yeah, let me get you something."

He opened, shimmied through, and closed his bedroom door carefully. While he was gone, Thom took the chance to examine the apartment more carefully. The TV stand bristled with wiring and consoles, including something that was pulsing with a lime green light, and there were open DVD and video game cases scattered everywhere. The kitchen was dusty—like most campaign staff, Clay probably ate most of his meals at or near the office. There was mail all over the couch, but also some pizza boxes, and a few controllers that looked like they matched the glowing green thing. It almost looked like he enjoyed spending time here, outside of the office.

"Here," Clay said, reemerging with a shirt that he tossed at Thom. Thom shook it out to examine it, but far from being some embarrassing graphic T-shirt, it was just a plain gray Henley.

He frowned at Clay. "Why do you wear your gross bargain-basement suits to the office when you could dress like this?"

"What, like I don't give a shit?" Clay said.

"Your hundred-dollar suits make it look like you don't give a shit," Thom said, whipping his slobbery shirt over his head. Clay blushed straight to the roots of his hair, and he actually seemed to consider turning his back on Thom for a second before he steeled himself and met Thom's eye. Thom just hoped he wasn't blushing too.

"It's a campaign," he added, tugging the Henley on. "As long as journalists aren't there, you can wear what you want. Especially if you're the tech guy." The shirt was too big, but surprisingly comfortable. He pushed the long sleeves up his forearms. "Now, once we win..."

Clay raised his eyebrows. "Well, right. Once we win, it'll be business formal, and I want to be ready."

"Clay," Thom said, "if we win, I'm gonna have to burn everything you currently own and take you shopping to get you something fit to be worn into the West Wing."

Clay seemed taken aback. "Okay."

Thom frowned. He didn't like the marker that had inadvertently been placed, but he didn't want to stick around long enough to dispute it.

"So, uh, thanks," he said, suddenly realizing that he was *wearing Clay's shirt*. The fabric was starting to warm as it collected the heat from his body, and his mind flashed to a vision of Clay pulling this same shirt over his head, smoothing it against his skin.

He was ready to leave. "Uh, bye," he said.

Clay nodded, looking just as uncomfortable as he was. "Bye."

Once Thom was home he pulled Clay's shirt off immediately, and took a shower to scrub off the last of the dog smell. He made a mental note to bring the shirt into the office as soon as possible and give it back to Clay. But it slipped off his bed where he'd thrown it while he was in the shower, and once it was on the floor, it faded into the background of his bedroom.

★ 16 ★

The one depressing thing that a job in politics and a job in tech had in common was that everyone was expected to be a workaholic. You were supposed to be so psyched about your job—so grateful to be there at all—that you'd basically be working all the time, even if there was no particular emergency or crisis to address. You just had to be Always On.

So it was not unusual for Lennie's office to be at least half-full on a Sunday, especially with her big announcement just under two months away. Still, Clay sighed as he looked out his window. It was a warm, lazy day—one of those days you felt vitamin-deficient just at the sight of sunbaked grass and the shimmer of heat waves above the highway. Lennie wasn't in, so there was no one in charge *per se*, but once the staff spotted Thom puttering around in his office putting things into his messenger bag, they started to pack up themselves with a quiet murmur of relief.

Clay was almost done with his work, but he made himself finish a few last spreadsheets before packing up. When he made it to the hallway by the elevator, the only person left waiting there too was Thom.

"Oh," Clay said. "Uh. Hi."

"Hm," Thom said, not looking up from his phone.

Clay cleared his throat as they waited for the elevator in silence. He was debating whether to make conversation when Thom stiffened with some kind of realization. "Shit," he whispered, glancing back at the office.

"Forget something?"

"Uh, my fucking internet's broken," Thom said, scrubbing a hand through his hair.

Clay frowned. "I was getting a signal just now—"

"Not here, at home," Thom said. "A tree fell on—something, I don't know. It went out last night and it's not supposed to be back by tomorrow. So I guess—" he sighed, and Clay realized with mild shock that even *Thom* had been looking forward to getting out of the office. "I guess I'll just stay here."

Clay thought back to the sight of Thom in his apartment the day before, with his slobbery shirt and spiky black hair, looking scornful and pitiful and just delicious.

Before he even knew what he was saying, he said, "You could come over."

Thom froze. "Uh."

"I mean," Clay rushed to add, "because I have Wi-Fi. And, y'know...this place is depressing."

Thom remained frozen for another couple seconds. Fuck, what had Clay been thinking inviting him to his place?

Then, surprisingly, Thom shrugged and said, "Okay."

Clay squinted at him. Was that a cautious *okay*? An...inviting *okay*? He could never read Thom.

When they got to his place, it was definitely awkward.

Thom glanced at his couch in open disdain, a hand curled over his messenger bag, and Clay rushed to sweep all the mail and receipts and stray clothing off it to clear a space for him. "So, the Wi-Fi network is CIA Van 3, and the password is POTUSParker."

Thom snorted. Clay ignored him. He dumped his work stuff on the kitchen counter and snagged two beers from the fridge. Thom had already opened his laptop and seemed focused on his work, which was good. It wouldn't be awkward if he had a reason to be here.

He huffed out a relieved breath and held a beer out to Thom. "Here you go."

"Thanks," he said absently, and grabbed it without looking.

As he did, his finger brushed the knuckle just below Clay's fingernail, a rough callous of skin that was somehow extraordinarily sensitive. He heard himself suck in a breath, and Thom glanced up too, his eyes dark.

"Uh," Clay said, yanking his hand back. "So yeah. Beer and Wi-Fi!" He smiled feebly. "And ESPN."

He sat hastily on the couch and turned the TV on as background noise. Thom went back to ignoring him, and Clay opened his own computer and pulled up what he'd been working on at the office. But it was impossible to concentrate with Thom right there next to him, the ghost of his touch lingering on Clay's hand. He wondered what Thom thought of his apartment. He wondered what Thom thought of him inviting him over. He wondered whether Thom was getting as little done as Clay was.

He became so lost in thought that he was startled when Thom shook his empty bottle and said, "Can I get another? I'll grab you one too."

"Uh, sure—thanks," Clay said, somewhat transfixed by the

sight of Thom moving through his apartment, sidling into his narrow kitchen and touching his appliances.

When he came back, passing Clay a cold bottle, he said, "You have a waffle iron?"

"Yeah. Why?"

"When have you ever made waffles?" Thom said, cracking open his own beer.

"I could."

"Uh-huh."

Abruptly Clay decided that he'd had enough work for the day. He tossed his computer aside and picked up a controller, firing up his go-to game for unwinding after work.

Thom didn't move his head, but even in his peripheral vision Clay could see his eyes darting to the TV screen, then back to his own laptop. "Uh, you know I'm still your boss, right?"

"Yeah, and I let you take shelter in my apartment."

That shut him up while Clay clicked through the opening screens. "Fine, goof off," Thom said. "It's not like you get much done at the office anyway."

Clay let him have that one and relaxed into the game, shooting at his enemies and rolling over towns in his heavily armored tank.

After a few minutes, Thom asked, "What *is* this?"

"It's called Battle of the Bulge," Clay said. "It's a WWII game."

"Why are all the players...donuts, though," Thom asked, his voice evenly split between curiosity and disdain.

"That's the bulge part," Clay said.

"But that was actually the name of the—" Thom stopped, watching Clay shoot up a person-sized chocolate éclair with a Gatling gun, spewing pastry cream across the bleak gray battlefield.

"Fine. Whatever," Thom sighed. A second later, he set aside his own computer and stretched. "I'm hungry," he announced. "You wanna order a pizza or something?"

"Okay."

Thom's irritated voice interrupted his game again a few minutes later. "Seamless and Postmates won't deliver here because you already have an account set up for this address."

"Okay."

"Okay, so will you get your phone out and order something?"

"In a minute," Clay said, eyes locked on the screen as he attempted to outmaneuver a strawberry sprinkled. Those fuckers were tough.

"Jesus Christ, you five-year-old," Thom said. Leaning forward, he grabbed the TV remote and shut it off.

"Thom!" Clay yelled, and dove for the remote. But it was too late by then—when the TV flickered back on, he was dead, his Boston cream's filling splattered all over the screen. "What the hell is your problem?"

"Relax, Cartman," Thom said.

"I didn't come over to your place and fuck up your shit!" Clay snapped.

"Fair," Thom said. He picked up one of the game consoles. "How about this. I'll play you, and if you beat me, I'll pay for dinner."

The sight of Thom holding one of his console controllers was bizarrely erotic. Clay cursed his fucked-up libido and said, "Ugh. Fine," as he queued up a multiplayer round.

"Don't you wanna know what happens if I win?" Thom asked.

He suppressed a shiver at the challenge in his voice. "Doubt I'll need to know."

"You cook for me," Thom said, with way too much confidence.

Clay rolled his eyes. "Okay then, Leave it to Beaver. Get ready to be pwned."

A multiplayer round in BoB was basically capture the flag—they each needed to recover an item on the other player's territory without getting shot. Clay started off ahead, easily picking off Thom's glazed infantrymen. But Thom got the hang of it pretty quickly, and he let out an excited whoop when he managed to find and boot up a panzer that had been hidden in a rusty supply shed. Five minutes later, he was rolling over Clay's guys and darting into his territory to snag the prize (the Ark of the Cruller).

"What the fuck," Clay said dazedly, sagging back against the couch. He wasn't sure if he was more pissed off or turned-on.

Thom stretched with a luxurious air and scratched his stomach. "So. Whaddya got back there, Julia Child?"

Clay threw his remote on the coffee table and stomped over to the fridge. The answer was basically nothing—he lived on takeout—but he knew Thom hadn't made the stupid bet to actually ensure himself a home-cooked meal. He'd probably sit and gloat in the living room for five seconds before going back to his work and ignoring Clay entirely, as long as his food was somehow en route.

But then Thom surprised him by following him into the kitchen and staring into the fridge under Clay's arm. "Ugh," he said when he saw what was in there. "Seriously?"

Clay shrugged. "Your stupid bet."

Thom started poking around the kitchen cabinets until he arrived back at the waffle iron. It had been a Christmas gift from his mom, and unfortunately, right there next to it was the bag of waffle mix that had come with. Thom turned to him with an evil grin.

"I am *not* making you waffles," Clay said.

Thom picked up the bag and shoved it at him. "I'm not eating whatever's under that pile of mold in the fridge."

"Just let me order something!" Clay said, exasperated.

"That wasn't the bet," Thom said smugly. He settled onto one of the bar stools at the breakfast bar and put his chin in his palms. "Do you have an apron or something?"

"Don't enjoy this so much," Clay said scathingly. Thom's grin just widened.

Clay had, in fact, never made waffles before. His mom had made them for him when he'd been a kid, and she'd probably thought that the gift was some sort of cure for homesickness. But Clay was pretty sure his waffles would turn out like crap, which would just bum him out more.

Weirdly, Thom made it easier by distracting him the whole time. He had opinions on how Clay was measuring, how he was mixing, whether it was weird that he didn't have syrup, if there was a store that might have syrup in walking distance (which Clay would of course walk to while the waffles were cooking—because *Thom* helping out wouldn't be *in the spirit of the bet*). It was infuriating, but at least it kept his mind busy.

And hanging out in his kitchen and hectoring him couldn't have been more fun for Thom than watching TV or playing the game more or even, Jesus, working. But for some reason he stayed put until Clay put a plate of only somewhat burnt waffles in front of him.

He made a show of tucking his napkin into his collar. "Dick," Clay said.

Thom made an exaggerated moaning noise around his first bite. Clay felt his face heat and turned away, pretending to be annoyed. "Glad I could be of service."

When he chanced a look at Thom again, he was smiling wickedly and brushing a crumb off his lower lip with his thumb. In a low voice, he said, "Thank you, Clay."

Clay began hastily cleaning up, throwing the waffle iron in the sink and brushing the counters off in rough motions.

When he'd invited Thom over, he'd been determined to keep things casual. Instead, they'd ended up horsing around all afternoon, and now he'd made Thom dinner.

He wasn't an idiot. He knew what it looked like when a guy was sniffing around for sex. Oh, he didn't think coming over to drink beer and goof around was some sort of seduction strategy on Thom's part. But he also wasn't sure Thom needed a strategy. And he wasn't sure *he* wasn't the one sniffing around.

Before he could stop himself, memories of the kiss at the fundraiser came flickering back to him, like shadows tugging at his thoughts. How he'd barely been able to see Thom's face in the dark. The chill of the night air at his neck. The rustle of their clothes, Thom's harsh breathing. The feel of Thom's hands grabbing at him, sliding over his skin, his soft mouth prodding Clay's to open, his tongue sliding inside. How little it had taken before Clay had gone out-of-his-mind desperate.

He couldn't believe how stupid he'd been, losing himself like that. But when Thom had put his hands on him, kissed him hot and slow and intent, every trace of common sense in his brain had blinked out like embers in a rainstorm. It had been a tipping point, leaving Clay exposed and unbalanced.

Except that Thom had gotten caught up in it too.

He balled his hands into fists on the countertop. He wasn't letting himself think about that. He wasn't letting himself think about how familiar they'd been getting, how most of the times Thom cursed at him lately had started to sound affectionate instead of biting.

This was so bad. Clay had had plenty of emotionless sex before, but his guess was that Thom didn't just *have* casual sex; he weaponized it.

Thom Morgan would chew him up and spit him out.

He glanced at Thom out of the corner of his eye. He was sopping up the last of the butter Clay had used in lieu of syrup with a satisfied look on his face. When he noticed Clay's attention, he grinned at him. Clay cleared his throat. "Good?" he asked hoarsely.

Thom nodded slowly. "Good."

★ **17** ★

It had been two weeks since Kerry Pham had come to see Thom in his office. He'd dodged a dozen calls from her since then, most in the first few days after their meeting. Then she'd gone dark for about a week. He should've known that wasn't a good sign.

Sometime between Tuesday night and Wednesday morning, the tweets started to roll in.

Not too many of them, and not all at once. Kerry was smarter than that. She didn't want to endanger the bill—not yet, anyway. But other smart and savvy activists—Kerry's friends and allies—were hinting that they'd noticed the swipe-fee issue. It wasn't percolating through to journalists and laypeople and the base just yet; it was a dim enough roar to ping only Thom's extremely sensitive radar. It was a shot across the bow.

So he met her for coffee at a quiet little place a few blocks from the office. He got a table that was outside but around the corner from the street and the rest of the building, so that they wouldn't be disturbed. Or seen.

Kerry smiled when she spotted him. Thom stood and gave her a hug, and they made polite small talk while Kerry waited for her coffee. Once the waiter was gone, Thom launched into his routine.

"So, Kerry," he said, "we looked into the swipe-fee issue. We've studied it in depth, put our best people on it—but unfortunately, there's just nothing the governor can do."

Kerry's fingers stilled where they'd been fidgeting with her mug. "Really."

"She doesn't write the laws," Thom said. "We can urge the legislators to drop the provision, but ultimately it's up to the Senate chairman what—"

"I know I'm just a physical therapist and not some hotshot political consultant," Kerry said flatly, "but I've got a grasp on the three branches of government."

Thom coughed. "Of course. But—"

"Lennie's the political muscle behind this bill," Kerry continued, talking over him. "She's the reason it's happening in the first place. If she tells them to take the provision out, it'll come out." She smiled coolly. "So why won't she?"

Thom kept his expression pleasant, but took it down a notch so she'd think she was making progress. "I hear you, Kerry. We can add in some loan counseling and subsidized financial planning assistance for those in trouble."

"So folks living paycheck to paycheck can learn about 401ks and health savings accounts that they can't afford to contribute to?" Kerry scoffed. "That's bullshit, Thom. My coalition can't support the bill with the swipe fees in there, and you know that." She squared her jaw and said what she'd come here to say. "That provision's got to come out, or we'll pull our support."

There it was. Thom had known it would end up here, but he'd come to the meeting with other offers and protestations because that was the polite thing to do when you were about to screw over an ally. Especially one so new to the game.

"It's not coming out of the bill, Kerry," he said. "I'm sorry."

"Really," she said, pinning him with a look that was sharp as steel.

"I know you view this as a betrayal—"

"No, it's not a betrayal," Kerry said coldly. "It's just step one. Step two is, I go to the press. I expose what you're doing. I tell people that the bill is a sham, that it'll hurt working people. That the governor doesn't care about helping anyone, just her donors and her own bottom line. And then step three is, the swipe-fee provision comes out."

"No," Thom said. "Step three is, the governor attacks you."

Kerry blinked. She hadn't been expecting that. "Me?"

"Yes. I write a speech for the governor where she extols all the good things the bill does, and attacks you as an ideological extremist who's damaging her own cause with purity tests and party infighting," Thom said. "Then step four is, the bill passes with the swipe fees, and Lennie gets credit not just for helping struggling students but for being unafraid to challenge her own base. A bipartisan, tough-talking dealmaker."

"A crook," Kerry countered incredulously. "People will see through that."

Thom shrugged. "Yeah, some. But not the ones who write the headlines."

A hard look settled across Kerry's features as the import of what Thom was saying sank in. "It'll still hurt Governor Westwood."

"Yes, it will. That's why I want us to work together,"

Thom said simply. It happened to be true. "But don't be naive. It'll hurt you more."

"Is that a threat?" Kerry asked.

"You don't want to get into a mudslinging fight with a presidential campaign, Kerry," Thom said quietly. "You're not ready for what that will dredge up."

Kerry shook her head slowly, sitting back in her chair. She stared at him like she was seeing him for the first time. "I can't believe…"

Thom waited, but she didn't finish her sentence. It didn't matter. He got the gist. Still, as he waited for her to regroup, he was irritated to realize that that hanging silence was bothering him. It was ridiculous—he was a professional; he didn't get rattled by idealistic young activists. It didn't matter what she saw in him, or what she'd thought she'd seen.

Ruthlessly, he pushed down his own sense of navel-gazing, morbid curiosity. "Look, we don't have to go there," Thom said. "You're still our ally. I know you're disappointed, but this is what politics is."

"No," Kerry said, her words quiet and clear. She still had that far-off look in her eye. "This is what people like you make it."

"Seriously, how can you not get this?" Thom said urgently, leaning toward her. "It's this bill or *no bill*. This is how it works. Take this progress, and come back at us about the swipe-fee thing in a year if you want. Or do it the next day! Loyalty is nothing in this business—alliances are, and they're built on what you can get, not what you want."

Kerry didn't respond. She was looking at the people walking down the sidewalk across the street from them, shopping and smoking and meeting up for brunch.

Thom sighed. It would be a shame to lose Kerry as a campaign asset—he'd had big plans for her, far beyond the push for this bill. More legislation, more events, and more of the intangible benefits that came with such a charismatic ally. Kerry would have done more than tee up exciting policy for them—she would have been a way for them to tap into the market of young voters, and, even better, young nonvoters.

Still. Getting one bill passed with her star power—even if she turned on it—would help Lennie. And they'd still probably use her picture on the campaign website, whether she stayed with them or not. She was pretty, even here and now, drawn and furious and refusing to look at him. And pretty got clicks.

He stood and dug his wallet out of his pocket, and put down enough to cover their bill. When she still stayed quiet, he said, "Pleasure doing business with you."

She said nothing, so he left.

★ 18 ★

Clay stormed into Thom's office Monday morning shaking with rage. Slamming the door behind him, he held up the letter he'd already crumpled in his fist and said, "Can you believe this shit?"

"Uh," Thom said to whoever he had on the phone. Clay tossed the letter onto Thom's desk and collapsed into a chair in the corner, then leaped up again. He was too frenetic to sit. "Mayor, would it be okay if I called you back? Minor crisis here on my end," Thom was saying. "Yes. Yes. No, under no circumstances. Yes. Okay, thank you."

He hung up and started picking at the crumpled-up letter, adding cattily, "That wasn't important or anything."

"Just read it," Clay shouted.

Thom smoothed out the letter enough to read it, but Clay couldn't stand to watch while he did so—just reliving the experience was enough to make his blood boil.

It was a goddamn *cease and desist* letter from Derek's stupid goddamn lawyer about Clay's fledgling map idea, the one about predicting where voters would settle after they'd moved. Derek was claiming that he had the rights to the program, that he functionally owned it. The letter said that Clay using the program, working on it, or even *accessing* it was theft of Derek's intellectual property.

"What the fuck?" Thom said, frowning thunderously. It instantly sapped some of Clay's anger, seeing it mirrored in someone else. He could feel his shoulders loosen slightly. "He can't be serious."

"Looks pretty goddamn serious to me," Clay grumbled, taking a seat again.

"He's saying *he* has the rights to your map thing?" Thom tossed the letter aside, leaning back in his chair. "You guys haven't worked together in years. You only started developing this, what, a few months ago?"

"A few *weeks* ago," Clay said.

"The balls on this guy," Thom said. "He's obviously full of shit. His lawyers probably talked him into letting them send this thing so they could charge for it. There's no way he wins a suit."

Clay groaned into his hands. *Another* lawsuit? "Why," he mumbled.

"Hang on," Thom demanded. "How does he even know about the idea?"

Clay frowned. How *had* Derek found out? The only thing he could think of was—

"Oh," he said. "Oh shit. I uploaded some of the documents onto our office Pinpoint account."

Thom's eyebrows rose. "He has access to that?"

"He shouldn't," Clay said. "Going through users' personal data? That's shady as shit."

"Could he have found out some other way?"

"No, man," Clay said. "This thing's barely off the ground, the only person I showed it to was—" He cleared his throat. "You."

He hadn't wanted to show it to anyone else until he was sure it would work. And honestly, the appeal of bragging about it, or anything else he'd been working on, had been dimming for him lately. He just wanted to make something that *he* thought was good.

And maybe Thom thought was good too.

"Well, *that* sounds like grounds for a countersuit," Thom was saying. "What did your lawyer say?"

"Uh," Clay said. "I, uh, still have to call him."

Thom nodded, scanning the letter again. "Gotta tell ya. Not a fan of this guy."

Clay's fury was draining away, leaving him more queasy than anything else. It had been stupid of him to store files about the map idea on Pinpoint. More stupid had been coming to Thom about this first, before he'd even called his own lawyer. He got out his phone and dialed the number, wondering if he should take the letter from Thom, but not wanting to disturb him. Now that he'd calmed down some, he actually felt kind of embarrassed that he had come to Thom for help. What was *he* supposed to do?

He got his lawyer's voice mail. Annoyed, he left a quick message and hung up.

Thom was shaking his head at the letter, incredulous. "How could he *possibly* think he owns your idea?"

"He thinks he owns everything," Clay said morosely. He felt like he'd been gut punched. It was bad enough that he and Derek had been fighting over Pinpoint for what felt like forever; now Derek was reaching into Clay's life and strangling the one new idea he'd had—the only *good* idea he'd ever had.

And maybe he was right to. Clay swallowed, flashing back

to that fateful night in Derek's office, when he'd demanded his fair share of Pinpoint and Derek had just laughed and laughed.

He'd thought that he and Derek were equals, and that Derek had just been hogging his share of the glory. Derek hadn't even noticed Clay was there.

He hadn't done shit for Pinpoint; Derek had made that much clear. Maybe the map idea was shit too, and that was why this was happening.

"Clay," Thom was saying, leaning down over his desk to try to meet his eye. "This guy's full of shit, okay? He's not gonna take your map thing away. In fact, him even sending this," he said, shaking the paper for emphasis, "shows it's a good idea. It means he thinks it's valuable."

Clay scrubbed a hand over his face. "Yeah. Maybe."

Thom had a weird look on his face, considering and careful. "Clay—"

Before he could say more, Clay's phone rang. His lawyer's number popped up on-screen. He waved the phone at Thom and stood up. "I should, uh, take this," he said. "Sorry for bothering you."

"It's fine," Thom said, leaning back in his chair. "It's gonna be fine."

"Yeah. Yeah," Clay said, feeling more like he was trying to convince himself, and opened the door.

He picked up before he'd made it to his office. When he turned and looked back through Thom's office blinds, though, it didn't look like he had gone back to work yet. He was sitting at his desk, looking right at Clay, with a determined look in his eye that sent a shiver down Clay's spine.

Clay flushed and looked away. He forced himself to concentrate on what his lawyer was saying, and shut his office door behind him.

★ **19** ★

"Oh my god," Thom said. "You have a *guitar*?"

It was the next weekend, and they were lazing around Clay's apartment again. It was slovenly of them to have not gone into the office, but things with the campaign had been slow, so Thom had told the staff they could work from home. Then it had just been a matter of pretending he wasn't waiting for Clay to text.

In the end it hadn't even been an invitation, just a selfie of Clay looking smug over a plate of waffles. Thom had shot back something taunting and probably sexist, and Clay had replied, and somehow they had sort of mutually agreed to hang out at Clay's place.

It made sense, anyway. Thom wasn't there because he liked video games or waffles—he was there to take pictures of them to post on Instagram, to keep the hashtag content going. He had a hunch that taking pics at someone's apartment would give the whole enterprise a feeling of intimacy that they'd been lacking.

And a picture of him fooling around on a guitar? That was *perfect*. He fumbled to find a good angle, trying out poses. Clay was still playing his dumb donut game and hadn't looked up when Thom discovered the guitar under a pile of dirty laundry shoved against the couch, but he finally threw the controller away in exasperation when Thom tried one pose too many.

"Gimme," he said, gesturing with his hand. Thom reluctantly handed him the phone, and Clay took a single picture before throwing it back at him. Thom was ready to complain, but then he looked at it—it was a surprisingly good shot, taken just a second before he'd gotten into position so that it was actually candid, rather than one of Thom's posed candids. In the photo, he was looking down at the guitar, his face relaxed, his fingers curled around the frets, and a shadow emphasizing the hollow of his jaw.

"Nice," he said, faintly surprised, and posted it to the Instagram account he'd set up for Clay that he controlled. Adoring comments started rolling in instantly.

"Remind me why we're doing this here, again?" Clay asked irritably, back at his game.

"I told you, doing it at an apartment feels more authentic."

"You have an apartment. I assume. Or maybe you just hang upside down from a door frame in the office like a bat."

"I have an apartment," Thom said. "It's too nice."

Clay scoffed. "Thanks."

"It's a compliment!" Thom said. "Your place has more of the vibe we're going for. Mine doesn't read…hipster enough."

"You mean human enough."

Thom ignored him. Clay hadn't ever been to his apartment—how would he know that that was true?

He was interrupted in his fumbling with the guitar when Clay's phone rang. He picked up, still mostly focused on his game, and said, "Hello?…Yeah…That's great." A few moments later he said, "Oh, don't be an asshole," and grinned widely.

It was a nice, warm smile, without even a hint of malice or smugness. Thom shook his shoulders to ward off the pleasurable ripple it sent over his skin. "Yeah, yeah," Clay was saying. With a smile, he said, "Fuck you too," and hung up.

"Who was that?" Thom asked.

"My grandma," Clay said.

Thom blinked at him. *Don't ask, don't ask, don't ask.* He was here for the content, not to get into Clay's weird…grandma issues. Or to stare at his smile.

Clearing his throat, he turned back to the guitar. When he finally strummed it, though, he immediately grimaced at the sound, slapping his palm on the strings.

"Yeah," Clay said. "I can never get that fucking thing in tune."

"Then why did you buy it?"

"I didn't know it was gonna be, like. Hard."

Thom rolled his eyes. "It's not hard."

It only took him about five minutes to tune the guitar by ear. It had been years since he'd touched one, and some of the fingering tripped him up, but pitch was instinctive. When he eventually had the strings sounding right he started to pluck out notes, then chords, then progressions. Clay glanced over at him as stray melodies began to float on the air, mostly stirred from Thom's muscle memory. "You can actually play?" he asked.

"Sure," Thom said, picking out a verse of "Don't Think Twice." "You would not believe how much chicks love guitar."

"Ugh," Clay said. "You're *that* guy?"

Thom played the riff from "The Man Who Sold the World,"

and Clay squirmed and quickly looked away. Thom smiled to himself. That one had always worked particularly well for him.

"Don't be a dick," he said. "I was gonna be a musician in college."

Clay glanced over at him again, like he knew he should ignore Thom for his game but couldn't quite do it. "What, like you had a band?"

"Not really." Mostly he'd been decent at guitar and desperate to get out of the small town he'd grown up in, and *musician* seemed like the fastest way. And then he'd met Caroline. "I mostly played backup for this girl I was with. She wrote the lyrics and sang."

"A girl?" Clay said. "I thought the whole point was to scam on chicks. Or was that why your little band broke up?"

"Uh, no," Thom said. "More like she scammed on me."

Now he had Clay's attention. "Oh. Shit," he said. "Sorry."

Thom shrugged. "She wasn't really cheating on me. We weren't together like that—she didn't do monogamy." Wiggling his eyebrows, he added, "She did everything else, though. And every*one* else."

He'd perfected the joking tone in which he told that story over the last fifteen years, but Clay didn't laugh. He was just staring at Thom, not even seeming to notice when his donut avatar in the game got a few more holes shot in it. "That sucks," he said. "Is that why you decided not to do the whole music thing?"

Thom laughed, more at himself than Clay's question. He didn't usually tell the rest of this story, but he could feel it bubbling up anyway. Something about Clay's apartment did that to him, he'd noticed—made him loosen up, say more than he should. "Actually—well, sort of. It wasn't like she ruined music for me or anything, but uh—I was thinking about how to get back at her, right? And I knew sleeping with someone else wouldn't hurt her. So I thought about everything she hated—and, uh, I ended up signing up for an internship with this local politician. And the rest is history."

He grinned at Clay, but Clay wasn't smiling. "Where is she now?"

Thom frowned. "Fuck do I know?" Clay seemed doubtful, so he said, "Seriously, I'm not upset. Look—" He sighed and ran a hand through his hair, unsure how he had ended up down this path with Clay of all people. "She showed up to an event we did once at the councilman's office. I don't even think she knew I was going to be there, or maybe she did, I dunno. But when I saw her in the crowd, protesting, I suddenly felt this, like, profound sense of relief. Like—rightness. I was so glad to be where I was. On the inside."

He could still see the crowd outside the councilman's strip mall office, waving their sad, handmade signs. He pictured it sometimes when he imagined himself as the White House chief of staff one day, in an office where all he'd see out the windows would be carefully trimmed greenery and Secret Service agents.

That daydream wasn't as calming now as it once had been, though.

The start screen of Clay's game was spinning impatiently. But Clay was still looking at Thom, like he was waiting for something. "She wasn't the love of my life, Clay," Thom said. "Politics is."

His phone buzzed, and he put down the guitar to check it. Clay got up and toasted him with his empty beer bottle as he walked by, saying mockingly, "To the happy couple."

"Make me waffles," Thom called after him.

"You didn't win BoB," Clay said.

"Yeah, well, you lost." Clay said nothing, so Thom said,

"I'll play for my dinner," and grabbed the guitar again, plucking out some "Infanta."

"Oh my god, the Decemberists? You're the worst," Clay complained, clattering around in the kitchen and muttering something that sounded like *calls me a hipster.*

"Yeah, like you have any taste," Thom said, stretching out on the couch. "Is this what you want?" He started up a new song, complete with the showy intro lick, and started to sing about sunrise on a dark day.

Clay came out from the kitchen, frowning. "Shit. Why can't I remember what song that is?"

Thom grinned. He kept singing, this time in Spanish, about taking his time. When he reached the cusp of the chorus, he looked at Clay expectantly, the melody hovering. Clay had the tortured look of someone with something stuck on the tip of his tongue. Savoring it, Thom played the notes of the chorus and sang, *"...muy rápido."*

Clay scowled at him. "That's not funny. C'mon, what's it called?"

Thom shrugged and played the chorus again, singing, *"Piénsalo..."*

"Thom!"

"Con cuidado."

"Goddamn it," Clay said, and headed for his laptop.

Thom shut it with one foot then put both feet on top of it, still playing. *"Dios mío!"*

Clay lunged for Thom's laptop and Thom finally abandoned the guitar to try to stop him, shouting out every four-syllable Spanish word he could think of. "Thom!" Clay shouted, in the tone of an aggrieved younger sibling. "Come on!"

They ended up on the couch with Clay on his back, hugging Thom's laptop to his chest, and Thom on top of him.

He dug his fingers under the computer, trying to pry it away, but Clay had a firm grip on the thing. For the moment, it was a stalemate.

Thom pushed himself up on one hand, taking a second to breathe. But as soon as he looked back down at Clay, he lost his breath again. Clay was half laughing, half wheezing from their tussle. His eyes were bright with excitement, his face open and relaxed, and his jaw curved into a smile.

Thom felt like he was drowning. He swallowed, desperately wishing he could remember a time when he hadn't found Clay attractive.

But he couldn't. And now that they'd paused, their struggle had lost its momentum and was starting to slide the other way, pulled along by the silence between them and their matched, panting breaths. Thom was sprawled all over Clay, his hand trapped between the laptop and Clay's warm chest, their legs entangled. With Thom above him, his hand splayed on the couch by Clay's head, his forearm brushing his temple, it was far too easy to imagine that they were—

Thom sniffed, then frowned. "Is something burning?"

Clay started. "The waffles!"

Thom sat back to let him get up, watching Clay sprint back into the kitchen and trying not to remember the feel of Clay's body beneath his. He grabbed the guitar again and cleared his throat, then sang, *"Desgarbado."*

"Aha!" Clay shouted from the kitchen. *"Despacito."*

"Using your phone is cheating," Thom called after him. Truthfully, he was thankful; he wasn't sure he could have gone another round of that game.

In his pocket, his own phone buzzed with comments accumulating on photos of him and Clay together.

★ 20 ★

It was late, and Thom was still at the office, but not for the usual depressing reasons. No, it was even *more* depressing: instead of being deluged with work, he was done with his work and still at the office anyway—spinning in his chair, swiping aimlessly through his phone, and trying his absolute hardest not to text Clay.

He needed to stop going over to his place. Sure, it was convenient; he could post content for their fake relationship, get some work done, and unwind all at the same time. But the part of himself that could still dimly remember what it had been like to be Thom Fucking Morgan, the pre-Clay version of Thom—that part of himself had some self-respect. Maybe.

He'd taken a picture of Clay yesterday after their little tussle over the computer, because his hair had been all mussed in kind of a cute way. He'd put it on Instagram and the damn thing had been breaking some kind of record, almost garnering as many likes as pictures of Thom did, which was border-line unacceptable. Thom was effectively the brand manager for their relationship, so he did take some pride in his promotional skills, but still.

He looked at the photo again, checking its stats. Clay was squinting in the picture, suspicious, and there was a blur in one corner that had probably been his hand trying to swat the phone away. It was just Clay's head in the shot, but Thom could remember how his shirt had looked too, all rumpled from their fight so that the scent of his laundry detergent had been in the air. Clay's apartment always smelled like that—dumb, domestic things that were mundane but also homey.

Thom shut the screen in frustration. Around him, the office was mostly dark, with just a few sharp points of light here and there illuminating the corner of a desk or an empty hallway.

He startled a little when Felicia appeared at his open door. He shouldn't have been surprised—if anyone would also have been working late, it'd be her. She held up a bottle of something—whiskey, it looked like—and wordlessly walked into his office to plunk two mugs from the kitchen onto his desk. One was from Lennie's first congressional run over a decade ago, and the other was a World's Best Boss mug someone must have gotten as a joke. Good thing Bex kept Lennie from ever seeing the kitchen.

As she poured, he asked, "Bad day?"

She sat in the chair across from his desk, taking her mug. "She's gonna go with ten percent."

Thom nodded. They'd been tossing around ideas for Lennie's climate platform. Felicia wanted her to go big and call for a fifty percent tax on various dirty emissions products. The donors had urged her to stick with something more moderate, like ten percent. Apparently Lennie had made her choice. "Your mistake was caring enough to have an opinion," Thom said.

"Ugh," Felicia told him. "Just let me drink in peace."

"You came to me!" Thom said.

"Why are you still here?" she asked.

He shrugged, like there wasn't somewhere very specific he could be right now. "Don't you ever just prefer work?"

"No," Fe said baldly. "I think we're just shitty with people."

"I'm *great* with people," he said.

She raised a dubious eyebrow at him.

"Are you kidding?" he said. "I've had girls *thank me* for breaking up with them over text. I'm smooth as hell."

"Yeah, you're real smooth," she said, her lips quirked in a small smile around the rim of her mug.

The flickering fluorescent lights of the office turned the white walls a sickening shade of bluish green this time of night. Thom took a sip of Fe's whiskey to warm up. "Maybe I do need to get out more," he conceded.

"Y'know the crazy thing?" Fe said wistfully, slouching in one of his chairs. "It never does distract me from work—dating, parties, any of it. Not really. It's always buzzing away back there." She gestured to her temple. "Polls. The stump speech. Calls I have to return." She sighed and downed what was in her mug, then poured another one. "No matter what."

He eyed the lines of her body. Under the wool and polyester, he could tell that it was lithe and strong. It was a body that deserved to be distracted every once in a while. "You're just not having good enough sex," he told her.

She smirked at him. "Is that so?"

Thom loosened his necktie button and held her look, saying nothing.

Her eyes widened, and she sat up in the chair. "Oh, no. Tell me you're not *hitting on me*."

"Of course not," Thom said easily. "I know that would offend your virginal sensibilities."

But his joke didn't work—Felicia was angry, angrier than would be merited by just an unwelcome pass. "No, you're offending my appreciation of your political skill," she spat. "If it gets out that you and Clay are fake, it will *kill* this campaign."

Thom went a little cold. He hadn't thought of that in a while. "Jesus, Fe, I wasn't hitting on you."

She shook her head, unconvinced and furious. "This *has* to work," she said. "It's not our fault that you signed up for an indefinite period of celibacy. That's the only way this works—we can't have a single hookup coming forward to contradict us, or it'll ruin the narrative."

"I got it," Thom snapped.

And he did. But it wasn't until this conversation that he recognized the tension in his muscles for what it was—an acute need to get laid. It had been a while. *Had* he been hitting on Felicia just now? Sometimes he did it without even noticing.

Then something else occurred to him. "Have you given this speech to Clay?" he asked.

There was a heavy pause underscored by Fe glaring at him flatly. Then she said, "You're an idiot," downed her drink, and left.

Clay jumped a little at a knock on his door late at night. He hadn't ordered any food, and he wasn't expecting anyone. Warily, he got up to answer it.

Thom stood at his threshold, holding a six-pack of beer. "Hey," he said. "Can I work here for a while? I can't concentrate at the office, it's driving me crazy."

Thom's suit was rumpled, but that wasn't all that looked off about him. He had a hand braced on Clay's door frame, and he looked sort of…slumped, in an odd way. Relaxed, except that on Thom, relaxed was a very weird look.

Clay felt weird too—it was late enough that he'd changed into a thin T-shirt and pj bottoms. He felt self-conscious about being so underdressed around Thom, but Thom didn't seem to care. "Uh," he said. "Sure."

He stood back to let Thom in. "Thanks," he said, handing him the beers. Clay took two, put the rest in the fridge, and joined Thom on the couch, where he was shedding his messenger bag and coat.

Despite his stated reason for being there, Thom took the beer Clay gave him but didn't reach for his laptop or his phone. Instead, he took a long swig and leaned his head back against the couch. He closed his eyes, his dark eyelashes fanning out over his cheeks. He really was ridiculously, unfairly handsome.

And tonight, he was uncharacteristically calm. Clay had never seen Thom get comfortable in his apartment without trying to play it off somehow. There was nothing distracting or preoccupying him; he was just *being*, and letting Clay watch him be.

Thom sighed, and his throat bobbed as he swallowed. Clay thought of how the sky turned dark before a lightning storm, and felt a distant call of thunder in his nerves.

"Am I working the staff too hard?" Thom asked.

Clay started. "What? No," he said. "We all want to work hard. Lennie's gonna be the president. What's cooler than that?"

"I dunno," Thom said. "A night off every once in a while. Getting a drink. Letting off steam."

What? "Okay, I know you don't actually think letting off

steam is cooler than working in the West Wing," Clay said, frowning.

"Even a top political operative needs some fun every once in a while," Thom said archly.

"Oh, yeah?" Clay asked. "You don't have enough fun?"

"Honestly, it's been too long. If you know what I mean," Thom said, sitting forward and giving Clay a *you know what I mean* eyebrow waggle. "Like…weeks."

"Of course you think everyone has sex every few weeks," Clay muttered, looking at his beer.

"C'mon," Thom said. "I'm just—I'm pissed off. On both our behalves."

"What?" Clay asked. "Why?"

"Because neither of us can fuck anyone until this charade is over," Thom said. "It'd be one thing if we got caught and people thought we were cheating—I mean, that'd be bad. But if it got out that it's fake? Cataclysmic."

He was not being subtle, but Clay tried to calm the rapid beating of his heart by telling himself that that wasn't where this was going. Thom took another long swig of his beer, then put it down on the table, pushing it away. He leaned back against the couch again, loosening his tie. Clay rubbed a thumb against his beer bottle restlessly.

"You know what else is gonna get us found out?" Thom asked, his eyes closed.

"What?"

"Our fake kissing," he said, looking at Clay. "It sucks."

Clay felt a self-conscious tingle that started in his scalp and swept to his toes. "Excuse me?"

"We've gotta get better at it. More relaxed," Thom said. "You're acting like it's our first kiss every time, and it's gonna get us busted."

Clay gaped as a flush of heat bloomed all over his skin. Of

course he wasn't relaxed when he kissed Thom—it *had been* their first (and second) kiss.

And it had been distressingly hot both times.

"Fuck you!" he managed to sputter. "You were tenting so hard at the fundraiser you were gonna knock over a topiary."

"Only because I hadn't fucked someone in weeks," Thom said. "Look, we should practice kissing the way real couples do."

Clay's heart hammered in his throat, making his voice come out strangled when he asked, "Like—what?"

"Boring," Thom explained. "Because they never fuck anymore."

"You want to practice kissing?" Clay demanded. "Boring kissing?"

"Jesus, Clay," Thom said, exasperated. "This is for *work*."

Clay just sat there, stunned and sweltering and still. Thom keyed onto the first two quickly, but it took him a second to notice the last one. When he did, he sat up, his expression tentative, and shifted closer to Clay. Clay still didn't move, though a part of him was screaming at him to run.

Thom leaned in and kissed Clay gently, just a soft press of lips with no tongue. Clay tried to imagine what this would be like if it weren't just their third kiss—and if it wasn't the first time they'd done anything like this when they were completely alone. He made himself relax back against the couch and meet Thom's lips softly, not too slow and not too fast. Measured, calmly, as if this were meaningless.

Thom withdrew slightly, changed the angle, and kissed him again, bringing a hand up to stroke Clay's jaw. Heat throbbed all through him, but Clay forced himself not to react. He made his muscles relax one by one. But he could hear himself breathing faster, and Thom's hand tightened on Clay's skin.

It kept going and going—an exquisite kind of torture, having to relax just as everything inside him was tightening with longing. As they kissed the heat grew, in his lips, under his skin, in the empty itch of his palms. He wanted to touch Thom, but he forced himself not to. He wanted to deepen the kiss, but he resisted. He wanted to let himself make noise, to gasp for breath like his body was dying to, but he could dimly remember that he wasn't supposed to. He couldn't remember why.

Before long Clay's entire body was churning, his brain fried and his hands shaking at his sides. Thom was muttering into Clay's mouth, but Clay couldn't make sense of what he was saying until Thom's hand clasped the back of his neck, a sudden white-hot shock. "We have to," Thom was slurring, "no one else can know, and it'll be good—so good, Clay, come on, it'll keep us sane, no one has to know…"

Bad idea. Bad idea, bad idea, chanted a voice in Clay's head, but the voice sounded drugged and distracted too as Thom crept closer and closer to him, their knees bumping and Clay's hands somehow already in Thom's hair. And really, hadn't it always been going here—not just since that day that Thom had slammed Clay against the wall, but before then, when Thom was the arrogant asshole whose dark eyes and soft skin had haunted Clay's dreams? When he'd wanted this for so long—before he'd even known he wanted it—how could he resist?

Thom hung on to Clay's neck and poured his words into Clay's mouth between kisses that were growing longer and deeper, until finally Clay shoved him back onto the couch and crawled on top of him.

They kissed wildly, wet and deep, their inhibitions completely gone. Thom reached up to yank Clay's T-shirt off, and Clay pulled Thom's dress shirt out of his pants, shoving two hands underneath it to get at his bare skin, nuzzling at Thom's neck even though his collar and tie were still in the way. Their hands bumped and tangled as they both tried to get Thom undressed at once, Thom undoing his shirt buttons while Clay almost strangled Thom in his fervor to get his tie off. The couch creaked as they lurched around, the only other sounds their frustrated grunts and frantic breathing.

Before long Clay was swatting Thom's hands away so he could lever himself down Thom's body. He pulled at the button of his pants and yanked down his zipper, then glanced up at Thom, who was red and gulping for breath. "Is this okay?" Clay asked raggedly.

"Yes. Yeah, yes," Thom said, nodding furiously, "Yes."

Thom's cock was just as mouthwatering as the rest of him, thick and hot and perfect. Clay gave it a few gentle, getting-to-know-you strokes, thrilled at Thom's hiss of surprise and pleasure. He breathed hotly over the head and licked out to taste him. Thom groaned, and all at once Clay was done with going slow. He swallowed Thom down as far as he could take him, pressed his palms to Thom's hips, and went for it.

Thom gasped and his back bowed, his eyes squeezing shut as if in pain. He made an unbearably hot picture from Clay's point of view, twisting and writhing with pleasure, his shirt hanging open and undershirt already damp with sweat. Clay moaned and sucked hard, loving the hot weight of Thom on his tongue. Thom's fingers burrowed into Clay's hair while he made tight, disbelieving noises, trying to muffle them against his other hand. Clay moaned again, unable to stop himself from rutting against the couch. He raked his nails down Thom's thighs and ran his tongue along his length and held Thom's hips down when he bucked up. Thom's fingers tightened against his scalp, digging in desperately. Clay never wanted it to end.

"Clay—" Thom panted, shuddering. "I'm gonna—"

Clay had just enough time to be surprised that Thom had good sexual etiquette, and then he was coming. He watched raptly as Thom shouted and jerked, keeping his throat loose to swallow easily. He gave him plenty of time to come down, then pulled back and wiped his lip while Thom lay there rebooting.

Clay sat back against the couch, panting. He was unbelievably hard, so turned-on he could barely see straight, but he didn't want to think about what would happen next. His mind was stuck on a loop of Thom's gorgeous, full-body spasm when he'd come, the addictive taste of him, and the sweet ache in Clay's jaw.

But his arousal was edged with trepidation. Because there had been some safety in getting Thom off. That had been fun, a hot-as-hell challenge that Clay had been more than willing to indulge—maybe even that he'd been craving for longer than he cared to admit. His crush on Thom had always been worshipful, so he felt no shame in having worshipped him. It had been like proving himself.

But Thom touching *him* would be different. Clay wouldn't be in control. He felt shaky, like a house of cards that would crumble from a single touch of Thom's fingers. There would be nothing left of his guard at all.

He wondered if Thom would just get up and leave without even trying to reciprocate. There would be some cold, predictable relief in that. Even imagining Thom reaching out to touch him felt too much like admitting something.

Thom blinked when he sat up, not trying to hide his doe-eyed languorousness. Clay felt his breathing go thin. Thom smacked his lips and put a hand on the couch near Clay's shoulder, but he didn't hurry him, didn't press. He shuffled closer like he was genuinely cold and looking for warmth, and started pressing kisses to Clay's temple, to his cheek. His breath gusted in Clay's ear, warm and wet. He was all soft, seductive sweetness now that he'd come, rubbing a hand down Clay's body and murmuring, "Hmm. That looks painful. Let me help."

At the first brush of Thom's hand against his cock through the thin fabric of his pajamas, Clay gasped like he was dying. "Let me," Thom said again, and heat flooded Clay's face, his entire body. The weight of Thom's eyes on him was too much, so he pressed his face into his neck and whimpered, nodding *yes, please*. Thom licked his hand and shoved it under the waistband of Clay's pants and, thank god, didn't fool around or tease at all—he gripped Clay tight and did it fast, giving him everything he needed. Clay made embarrassing noises into Thom's throat and breathed in the scent of him and gripped his thigh so hard he probably left marks.

His orgasm was as white-hot and all-encompassing as he'd known it would be. It left him in a stupor, slumped against Thom. He might as well have been snuggling him. It was abjectly humiliating, but undeniably peaceful. He drifted.

Then Thom said, his voice winded but casual, "See? Now we're not stressed anymore."

Clay pulled back and looked at him. Thom was wearing his consultant face, the blankly affable look that said, *Don't worry, none of this matters*. Clay had seen it at the office hundreds of times before—it was Thom's default state—but it was still shocking to see here, now, when his skin was still chilly with sweat and there were come stains drying on his pants.

Clay stared at him, and Thom held his look. His answer to Clay's unspoken question was clear.

Then Thom glanced down at his hand. "Aw, gross," he complained, and got up from the couch, heading for the bathroom.

Clay was still tingling. He felt winded and wrung-out in the best possible way. But that edge of fear he'd felt before settled into his bones, a quiet dread that chased off the post-orgasm haze.

★ 21 ★

It kept happening.

This was, literally, exactly what Clay had feared. He'd fucked Thom, and it had been even better than he'd fucking expected, and now there was no way it wouldn't all end in shit. Thom was a relationship white walker—he could go through the motions, but emotionally he was a rotting corpse. He'd made it quite clear that he viewed Clay's dick as his own personal stress squeeze ball, and Clay himself as nothing more than an agreeable squeeze-buddy. There was no one less worthy of sex-based emotional entanglement than Thom, and no one more primed to extract it anyway—with his intoxicating smile, his infuriatingly perfect body, and his easy charm. Clay had known hooking up with Thom was a bad idea before they'd done it, and he knew it was a bad idea to keep doing it now.

Yet it kept happening. Apparently, Clay was easy enough for Thom Morgan that his resolutions only ever lasted half a day, because every night he came home from the office determined not to let it happen again, and then he'd sit on the couch playing BoB with Thom on his laptop next to him bitching about how distracting it was while he was trying to work, and Clay would congratulate himself on his smart choice to not fuck Thom anymore because he'd rather fucking kill him. Then Thom would get up for a beer and Clay would watch the long lines of his legs and back as he walked away, and when he'd sit down again Clay would get a hint of his cologne mixed with sweat from a long day, and a few minutes later Thom would put a hand on his thigh, cold from the beer, and—

And so it went, over and over. They traded blowjobs and handjobs every night that week, always on the same couch that had spelled his doom in the first place. Clay was getting way too good at it—he was learning Thom's noises, his most sensitive spots, how to tell when it was a night he'd let Clay push his clothes off slowly and dick around kissing his ears or the soft skin under his belly button, and when he'd want Clay to scrape his hand raw on the zipper of his pants, he was so desperate for his touch.

And Thom was improving too. It was clearly his first time with a guy, but he never seemed shy or nervous—it was more like he was aware of what he already knew how to do, and happy to stick to his comfort zone. But he broadened his horizons the more time they spent naked together, and he had a voracious appetite. All he had to do was flick a glance up at Clay through those eyelashes as he was trailing his mouth down his skin, and Clay forgot every doubt or fear he'd ever had, lost in the fever of Thom's hands and tongue. The memory of it would distract Clay sometimes at the goddamn office, and he had *never* been one of those people.

After the first few nights of Thom Uber-ing back to his place every night at one a.m., he'd finally started sleeping on Clay's couch—brushing his teeth at the office and showering at the gym, Clay assumed, because he never saw Thom doing anything that suggested he actually *lived* in Clay's apartment except nodding off next to him after sex.

Then again, Clay didn't *see* Thom being domestic—but he was beginning to notice the telltale signs scattered around his apartment. Thom would bitch about the unopened mail strewn all over the place, but not do anything except angrily brush it to the side while Clay was there. In the morning, though, there'd be a neat stack of bills on his coffee table, and all his catalogues in the trash. Clay's kitchen counter was usually a jumble of appliances, but a few weeks after Thom started coming over, he found that someone had combed out all the power cords and positioned the waffle iron to be especially free of interference.

And Clay's mom had sent him a plant when he'd first moved in—a short, stubby little thing that had started turning a sadder shade of green almost immediately. The back of Clay's apartment was a big sliding glass door, but it faced a dark, dingy storage area that was open to the street above, so he had to keep thick curtains up all the time to ward away creepers. With no sunlight, that had basically been it for the plant. Until Clay noticed one day that the farthest-right part of the curtain had been tied in a knot at the bottom, and the knotted fabric tucked into a wrought-iron bar running vertically next to the window. It created a perfect little triangle of sun for the plant, while still shielding the apartment from view from the street. It was an elegant solution, and Clay could picture Thom doing it. He wondered how long it had taken for him to notice. The plant already looked greener.

His entire apartment looked like it was slowly coming to life.

Thom was getting used to Clay's apartment. It was sunken and small, which annoyed Thom at times, but it was also warmer than his apartment—not just literally, but in the crumbled brick walls, the dark furniture and the deep green fabrics. Somehow, the effect of the colors and the cramped space made it feel cozy, like being cocooned away from the rest of the world.

He'd still never been in Clay's bedroom, and he wasn't planning to be. Hooking up regularly on the couch was intimate enough for Thom; there was no need to make things confusing.

Because aside from the potential for confusion, things with Clay were going surprisingly well. It had been a while since he'd had a fuckbuddy, and it had rarely been an actual fuck *buddy*. He'd had standing sex appointments with political allies, and political rivals he'd met up with for sporadic hate sex. But the comfort and familiarity of having someone whose apartment he'd effectively colonized, whose schedule he literally had at the press of a button, who'd be there whenever he wanted him, who he enjoyed spending time with—

Scratch that. He did *not* enjoy spending time with Clay. It was just that the fuckbuddy setup was going well, which meant that Thom was getting laid regularly, which was putting him in a better mood than he'd been in in a while, which meant that he was getting along better with everybody.

It was definitely, positively not Clay. Spending more time with Clay just meant learning more than Thom ever needed to about his dopey, bro-ish interests, like sports and the donut game and why he liked bars that had games in them like Skee-Ball. Thom had tried to explain to Clay once that the only bars worth going to were the ones where you were guaranteed to be seen by reporters, but Clay had just laughed and promised to take him to play air hockey sometime. Thom couldn't remember if he'd said yes.

The point was, the sex was incredible. If anything, it was getting better over time, hotter, as if they needed it more the more they got. Hooking up on the couch did make Thom feel depressingly like he was back in high school, except that he was sort of into it sometimes—that messy, crazed feeling, like he would die if he didn't get Clay's hands on him. It was the perfect antidote to the tightness that crept into his shoulders and the small of his back after a long day at the office—Clay pressing him down into the couch cushions, his hand in Thom's hair to pull his head back so he could lick and suck at Thom's throat, his other hand pawing at Thom's clothes, his thigh grinding down between Thom's legs.

Maybe it was only so good because it was his first time with a guy—kind of like trying a new food. The first time Thom had tried Thai, it had been like, *Oh my god, where has this been all my life*, and he'd ended up ordering drunken noodles so often that he was pretty sure the hostess at Monsoon Siam would report him as a missing person if he ever stopped. But after a while the novelty had worn off, and it had become plain and ordinary. He was sure that would happen with Clay soon; he'd become just another menu buried at the bottom of Thom's kitchen drawer.

In the meantime, he was happy to be the recipient of Clay's relative expertise. Clay had actually teased him about it once—right after Thom had come, while he was still limp and boneless on the couch, Clay had handed him a fistful of paper towels from the kitchen and said, "I kinda feel bad."

Thom was still trying to get his brain to restart. He pawed ineffectually at the paper towels. "Huh?"

Clay grinned and nipped him on the ear, which made Thom's still-tingling bits throb with approval. "I feel like I've been taking advantage of your, uh…virginity."

Thom raised an eyebrow. "My what now?"

"Your *gay* virginity."

Thom laughed. "Yeah, okay. I don't think that's a thing, but thank you. I know what I'm doing."

Clay frowned. "You've been with other guys before?"

"No, but, y'know," Thom said, drying himself off. "When I got this assignment, I…did my research."

Clay's eyes darkened, and he leaned into Thom's space. "You've been watching gay porn?"

Thom's heartbeat sped up, even though he knew for a fact that he'd be out of commission for the next hour at least. But Clay was watching his lips, and the unmasked lust on his face had an answering need unfurling beneath Thom's skin. It was so stupidly good with Clay every time, and so *easy*. He was comfortable here.

Comfortable with Clay.

So he scoffed, and made his voice light. "Yeah, for *work*."

Clay blinked and sat backward. "Right."

Thom fumbled his phone out from between the couch cushions. "It's late. I should go."

"Yeah, okay," Clay said, trying to make himself sound distracted. Thom was merciful and never called Clay out on it when he had trouble with the rituals of casual sex. He was obviously less used to it than Thom.

Once he'd ordered an Uber, he put his phone in his pocket

and started gathering his things. "Wanna wait in here?" Clay asked casually. "It's windy out."

"Nope," Thom said. "See you tomorrow."

Thom waited on the curb as he watched the car icon on his screen inch closer. It *was* cold outside, but it was more comfortable than it would have been inside.

Less confusing too.

★ 22 ★

When Thom got to the office on Tuesday, he was surprised to find himself walking in next to Clay. With an irritated glance at him, he asked, "How is it possible we're getting here at the same time?"

"Hmm?" Clay asked blankly. "I don't know. Why wouldn't we?"

Because I had to Uber back from your place at five a.m., work out, shower, and get ready first, Thom thought. But he only said, "Because I had more to do."

His gruff tone seemed to clue Clay in to what he was talking about. Defensively, he said, "I like sleeping in! I need my beauty rest."

Thom rolled his eyes. They got onto the elevator together.

When the doors closed, Clay asked, "Besides, what's the problem? Are you worried that if we get here together people will think…that we're sleeping together?"

He had a point. Thom grimaced but said nothing.

"We should be even *more* obvious," Clay continued, starting to grin. "Come in wearing each other's clothes. Get matching coffee cups. Maybe I should give you a hickey."

"Don't even think about it," Thom said darkly.

Clay just ignored him, sidling closer so he could pretend to inspect Thom's neck for a good hickey spot.

"Ugh," Thom said, fending him off with his messenger bag. Annoyingly, though, he could feel himself starting to smile. "Don't!"

"It'll help sell it," Clay said, making awful, gawp-y mouth sounds at him. "C'mon, let me!"

"Stop!" Thom said, an inadvertent laugh scraping out of him. He shoved Clay away just as the elevator doors opened.

They revealed Felicia, who did not seem amused by their antics. Thom cleared his throat and straightened his tie. "Morning."

She arched an eyebrow at him. "The meeting?"

"Oh, crap," Thom said, glancing at his watch. "Right, okay—let me just grab some files from my office and I'll be right there."

Felicia gave him a flat look and walked off without another word. Thom turned to Clay and had the fleeting, utterly bizarre impulse to kiss him before leaving. Clay was looking at him too, laughter still fading from his eyes, a small smile on his face.

Thom blinked and stuffed the strange feeling away, turning to leave and muttering, "Bye."

He was, in fact, several minutes late when he got to the conference room, where Felicia and a few of the junior policy and communications people were waiting. Thom put his files on the table and said, "Alright everyone, let's get started. As you all know, the student loans bill is about to pass, so we need to make sure we're ready for our victory lap, i.e. our media rollout." He flicked open one of his files. "The first thing to know—"

"Uh, Thom?" Felicia interrupted him delicately. "I called this meeting. Remember?"

Thom frowned. "Yeah. I thought you called it to have me brief everyone on the bill to set up the rollout."

"Partly," Fe said, standing. "But mostly I wanted to talk about Kerry." She clicked a button on the remote she was holding, and a slideshow fired to life on a pull-down screen on one wall. The first slide was a large picture of Kerry, along with logos of media companies and a bulleted list that read: *activist, Woman of Color, good narrative, local roots.*

"Uh," Thom said uneasily, sitting down. "What about Kerry?"

"Like you said, we're about to take our victory lap on the student loans bill," Felicia said, addressing the room as a whole. "And Kerry is the face of the bill—well, the other face, aside from the governor's. So far we've only been partnering with her on local media, but soon we'll want to raise her profile on the national stage. We have to make sure she's ready."

"You want oppo?" asked one of the junior staffers, scribbling down notes.

"No, Thom's already done all that," Fe said. "I'm thinking more media training, plus some brainstorming about the best way to package her." She clicked over to the next slide, which showed a set of polling results. "We included a few questions about Kerry in our last in-state poll, and the results show that people really—"

"Um," Thom said lowly, leaning toward Felicia. "I'm not sure that we should bank on Kerry being a surrogate for the bill. Or us."

"Why not?" Felicia asked, frowning. "This is her whole thing."

Thom glanced at the junior staffers and lowered his voice another notch. "Yeah, but, uh…the thing is…"

Felicia's face darkened. *"What."*

He was saved from having to answer when everyone's phones started buzzing at once. As soon as he realized why, however, he lost all sense of gratitude. His heart sank when he saw the words *Westwood* and *leaked audio*. "Christ," he said. "Not again."

There was a clip circulating online, apparently a leaked recording of Lennie on a phone call with a major donor. One of the junior staffers had already started playing it on her phone, the volume loud enough so that everyone could hear Lennie's echoing, disembodied voice saying: "Well, I don't know why you weren't invited to the breakfast, Steve. Listen, that was my staff's fuckup, I assure you, because with the amount you've given, I mean, I'll make up the guest bedroom for you, you can move in!"

The tinny sound of Lennie's laughter punctuated the end of the clip. Felicia closed her eyes, her expression pained. The audio started looping around again on the staffer's phone. Thom glared at her and she jumped, fumbled with her phone, and tapped at it a dozen times until the sound finally died away.

"Fuck," Thom hissed. Any type of leak involving donors was always terrible—voters got to see how the sausage was made, and that was never a good thing. This particular clip made it sound like Lennie would sell the state of California for a big enough donor check. "How the fuck does this keep happening?" he asked.

He glanced at Fe, who still had her eyes closed, a hand pressed to her temple. "Where's the governor?" he asked.

She sighed and got out her phone. "At a fundraiser," she said, typing. "I'll make sure Bex takes her phone and keeps her calm until she's somewhere private."

"And make sure it actually is private," Thom said. "We're gonna have to get Bex one of those stupid things that picks up radio signals to scan for bugs." A staffer started typing on his phone, and Thom snapped, "Don't write that down!" Pointing to another staffer, he said, "You—get me a full report on this story—the full quote, who she was speaking to, who's running it, any responses from Warhey, everything. I want it in ten minutes. Go!"

The junior staffers all jumped up to leave. Thom sat forward and put his head in his hands, already beginning to feel a stress headache coming on. It was just one thing after another: the hair gaffe, the Bash limousine leak, now this. He glanced at Fe's slideshow, showing Kerry's smiling face, and felt another throb of pressure.

Clay poked his head into the conference room. "You guys okay?" he asked. "I saw the others race out of here."

A few months ago, Thom would have screamed him out of the room. Today, though, the sight of him ratcheted down his thudding heartbeat. "Close the door," he told Clay tiredly, and he silently obeyed.

Thom sat back in his chair and asked Felicia, "How do you want to handle this?"

She rubbed at her face. "Can we get the student loans bill out in time to step on it?"

Thom shook his head. "It's still in markup."

"Fuck," Fe said. "Okay, what other policy do we have ready to roll out?"

"Uh..." Thom said blearily. Clay closed the door and sat down next to him. "Not much."

"What, really?" she demanded. "We have student loans, and nothing else?"

"Student loan reform is going to be our signature issue," Thom said. "We've been putting all the policy staff to work finalizing it."

"They can only work on one thing at a time?"

"They're junior policy staffers," Thom said. "They can barely work on one thing at a time."

"C'mon, be serious," Felicia said. "There has to be something. Even something small—some issue we can harp on to refocus the press."

"I am serious," Thom said, slightly irritated. "It's not like we can just cook something up in an hour—policy takes time. Besides, it's not like we have a huge bench of policy experts. Most of the money's been going to paid media, direct mail, and those consultants who are coming up with the whole digital media campaign. Y'know, the Twitter hashtag and whatever."

Felicia blinked at him. "Right," she said, slowly folding back into her chair.

Clay piped in next. "What about an interview?"

Thom frowned. "An interview? With who?"

"I dunno," Clay said. "But, like, get her on TV. That would change the narrative, right?"

"To what?" Thom asked. "They would just ask her about this." He leaned back in his chair, sighing. "God, where's a natural disaster when you need one?"

"Uh, okay," Clay said. "What if…she got a dog?"

"You want her to get a dog," Thom said flatly.

"Or, I dunno," Clay said. "What about a meme?"

"A meme?"

"Yeah, she could do something funny on Twitter, go viral."

"Why didn't I think of that? Let's just make our political candidate popular on the internet!"

"You know what Thom, I'm trying to help."

Thom rubbed his face with his hands. "It just needs to be something, anything, to reset the news cycle. What if...what if she got a new haircut?"

Felicia burst into laughter, making Thom jump in his seat.

"A new haircut!" she said in a strangled, high-pitched voice. Thom glanced at Clay, whose eyes had gone wide.

"Uh, Felicia," Thom said. "You alright?"

"Yeah, I'm great," Felicia said, throwing her head back. "A new haircut. A new *haircut*."

"It's just an idea," Thom said.

"No, you're right, it's a great idea," Fe said. "She's running to be the most powerful person in the world, in charge of three hundred million people, a trillion-dollar economy, and enough nuclear weapons to end life on earth dozens of times over. Why doesn't she try bangs?"

"Felicia—"

"I'm fine," she said, tilting her head down and pinching the bridge of her nose between her fingers. The laughter was abruptly gone from her voice.

The silence sat awkwardly for a moment. "I like her hair," Clay offered.

Felicia's head snapped up, a fake smile plastered on her face. "Hey, there's an idea," she said. "Why don't you two do something?"

"Uh," Thom said, sharing another uneasy glance with Clay. "Us? What do you mean?"

She shrugged tightly. "Your little dates have been the best moments this campaign's had over the last few weeks," she said. "That's what we did the last time there was a crisis."

Thom looked at Clay. Neither of them said anything. After

a moment, Thom said, "I guess we…could do that. What did you have in mind?"

"I don't fucking know," she said, getting up and turning her back to them.

Another bleak silence fell. Thom stared at his shoes so he wouldn't look at Clay. The truth was, he didn't need any suggestions from Felicia—he already had way too many ideas for things they could do—inane, unproductive things, like trying new restaurants or walking around the city. He just wanted to spend hours with Clay doing something stupid and utterly pointless. He was starting to crave it.

He shook his head and tried to focus on real, substantive ideas for how they could move past the gaffe, but his political consultant brain wasn't firing up. Instead of generating workable ideas, he was stuck on the memory of Clay's laughter as he'd tried to pin him in the elevator, and the stupid faces he'd made, smacking his lips together like an idiot.

Clearing his throat, Thom said, "Are you sure it should be us? The distraction thing will only get us so far. It really feels like we should do something focused on Lennie."

Felicia said nothing.

Clay, looking as uncomfortable as Thom, said, "Hey, uh—what about Bash?"

"Bash?" Thom asked incredulously.

"Yeah," Clay said, shrugging. "I mean, you want to change the conversation—why not do something, like, mother-son, just the two of them."

"More media attention to Bash is the last thing we need right now," Thom said drily. He turned to Felicia, who had gone very still, a small frown on her face. "Fe? Want to back me up here?"

Felicia glanced down at her phone, then back up at him. "What?"

Thom raised an eyebrow. "You want to explain why Bash is not a solution?"

Felicia looked lost in thought for another moment. Then she seemed to come out of it, saying quietly, "Yeah, he's not."

"So what do we do?" Thom said.

Felicia put her phone back in her pocket and crossed her arms. "We do nothing."

"Nothing?" Thom asked.

"We power through it," Fe said grimly. "We don't have anything to throw out as a distraction—nothing worthwhile, anyway. So we just…wait."

"You think that'll work?" Thom asked.

"It has to," Felicia said. "And I'm going to make sure it doesn't happen again."

"What?" Thom said. "How?"

"Just trust me," Felicia said distractedly, and left the room.

Thom glanced at Clay, who looked as lost as he was. "At least we're off the hook?" Clay said tentatively.

"Right," Thom said.

He wished that made him feel better.

★ 23 ★

It was very weird, Clay thought, how often Thom pretended he wasn't spending time with Clay when he actually was.

He'd stopped by that Saturday morning for sex, armed as usual with some flimsy speech about how he was going to leave as soon as they were done. But once they were done, he'd declared that he was too tired to move, and then he'd just wanted to check his phone quickly, you know, just to scan the headlines, and soon enough he'd gotten hungry, so they'd ordered food.

They'd ended up whiling the day away watching the news and complaining about work. Lennie was still trailing Warhey in the polls by about as much as she had before Clay had joined the campaign, and he thought she should've gained some by now if Thom was doing his job right, and if their fake relationship was really as popular as it seemed to be online. Thom had some complex argument about how Lennie holding steady was actually as good as gaining at this stage of the campaign, and also how Clay should shut up about it if he was going to blame Thom.

By the afternoon they were both feeling restless and sun-starved, so they walked to the Starbucks around the corner from Clay's apartment. On the walk over, Clay pitched Thom on an idea he'd had about how Lennie could overtake War-hey in digital ad space. Thom told him that every aspect of his idea was shit, but he still listened to it, which was new.

Their whole dynamic that day was new, Clay realized. For all the big, weird, theatrical changes in his and Thom's relationship over the past few months, the low-key strangest change of all was that they'd become…well, if not friends, then at least coworkers who didn't entirely hate each other. He knew how rare it was for Thom to actually listen to anybody that he worked with, or really anybody at all.

But it was still Thom, so anything that could even remotely be considered a sign of affection always had to be tempered with plausible deniability. As soon as a lull fell in their conversation as they were waiting for their drinks, he whipped his phone out, clearly trying to put some distance between them by pretending that he had to focus on work.

Clay decided to distract him. "Ooh," he said, grabbing something random off a nearby shelf of merchandise. "I should have gotten a mug to go with my coffee."

Thom only glanced up from his phone, clearly unimpressed. "Mugs are the only kitchen item you already have."

Clay put it down and pivoted to the next nearest tchotchke. "Oooh," he said, "I should have gotten a little bag of cookies."

The plastic wrap around the cookies crinkled temptingly between his fingers, but Thom only said, "Meh," and looked back down at his phone.

Clay turned back to the shelf. "Ooooh, here it is," he said confidently, grabbing an item and shoving it between Thom's phone and his face. "A CD of cool coffee shop songs!"

"You're kidding, right?" Thom's tone was scathing, but as he spoke he slid his phone back into his pocket. Clay fought to hide his triumph.

"I could put it on at home," he said instead. "And pretend I'm at a coffee shop, and get work done."

"A, you don't work. Two, you could just *go* to Starbucks, and also," Thom said, and paused doubtfully, "you have a CD player?"

"No," Clay said, smiling. He put the CD back on the counter and took a step closer to Thom. "You know you did the numbers wrong?"

"Yeah, I was being funny," Thom muttered, a small smile fighting its way onto his face. He didn't move away when Clay drew closer, just craned his head back.

"Not that funny," Clay breathed.

"Shut up," Thom said, and leaned up toward him. Clay's heart thumped with surprise—Thom wasn't really the type to kiss outside of sex. But still, he was tilting his face toward Clay's, his eyes gone dark, and Clay could smell his cologne—

And then his phone buzzed between them. "Leave it," Clay said breathlessly.

Thom looked down. "It could be important."

Or it could be an excuse for you to leave just when things are nice, Clay thought. The barista dropped their drinks off at the counter, and he sighed, turning to get some cardboard sleeves.

As he did so, he moved one of their coffees too close to the edge of the counter, and it tipped over. He fumbled to save it, but ended up overcorrecting and jerkily spilled the coffee all over himself.

Thom snorted, looking up from his phone. "You think they sell Starbucks T-shirts?"

"Ha ha," Clay said, pulling his hoodie away from his shirt to try to salvage it. "Aw, man, it's everywhere."

He unzipped the hoodie and pulled it off, throwing it over his shoulder as he tried to sop up the spilled coffee. "Can you get me more napkins?" he asked Thom absently.

When Thom didn't answer, Clay threw his empty coffee cup and the sodden napkins into a nearby trash can and turned around. Thom was eyeing him with a grim expression. "What?"

"What *is* that," he asked, disgust heavy in his tone.

Clay glanced down at his T-shirt, which was now on display with his hoodie off. "It's the original BoB characters," he said, pulling the shirt out so Thom could see. Admittedly, it was old and a little ratty even by his standards—the fabric had probably been more white than yellow when he'd first gotten it. And it did clash a little with his maroon gym shorts and lime green sneakers.

The longer Thom looked at him, the more appalled he seemed by Clay's entire outfit. Thom, of course, looked incredible in his perfectly tousled casual clothes: a dark blue T-shirt, slim-fitting camel-colored slacks, and blindingly white sneakers. Even his hair was artfully untidy, a few black locks falling over his forehead like he'd just rolled out of bed.

"I didn't even notice," Thom said, shaking his head. But he looked more disappointed with himself than with Clay.

"It's not that bad," Clay said defensively.

"No," Thom said, standing up straighter with a determined set to his shoulders. Apparently, he'd forgotten all about the supposed work he'd been using as an excuse to leave. "I can't believe I've let this go on for so long, but I'm not getting photographed with—" he gestured to Clay "—*this*, anymore."

It was probably a bad sign that none of that had offended Clay. He just sighed and said, "So get your own coffee next time," and turned back toward the register.

Thom stopped him with a hand on his elbow, tapping at his phone one-handed. Clay frowned as he saw him calling an Uber. "Oh, no," Thom said. "We're fixing this today."

"Fixing it?" Clay asked apprehensively. "What do you mean?"

"Thom," Clay hissed, blanching when he turned a tag over. "These clothes are too expensive."

"Stop buying downloadable content for your donut game," Thom said, flicking through blazers that each cost more than Clay's phone.

"I liked the Blintzkreig DLC," Clay grumbled.

Thom had taken them to some kind of chichi boutique that seemed to only stock two colors of everything and probably charged people to browse. It was clearly somewhere Thom shopped, and also the kind of store Clay would have burned his own skin off before voluntarily stepping inside. He could feel the salespeople judging him.

"So make more money," Thom replied.

"Tell Lennie to pay me more."

"I would," Thom said, "if you hadn't just told me you'd rather spend that money on video game add-ons than professional attire."

"These are *jeans*," Clay said, "not professional clothes."

"These clothes are for when you're seen with me," Thom said lowly, "and that's work." He shoved a massive pile of clothes into Clay's arms while waving down a saleswoman. "Hello? We're ready to see a room."

The clothes may have been expensive, but apparently the store couldn't be bothered to spring for real fitting rooms with proper walls. Even after Thom latched the door behind them, Clay could still hear other customers and salespeople talking as if they were right there. He kept his voice soft as he complained, "I still don't get why we have to do this. My clothes are fine."

Thom snorted, and Clay reluctantly peeled off his T-shirt so he could try on one of the shirts Thom had picked out. "Where do you even shop?" Thom asked, eyes flicking over Clay's torso. "Target? T.J. Maxx?"

"I dunno," Clay said. "Old Navy."

"Oh god," Thom said. "I'm sorry I asked. Here, try this one."

Clay rolled his eyes and pulled on the sweater Thom had handed him. When his head emerged, he saw Thom taking a picture. "What the hell?" he asked.

"What?" Thom shrugged, unrepentant, though his face looked a little red. "This is good content."

At least Thom had the courtesy to show him the picture, and Clay could begrudgingly admit that it looked cute—his elbows were poking around in the sweater as he got it on, and the little strip of his stomach showing at the bottom actually looked kind of hot. He gave Thom the go-ahead to post the picture, and turned around to look at himself in the mirror.

The sweater did look nice, although it clashed with his basketball shorts. Thom nodded in approval, and Clay shrugged it off quickly, muttering, "The internet liked us just fine when I could still afford food."

"Relax, you baby. You can write this off as a business expense."

Clay frowned. "Can you?"

Thom shrugged. "I don't know. Here, try this…" He handed Clay a T-shirt and a bulky cardigan. "And these," he added, fishing a pair of jeans out of a different pile.

Clay felt his face heat as he stripped down to just his boxers, pulling on the clothes Thom had handed him. Thom wasn't ogling him as he got undressed, but the calm focus of his gaze had Clay's heart beating faster anyway. Any and all of Thom's attention aroused him, whether personal or professional. It made him wonder what Thom would do with him, how he would provoke him next. As if he'd prompted him with his thoughts, Thom stepped forward once Clay had zipped up the jeans, twitching the T-shirt right where he wanted it and tugging the sides of the cardigan into place.

When he was done, he nudged at Clay's shoulders, turning him to face the mirror, and stood behind him to take in his handiwork. "There, see?" Thom said lowly. The clothes didn't look like what Thom would have worn—they were too slouchy and grunge-looking. But they weren't exactly what Clay would have chosen either—they were too self-consciously trendy. Clay liked his old, shabby house clothes. The guy in the mirror now was Thom's version of Clay, suitable for public release.

But the inauthenticity of it didn't bother Clay as much as it should have. Instead, it was turning him on—like the clothes Thom had picked out were Thom's hands running all over him, cradling him and presenting him to the world. "Looks fine," Clay said, his voice a little unsteady. "I dunno if it's worth the money."

"Hmm," Thom said with a small smile, as he turned Clay back around to face him. "Well, there's another perk."

Thom leaned in to kiss him, and Clay huffed out a relieved breath, pulling Thom close. It really was appalling that he wasn't at least growing immune to Thom over time. They'd had sex dozens of times now, but his brain still flickered off every time Thom got close, and he was still driven to distraction by the touch of Thom's skin to his.

Thom pressed him back against the fitting room wall and undid his belt. Clay swallowed and looked away, tipping his head back against the wall. He could hear other people in the store just inches away, and the illicitness of it made him burn even hotter. He had to press a fist to his mouth to keep from gasping when Thom sank to his knees.

But it wasn't just the fact that they might get caught. He and Thom were publicly—but not really—together, and now they were having *sex* in public but trying *not* to let anyone find out. Clay felt like he was made of paper, on display and twisted up like an Escher painting or some shit. Thom's mouth was fire-hot and slippery-wet, and Clay's head was spinning with the overlapping, contradictory narratives, and Thom's hair was so soft between his fingers, and he was light-headed and he wanted Thom so badly and the confusion of it all was just turning him on more—

Clay muffled a moan against his hand as he came, the nails of his other hand scratching against the dressing room's cheap textured wallpaper.

He slumped backward as Thom pushed to a stand again, twisting and stretching his cramped muscles. Feebly, Clay asked, "Want me to do you?"

"Nah," Thom said, wiping his lip with his thumb. "I don't want them to get suspicious. It can wait till we get home."

Clay froze. Thom squinted, and corrected himself. "Back. Till we get *back* to your place."

"Right," Clay said, nodding uncomfortably.

Of course, as soon as they got back Thom tried to leave, claiming some obviously bullshit work emergency. Clay ignored him and pulled the shopping bags out of his hands, throwing them on the floor and pushing Thom back against the front door to close it. Thom murmured a halfhearted objection and Clay ran a hand up his side under his shirt, leaning in to suck on his neck and say, "But I wanna pay you back."

Thom gasped and said something about an urgent memo, and Clay raked his nails down Thom's back, gently biting the thin skin of his throat, and Thom's hips arched into Clay's, his complaints dying off.

They ended up on the couch, where Clay gave him a long, languorous blowjob that Thom kept trying to hurry along, a hand in Clay's hair urging him to a faster pace. But his hand would drop away every time he got swept up in it, and it went on and on, alternating fast and slow, until Thom came with a shudder and a helpless whimper that was almost a sob.

Clay slid down onto the floor, his back against the couch. The bags from their shopping trip were lying crumpled on the ground, and his jaw was sore. But Thom was still non-verbal, slumped in place, panting and shiny with sweat. Clay allowed himself a small, private grin.

His stomach growled, and he realized how hungry he was after their day of errands. He hauled himself up and wandered over to see what he had in his fridge. "You want leftovers?" he called to Thom.

Then he heard the clink of Thom's belt buckle. Turning around, he saw Thom standing by the couch, almost fully dressed already. "You're going?" he asked, incredulous.

"Yeah," Thom said. His voice was hoarse, but he was looking down at his phone. "Gotta be getting home."

He put a little too much emphasis on *home*. "Right," Clay said. "Yeah. Okay."

He kept his head bent down into the chilly air of the fridge until the door slammed shut behind Thom.

★ 24 ★

Because Thom was very important and influential, he got invited to participate in a lecture series on political communication sponsored by a local university. He'd gotten the invitation a few months ago, though, when he was just a successful, handsome, somewhat-famous political operative. Now he was a successful, handsome, slightly-more-famous political operative in one of the internet's favorite couples, so the spotlight was shining on him more harshly than ever. He loved it, but he was also feeling the pressure.

"Relax," Clay said, "you look fine."

They were in the greenroom backstage, which wasn't actually a greenroom but just a classroom the event was using for that purpose. Still, there was one of those cheap Ikea overdoor mirrors in a closet, and Thom was twisting in front of it, trying to make sure his suit looked good from all angles. *"Fine?"* he asked, deeply affronted.

Clay rolled his eyes from where he was sitting in a chair against the far wall. "You're ridiculously good-looking, you know this."

"Well, yeah," Thom said, straightening his tie again. "Besides, I am relaxed."

"No you're not. You always rub your thumb along your jaw like that when you're nervous," Clay said. He wasn't even looking at Thom anymore, he was fiddling with his phone instead, so Thom wasn't sure how he'd seen him doing that thing with his thumb.

Thom walked over to the door and peered out through the narrow gap where it had been left ajar. In the hallway, people there to see the panel were milling around and making their way to the auditorium to take their seats. Most of the people were on the younger side and fairly serious looking, with lots of hushed conversation and furrowed brows. It wasn't exactly his crowd, but it was close.

Then again, this wasn't exactly his kind of event. There would be cameras, which was enough to get him there, but the other two panelists that had been invited were an activist and a blogger—more of the serious, furrowed-brow types. Thom was here to bring the star wattage, and he was fine with that.

He caught himself running his thumb along his jaw and hastily jerked his arm down to his side. Turning back to the room, he glanced at Clay. He looked good; he'd selected Clay's wardrobe exclusively from the clothes they'd bought last weekend, knowing they might get photographed together. He'd ended up choosing dark blue slacks, brown shoes, a white button-down, and a blue jacket with a wide checkered print that was deliberately retro-chic. His brown hair was neatly tamed again, and he sprawled in his chair with a relaxed, languid vibe Thom had noticed in him more and more lately. With his blunt features relaxed into a nonthreat-ening, nonsmarmy expression, he was undeniably handsome.

Fuck it. He was hot.

Thom shook himself a little. He was *not* about to start get-ting starry-eyed over Clay.

Still, it was good that he was here. Even if Thom screwed up and said something horrifying onstage, there'd be one person in the audience who wouldn't give him shit about it. Well, Clay would definitely give him shit about it, but it wouldn't be nearly as bad as what Felicia would do if he did anything today that hurt the campaign. They had just started to move past the stormy couple of days prompted by the donor call leak, and had finally regained some forward momentum. Nerves crept up the back of his throat again.

He shook his head, trying to chase out the scuttling anxi-ety. "You should get out there," he told Clay.

"'Kay," Clay said, unfolding to his feet. "Don't be nervous, you're gonna be great."

"I know," Thom said, mentally running through his list of talking points.

Clay grabbed his shoulders, startling him into looking at him directly. His eyes softened when he saw he had Thom's attention, and he said lowly and emphatically, "You're going to be great."

Something unlocked around Thom's lungs, and he took a deep, settling breath. The ground firmed up a bit beneath his feet. "Yeah," he said, sighing a little. "Yeah."

He was really thankful Clay was here.

Seeing that he had relaxed a little, Clay put on a big, sweet smile. "Just be as fake and emotionally manipulative as pos-sible."

Thom laughed. "Obviously."

Clay's smile faded a little, the teasing leaking out of it until only affection was left. And then Thom was seized with the impulse to kiss Clay for good luck—or fun—or courage—but he ruthlessly squelched the feeling.

"Um," he said awkwardly. "You should—"

"Right, right," Clay said. He smiled, clapped Thom on the shoulders one more time, and said, "Good luck," before slipping out the door.

Thom took a few deep breaths and paced the room, reading his phone until one of the staffers for the event stuck his head in the room to let him know it was time.

He was led backstage and introduced to the fellow panelists and host. The crowd roared as they were announced and walked onstage, and Thom got comfortable in one of the wide leather chairs they'd set out. There were few things he loved more than the feeling of a microphone in his hand.

Still, he felt some residual jitters as the host began her introductory remarks. Tonight was the kind of event he'd wanted to be invited to for a long time. He didn't want to blow it.

The lights made it hard to see anyone in the audience, but just under the horizon of the harsh glare, Thom could make out the first few rows of seats. Clay was there, off to the right, mostly in Thom's peripheral vision. Still, seeing him there, his hand on his chin like he was already absorbed in what was happening, made Thom calm down a little. It reminded him that this was political theater, like every other aspect of his job.

Thom was a performer. He'd be good at this.

He was not good at this.

The panel was more than halfway over, and he was not doing well. It wasn't anything in particular that he'd said or done; he hadn't been booed by the crowd or pronounced canceled. It was more a general sense he had that he just wasn't impressing anyone. His comments never seemed to coax much of a response from the audience, and his ideas never seemed to influence the conversation. He had a feeling he was coming across as canned and cliché, where the other panelists seemed earnest and serious. He wasn't making an impact.

Itching with restless energy, he looked out at the crowd as one of the other panelists spoke. He didn't want to let this opportunity slip away from him without making something of it. He needed to step up his game. He needed to seem authentic.

They were in the middle of a discussion about political rhetoric and communication, and one of the other panelists was talking about breaking the traditional rules of political speech. "It's easy to say *Connect with people*, but what does that mean?" he asked. "How do you motivate people about problems that seem insurmountable, like climate change or voter suppression?"

The other panelist nodded. "Keeping your audience in mind is so crucial," she said. "It's not so much about, what do you as a politician want to say. It's about, what are these voters ready to hear?"

Thom glanced into the audience again, and spotted Clay off to the side. As their eyes met, Clay smiled at him encouragingly. A random image popped into Thom's brain, and before he could help it, he laughed.

Both of the other panelists glanced at him, confused, and the room went quiet.

"Uh, sorry," he said. "It's just..."

As he wondered why that memory of Clay on the phone with his grandmother had just come to him, he realized why he'd made the connection.

"This is so random," he explained, "but—um, you know

how, when you spend a lot of time with someone, you end up eavesdropping on some of their phone calls? Well, this is how I discovered that when my partner calls his grandma, they curse at each other a lot."

The audience wasn't sure how to react—there were some giggles, but also a few gasps. "Yeah, I know, it's really weird, right?" Thom said. That got a few more laughs, and as the audience relaxed into the story, Thom did too. "Apparently Clay got his foul mouth from his grandma. And I'm not talking TNT after ten p.m. foul, I mean like HBO foul. They just lay into each other, all this screaming and cussing, and then at the end it's, *Oh, I miss you, I love you too.*" The other panelists chuckled, and Thom waited a beat before continuing. "But when I asked him about it, he told me…his grandma has to go to the doctor about once a week to get some tests run. She's really nervous every time she has to go, because she's always afraid she's going to get bad news. And that's when I realized, he curses at his grandma to try and distract her. That's how they've always talked to each other, and he's just…trying to keep her in a good state of mind."

A big rippling *aww* swept through the crowd, and Thom tried not to look too triumphant. "So—yeah, I think you're absolutely right," he finished, addressing the other panelist. "I think when people need it the most, that's when it's most important to throw out the rulebook for how we talk to each other. Because that's what political rhetoric is supposed to be, right? Making a connection that makes it possible to do what seems impossible."

He had *no* idea how he'd pulled that line out of his ass, but it worked. The audience murmured approvingly, there were some admiring whispers, and even the fellow panelists seemed touched. Thom sat back in his chair in satisfaction.

Afterward, backstage, Clay pulled him into a big hug.

"Congratulations, man!" he said, thumping him on the back a few times. "You fucking killed it."

"Thanks," Thom said breathlessly. He'd already thanked the hosts and the other panelists, and although there were some other staff milling around and people picking up their things to leave, he didn't think they'd be overheard. Leaning in so he could lower his voice, he asked Clay, "You're not upset about…"

Clay frowned. "What, the thing with my grandma? No, that was fine. The audience loved it!"

He was grinning widely, practically drunk on Thom's success. But Thom was seeing Clay's face when he'd been on the phone with his grandma, and how fond he'd looked as he'd told her she was an asshole for putting off her next appointment. How he'd been hesitant to open up to Thom about her health problems, because he was so clearly unwilling to think about them too hard himself. How vulnerable he'd looked when he'd finally laid it all out, his eyes dark with worry.

Suddenly Thom regretted having told a whole auditorium full of people that story. The fact that Clay had confided all of that in him made it feel wrong, like it had been something between just the two of them. Something…private?

Oh no. Thom swallowed. "Right. It was awesome."

Clay grinned at him, oblivious to his inner turmoil. "Yeah, yeah, you're a rock star," he said, wrapping an arm around Thom's shoulders. "Ready to go?"

"Yeah," Thom said faintly, and tried to ignore the lump in his throat.

★ 25 ★

They were hanging out at Clay's apartment that weekend when Thom's phone rang. Clay thought it was pretty annoying, since they'd just finished some Thai takeout and Clay had finally convinced Thom to play BoB with him without any stupid bets that would involve him having to cook. Still, he paused the game without complaining. Thom stood up as he answered the call and walked over to the kitchen, which was about as much privacy as Clay's apartment would allow.

"Hey," he said easily. "Yeah, man, how are you?"

Clay had seen Thom exhausted, depressed, pissed off, and cranky, but his political persona was always effortlessly charming, like it had its own energy source that existed outside of him. He was just a natural when it came to putting other people at ease, helping to lower their guards so that they wouldn't see the knife coming. But as easy as it was for him, Clay had spent enough time around Thom by now that he could see how that part of him swam over his surface like oil on water, shimmering and slick. His voice was all charm and no warmth, all humor and no smile.

"Oh, yeah?" he said, a hand braced on Clay's countertop. "That's great, congratulations."

Clay wondered who he was talking to. *Congratulations* could be because some bill had passed, or maybe some minor rival of Lennie's had gotten screwed over. He was pretty sure it wasn't Felicia on the other end—she seemed to be the only other person Thom dropped his act with, besides Clay.

"Uh-huh. Uh-huh," Thom was saying. "Well, better than your sorry ass."

There was just a hint of familiarity in Thom's voice that gave Clay pause. And yet it seemed to be for the benefit of whoever was on the phone, not Thom. He was pacing the kitchen slowly, and when Clay caught a glimpse of his expression, it was cool and tight, the usual mask he wore around the office.

"No, that's great," Thom said. "Sure. Sure. Hey, text me your address, I'll send you something. No. No, really. Yeah. Okay. Bye."

He hung up and settled back on the couch next to Clay. Clay let it lie for a minute as Thom picked up his controller and unpaused the game. Then he asked, "What was that?"

"Nothing," Thom said. Clay waited him out, and a few moments later Thom shrugged. "My brother. Had his third kid."

It hit Clay kind of like a far-off boom—quiet but rattling. "That was your *brother*?" he demanded.

"Yeah," Thom said. After an awkward, silent moment, he caught Clay's eye and said, "What?"

"Nothing," Clay said, keeping his eyes on the TV.

"What," Thom said flatly.

Clay's head felt like it was filled with a series of question marks and commas. That call had sounded like an awkward catch-up with some acquaintance from college or a distant relative you weren't crazy about—not a *brother*. "You guys aren't close?" he asked.

"You know who I'm close with, Clay? My Twitter followers," Thom said. "Actually, no, scratch that—my Twitter *mutuals*."

"Oh, good," Clay said drily. "Important clarification."

They played the game in silence for a minute or two. Then, casually, without real interrogation or emphasis, Clay asked, "Why aren't you close?"

Thom dropped his head back against the couch. "God, Clay—"

"Okay, fine, whatever."

"We're just not, okay?" Thom said. "We have fuck all in common."

Clay shrugged. "You don't have to have a lot in common to be close with family."

Thom frowned. "Yeah, you do."

Huh. "What do you mean?" Clay asked.

Thom made an annoyed face again, but Thom was annoyed by lots of things. This particular expression seemed worse, like it pulled tighter at his features. It was a bitterness that looked worn into the grooves of his face, the clench of his jaw and the dark corners of his eyes.

"Because otherwise…" Thom trailed off, sighed, and then started again. "Theo—my brother—he's like my parents. They're…suburb people. They like team sports and chain restaurants and CBS."

A sarcastic reply floated through Clay's brain, something like *Sounds rough*, but he didn't even contemplate saying it out loud. Maybe the old Clay would have—back when he and Thom were just work rivals who'd given each other shit all the time. But now, just the idea of teasing Thom about this was horrifying. It would be like shoving a kid or sneezing in church. Thom was *talking*—talking about something *real*. Clay couldn't imagine cutting him off.

"Obviously, I wanted out of there," Thom was saying. "Even before I was into politics—for as long as I can remember." He was still looking at the screen, but Clay didn't think he was seeing the game. He kind of sounded like he'd forgotten he was talking out loud.

"I wanted more," Thom said simply, "but they didn't." A small frown was tugging at his brows. "That was enough for them. They were all just...happy, all of the time, for no reason. Like, they'd all be over the fucking moon when Theo won a middle school soccer game, and *I'd* be the weird one for—"

He cut off abruptly. His chest rose and fell, like he'd been breathing harder. Clay said nothing.

The weird one.

He thought he might be starting to understand. Lots of people grew up in places that weren't enough for them. Lots of people left a sleepy suburb behind for the big city or a grand adventure.

Lots of people felt out of place in their hometown. Not everyone felt out of place in their *home*.

Clay thought about his own childhood, about how his mom and dad had made him feel like he hung the moon no matter what dumb hobby or interests he'd developed. What Thom was describing was barely less than that—it was hardly neglect or abuse.

But he could picture a young Thom at some Little League game, everyone else there happy and content. And he could understand with perfect clarity how it might feel to be the one person there itching to get out, and to have your parents meet that feeling not with sympathy, or even anger, but with distant confusion...or disinterest.

That kid would learn to fool people pretty quickly.

"Did you guys fight a lot?" Clay asked.

Thom snorted. "No. I just pretended to like all that shit, and then got out the first chance I had."

There was a pit in Clay's stomach, sort of like how he felt when he'd eaten too much junk food—oppressively empty. "So," he said, clearing his throat. "You're not gonna go visit them? Meet the new baby?"

"Fuck no," Thom said with a mocking smile. "Do I seem like a baby person?"

Clay pictured Thom gently cradling a newborn, and the pit in his stomach became a sinkhole. It was a stupid, pointless feeling he tried to push away.

But his vision kept filling up with images of Thom—as a child, with a child, at home with his family. If he went back now, would his family be surprised that he had shown up? Would they be chilly? Awkward? Happy, unsure, regretful? Thom wouldn't have any idea what to say or how to act, Clay was pretty sure. Or maybe he'd know all too well, and would fall back into his typical assholic routine, squandering his time there. He would have no fucking clue what to do with a baby. Who would prompt him to make an effort? Who would smooth things over with his family? Who would get him to laugh when they were bugging the shit out of him?

Clay stared at his video game determinedly, trying to ignore everything he was feeling, and the way it was coalescing into words that he kept trying to swallow down. It would be so stupid, so presumptuous, like fumbling around in a dark room unafraid of what he might knock over. But before he could stop himself, he blurted out, "Maybe it wouldn't be that bad…if I went with you."

Thom went very, very still. He was still fiddling with his controller, but Clay could feel the way the core of him had gone leashed and frozen. After a second, he got up to take his empty takeout box into the kitchen. He threw it in the trash, walked over to the sink, and turned the water on.

With his back to Clay, over the rushing of the water, he said, "Why? No cameras at my parents' house. No coverage. No benefit to Lennie."

Clay felt like chunks of him were breaking off and disappearing down that cold, dark pit in his chest. "We could take some pics," he said hollowly. "Post them."

There was a scrape of dishes from Clay's sink. Thom still hadn't turned around. "A lot of shit to suffer through for the content," he said, his voice barely audible.

"Yeah," Clay said.

Thom's hands were braced on either side of the sink, his knuckles white, his shoulders bunched up around his neck. Clay cursed himself for ruining their chill night with his intrusive bullshit. He turned the volume up on the TV so that Thom would hear the tinny video game music and understand that Clay was done making him feel weird.

Thom stayed by Clay's sink, breathing slowly.

★ 26 ★

Thom was packing up his things late at night when he spotted Felicia pacing in her office. He hadn't seen her much the last few days, ever since their panicked meeting about that leaked audio of Lennie's donor call. In the end, nothing much had come of her cryptic pledge to make sure it wouldn't happen again. It hadn't been a pleasant news cycle, but they'd mostly gotten past the worst of it. He'd been a little curious about what she'd been up to, but he was far more afraid of actually asking her and possibly setting off another mini-breakdown, or whatever had been going on with her that day.

Right now, she looked as if she might be on the verge of another breakdown, pacing back and forth frantically. He probably should have just left, but the one, tiny spark of compassion he had for Felicia had him stopping in her doorway, asking, "Hey. You okay?"

She stopped pacing abruptly and glanced behind him. Her eyes were wide. "I'm fine."

"Yeah, you seem fine," Thom said. He shut her door. "What is it? Did something happen?"

Distantly, she said, "I have this...crazy idea. And I don't know what to do with it."

"Okay," Thom said slowly. For a second he worried that whatever she was freaking out about had to do with him and Clay, but then he reminded himself that not everything was about them.

The silence stretched as Felicia kept at it with the thousand-yard stare. The more it did, the more Thom worried that maybe this *was* about him and Clay. His heart beat uncomfortably. He was just about to ask, when she said, "The leak."

He frowned. "What?"

"The other day," she said nervously. "The donor call."

Now she had his attention. "Yeah? What about it?"

Lowering her voice to a minuscule whisper, she said, "It was Bash."

It took Thom a moment to figure out what she was saying. "What do you mean, it was Bash?"

"It was Bash," she repeated. "He did it. He recorded Lennie on that call, and leaked it."

He felt himself blinking a lot. "I'm sorry, we're talking about Bash?" he asked. "The guy couldn't tie his own shoelaces unless you made him dry out for a week."

"It was Bash," Felicia swore. "And I think he was the limousine leak too."

"Wait, what?" Thom asked.

"Think about it," she said. "We looked for spyware on his phone and Lennie's, and we didn't find any. We assumed that meant someone bugged the limo, but who does that? It wasn't a bug. It wasn't spyware. It was him."

The last time Thom had seen Bash had been in the office that day after the fundraiser. He had handed over his phone for them to examine without even a peep of protest, which in retrospect was...somewhat odd. But it was still *Bash*. Thom shook his head. "That—"

"And the call with the donor," Felicia continued, conspiratorial and intense. "Why can't you hear the donor's voice?"

The audio clip had only featured Lennie's voice, not whoever she'd been talking to. "Probably because *they* leaked it and didn't want to incriminate themselves," Thom pointed out.

"Yeah, but listen to Lennie's voice." Felicia had her phone in her hand already, the recording all queued up. Lennie's voice was a little hard to hear, distorted somehow, even though the words were clear enough. "It's echoing," Fe said. "Because this isn't a recording of the call, it's a recording someone made of Lennie while she was on the phone. At her house. By Bash."

It still didn't make any sense. "What are you saying?" Thom said. "Bash is, what—trying to tank her campaign?"

Felicia's gaze had been skittering around the office, but at this, she looked straight at him. "Can you imagine growing up with Lennie as your mother?"

He flashed back to that day in the office again—to Lennie throwing Bash's phone against the wall, the glass scattering everywhere. A chill went down his spine. "That's... still a big leap," he said.

"What do we do?" Fe asked. "We can't tell her. She'll kill him."

"If it's true, we can't not tell her," Thom said. Fe gave him a sort of pleading look, and he frowned. "Hang on, you can't actually be—" As he focused on her, he felt as though he was seeing her for the first time—her jittery agitation, the haunted look in her eyes. "Are you—*siding with Bash?*"

"I don't know!" she said, throwing her hands up. "I mean, Jesus, I always guessed her home life was pretty messed up, but this—"

"Felicia," he said sternly. "You've got to get your head on straight. If Bash is doing this, we have to—"

He cut off, and she gave him a look that said, *Well? What are we going to do?* What could they do? He remembered his number one rule—Don't Mess with the Family.

"That's why I've been going crazy," Felicia said, pacing. "My whole job is fixing these kinds of problems, but I have no idea how to fix this if Bash is the problem. And if it is Bash..." She trailed off, looking anxious and adrift.

"What?"

"I just," she said. "The gaffes. The polling. We barely have a policy portfolio. And now—if her own son is trying to sabotage her... I mean—" She laughed under her breath and asked desperately, "Is anything about this campaign *real*?"

Thom thought about Clay asking him about his brother, letting Thom continue to play video games while they talked so it didn't feel as intrusive. Listening to Thom's life story, even though it was stupid and mundane, and didn't really explain anything about why Thom was...the way he was.

Offering to go home with him. So he wouldn't have to make the trip—and see his family—all alone.

"I don't know," he said quietly.

Felicia was staring out the window, looking impossibly tired. "Get some sleep," Thom told her. "Maybe you're wrong—maybe it's not Bash."

"Yeah," she said. "Maybe."

They walked out together once Fe had gathered her things, and waited for the elevator in silence.

★ 27 ★

Clay was at work when his phone started blowing up. He was a little confused, because usually he was with Thom when that happened—because Thom had just posted a picture of them or tweeted something cutesy at Clay that he'd already scripted out an equally cute reply for. The other day he'd done a whole tweet thread about them watching a movie together—mostly complaints about Clay's bad taste in movies and movie snacks—and the internet had gone wild over it. Clay had been distracted the whole time because Thom had been slumped against him as they'd watched, his back against Clay's side and head on his shoulder. Clay had suggested they take a selfie of their pose to add to the thread, but Thom had just shrugged off the idea. It made Clay's heart beat a little faster just thinking of it.

But this time his mentions weren't going off because of a picture or some other couple-y thing. Today, everyone was tweeting a *Recode* story at him. His eyes widened as he scanned the headline.

Pinpoint Accused of Monitoring Users' Private Data.

He dropped his feet from the edge of his desk and sat forward, scrolling through the piece quickly. It was brutal—the allegations were damning, and the article made it sound like Pinpoint had been rocked by the news, with rumors of an emergency board meeting and infighting among the staff. An inset picture showed Derek staring downward, his mouth twisted in an ashamed little moue. Clay's heart pounded with ugly, triumphant joy.

Then he stopped, arrested, at a paragraph toward the bottom:

Staffers for California Governor Leonora Westwood, speaking on the condition of anonymity because they are not authorized to comment on the ongoing investigation, say they became aware of Pinpoint's data monitoring practices when former CEO Derek Keating sent Westwood data analyst and former Pinpoint staffer Clay Parker a cease and desist letter over a program Parker had been developing on the campaign's private Pinpoint account. "First they tried to steal one of our people's ideas, and then in the process they tip their hand that they've been spying on users' accounts?" said one Westwood operative. "It's like the Streisand effect but much, much dumber."

Clay was stunned. He stood up on autopilot and strode over to Thom's office. He didn't even knock before walking in, his jaw still hanging open dumbly.

Thom was sitting at his desk, leaning back in his chair, hands folded over his stomach, looking smug as fuck. His grin deepened as Clay walked in. "See anything interesting lately?" he asked.

"You—you," Clay sputtered. "How?"

"Hey, this was barely me," he said, standing up and putting his hands in the air. He looked even guiltier when he was trying to look innocent. "Derek did this to himself with that nutjob letter. Did you finish reading the article?" Thom was practically bouncing on his feet with excitement, leaning over to look at it on Clay's phone. "This could get really bad for them. The stock'll take a hit, Congress might want to investigate. Hell, they could be looking at a criminal probe."

Clay glanced at the article again, filled with vicious satisfaction at how bad this would be for Derek.

And it was all because of Thom, who was smiling back at Clay with that same vicious glee. He'd done this—he must have taken the letter Derek's lawyers had sent Clay about his map idea, figured out the shady shit Pinpoint was up to, and gone to a reporter. He'd made this whole thing happen. Clay kind of wanted to throw his phone over his shoulder, shove Thom up against his desk and ravage him right here.

Thom had done this. For *him*?

"Did you see that part at the end?" Thom asked casually. Clay swiped to the end of the article and found a paragraph that briefly mentioned the program Clay had been developing on Pinpoint, the one Derek had tried to steal. The article made clear that it was, in fact, Clay's idea, and it made him sound amazing—like a brave, innovative entrepreneur being unfairly attacked by a bitter, pathetic has-been. There was also a subtle dig at the Warhey campaign for having hired Derek.

"Yeah," Thom was saying, "I had to burn a few favors to make sure they printed all the stuff about Warhey. Still, it'll be worth it. The Warhey campaign will have to issue a statement—this makes them look like they're caught up in a data breach."

"Yeah," Clay said, a bit of his enthusiasm dimming. He smiled at Thom. "This is great for Lennie."

"And bad for Derek," Thom said meaningfully, grinning up at Clay. His dark-rimmed eyes were alight with mischief and excitement. Clay's pulse picked up. Maybe he *would* shove Thom up against that desk.

Of course, that was when Felicia came into Thom's office. "Uh, wow," she said, looking at her phone. "This is incredible."

"Thank you," Thom said. He gave Clay a brief, private look that seemed to suggest there would be victory sex of some kind later. This day was so awesome.

Thom had done this for him. He knew he shouldn't be thinking that, shouldn't have been nearly so sure of it, but he was—stupidly, recklessly sure, drunk off the looks Thom was giving him and the proof he held in his hand. If Thom had a love language, it would be ratfucking—settling scores and taking out hits on behalf of the people he cared about. Thom had schemed and plotted behind the scenes to make this article happen, to get vengeance for Clay—because he cared about him, at least a little. At least enough to do this.

Thom and Felicia were analyzing the reaction to the article on their phones, reading off particularly good tweets, when Lennie appeared in Thom's doorway. "Thomas," she said. "I think congratulations are in order, you little snake."

"Thank you, ma'am," Thom said, practically preening. "I'm glad you liked it."

"This is going to infuriate that old fart," Lennie crowed. "Warhey can barely turn on a computer, and now he'll have to explain why his golden boy was involved in, ah—what is it, again, Felicia?"

But Felicia was distracted by something on her phone. "Wait a minute," she said, looking at Thom. "You did an add-on too?"

"What's an add-on?" Clay asked, still breathless with excitement.

"It's like another story about the first story. A media blogger at *Politico* is doing one—a Twitter thread with behind-the-scenes details on the *Recode* article," Felicia said, reading off her phone. "'I'm hearing that a major source for the Pinpoint exposé was Thom Morgan. I guess if you come at the king's boyfriend, you best not miss.'"

Lennie looked confused. "I don't get it," she said.

"Thom leaked that he was the source of the Pinpoint story," Felicia said. Clay frowned.

"Isn't that bad?" Lennie asked.

"No, because the story's barely about us anyway," Felicia explained. She gestured between Clay and Thom. "But Thom managed to spin that story into an extra story about him and Clay."

Clay's stomach sank. Thom wasn't looking at him anymore. "This is so cute," Felicia said. "Your fans are loving it. This one girl says you coming to Clay's defense has cleared her skin and watered her crops, Thom."

Clay felt like shivering, suddenly cold all over. Felicia was chuckling as she read off more adoring comments from their shippers. With each one, some of Clay's giddiness drained away. Each one was a random internet stranger who'd come to the same conclusion Clay had, and each one made him feel more like an idiot.

Thom hadn't done this for him. He'd done this so people would *think* he'd done it for him.

So it would *look like* Thom cared.

"Wow," Felicia said, scrolling. "I mean, I know this is fake, and even *I'm* kind of touched by your romantic gesture, Thom."

"It's like a fricking soap opera," Lennie said, impressed. "This is great. Well done."

Their words bounced off him as Clay remained sunk in his misery. For the first time in a long time, he wondered how long his fake relationship with Thom was supposed to last. They'd never talked about an end date, but it would have to end at some point, wouldn't it? It wasn't like the campaign would last forever.

Come to think of it, they had never talked about *how* it would end. Would they put out a statement? Stage some sort of fight? Or would they eventually just stop—quietly stop everything they'd been doing; stop going through the motions; stop pretending?

Who would decide when they were over? Him or Thom?

Whenever and however it ended, Clay wanted to be ready. Maybe he'd ask Felicia about it, so he would know. So he could prepare.

But he knew that he wouldn't.

"Good job, man," Clay said lightly to Thom.

Thom looked up at him, surprised. "Thanks," he said. He seemed tense, like there was something more he wanted to say or do, but was holding himself back.

After a moment, Clay nodded and walked slowly back to his office. He felt hungover, his brief emotional high completely burned off. And there was an ache in his chest that was all the worse because it wasn't even for himself, not fully.

He was just so sad for Thom. Sad that he was like this. Sad that he so clearly viewed emotions as a weakness to be exploited, not something to be embraced. Or cherished.

Sad that it was all fake, through and through and through.

He sat in his chair and looked back at Thom's office across the bullpen. Lennie and Felicia were still there, no doubt planning how to react to the article and capitalize on it. Thom was sitting behind his desk. When Clay looked at him their eyes met, but after a moment, Thom looked away.

★ 28 ★

When Thom stopped by Clay's apartment on Sunday morning, Clay was out but the door was unlocked. So Thom let himself in, helped himself to a beer, turned the TV to something boring he could listen to while working, and locked the door.

He smirked about twenty minutes later when he heard Clay trying to get in and cursing in frustration when he couldn't. He was about to shout some sort of taunt in reply when he realized that Clay was on the phone.

"No, you're not a piece of shit, Mom, my—my door is," Clay said, glaring at Thom as he fumbled into the apartment, keys in hand, phone pinched between his ear and his shoulder, and his arms full of groceries. Thom made a mental note to yell at him if there wasn't at least one thing of syrup in those bags—they were running low.

Clay was running low, he mentally corrected himself. He really needed to stop doing that.

As annoyed as Clay clearly was at the door thing, he didn't seem surprised to have found Thom at his place. Was he really here that often? The thought made him embarrassed, so he decided to compensate by not helping Clay put away the groceries.

This turned out to be a good move, because Clay's conversation with his parents was a stem-winder that took him the entire time. He had just put away the last of his shopping bags when Thom heard his voice turn oddly veiled as he said, "Uh—yeah, Mom, yeah. He's—he's fine."

Thom's ears perked up. "Yeah, just working really hard. We both are," Clay was saying. "Well, yeah, like, sometimes. Enough."

He glanced at Thom from the kitchen, something inscrutable in his expression. Clearly he was uncomfortable, but Thom wasn't sure if that was because he was talking about him while he was there, or because he was lying to his mother.

"Yeah, it's great," Clay said hurriedly, sitting on the other end of the couch and not looking at him. "I'm really happy. Yes. Yes. Okay, talk to you later. Love you."

He tossed the phone next to him as he sank back into the couch. "Aww," Thom said. "What'd you tell her about me?"

"Nothing! I stuck to the script. Y'know, we're crazy about each other and all that."

"Good. I don't need your mom leaking to Drudge that we're fake."

"Okay, fuck you, my mom doesn't read the fucking Drudge Report," Clay retorted hotly. "She's a classy lady."

Thom rolled his eyes. "Sure."

Clay fiddled with his phone for a second, then said, "She asks about you a lot."

"Okay," Thom said doubtfully.

"I don't tell her much," Clay said, already defensive. "I mean, there's not much to tell, besides work stuff."

"Are you asking me to give you stories you can tell your family about me?" Thom asked.

"No. I don't know." He dropped his phone and promptly started fiddling with the TV remote. After a second, he asked, "What *should* I say when she asks about you?"

Thom blinked at him. "I don't know, Clay. Whatever it takes to keep her off your back."

Clay rolled his eyes. There was another pause that was probably more awkward for Clay than for Thom, and then he asked, "Do you talk to your parents about me?"

"We don't really talk, remember?" Thom said.

"Right," Clay said, nodding and not looking at him. Then he asked, frowning, "Do you talk to anyone about me?"

"What, like a therapist?" Thom said.

"No—although, there's an idea," Clay said drily. "But seriously, I meant like, friends. Do you *have* non-politics friends?"

"Non-politics friends? Not really," Thom said. "Some friends from college, but we don't really hang out much anymore."

"What's not much?"

Thom shrugged. "I dunno. It's been a few years."

Clay raised an eyebrow. "Anyone else?"

Thom squinted as he thought about it. "My weed dealer."

"Your *dealer*?" Clay said, unimpressed. "Dude, this is California. Go to a dispensary like everyone else."

"Uh," Thom said. "Okay, I used to have a regular barber."

"Used to?" Clay asked.

"Yeah, well," Thom shrugged. "When I started working for Lennie I found another place closer to the office, so."

"So you had a nonwork friend that you dumped because of work," Clay said, disapproval all over his face.

Thom snorted. "Yes, Clay. Most of my friends are from work."

"Okay," Clay said doubtfully, and subsided back against the couch with that same disapproval fairly wafting off him.

"Look, Clay, if you want to play on my level, that's probably what your life is gonna look like," Thom told him. "Fewer friends from college, more friends on TV, and in the Senate, and on Wall Street."

"On your level," Clay muttered. "Yeah."

Thom was irritated to realize that Clay seemed more annoyed by this conversation than the one with his parents. "What?"

"I dunno if I want to be on your level," Clay said.

"What does that mean?"

Clay shook his head, looking down at his hands. "Did you know I used to want to be you? Actually, I thought I *was* you." He picked at the wrapper on his sweating beer bottle. "Then I realized I didn't want to be. And then I realized I didn't want you to be either."

He'd said it with the cadence of an insult, and Thom scoffed at him in reply.

But that didn't stop him from hearing what he'd actually said. The only thing he could've really meant.

Clay was taking a long swig of his beer. He wasn't looking at Thom anymore.

He'd heard it too.

He looked vulnerable, almost despondent, sitting hunched forward on the couch, trying to power through the awkward lull in their conversation. Thom should've jumped in to change the subject, but for once he felt lost for words too. There was a shifting current inside him, too churning and

241

chaotic to put into words. Part of it felt like anger at Clay. Part of it felt like shock. And part of it felt like an unsettling desire to put his hand on Clay's back, to feel the warmth of his skin and the hum of his body. To know that he was still there, and to show him that Thom was too.

That would definitely be the wrong move. Thom had heard this kind of thing before. Usually it came from women he knew were lying, who were telling him what they thought he wanted to hear. But sometimes he'd gotten the feeling that it was genuine. Or as genuine as anyone's feelings for him could be.

That never changed the outcome. Sooner or later, they always realized what a mistake they'd made.

Clay would realize it too. He was probably just confused. Hell, he'd basically called Thom heartless. He wasn't operating under any illusions.

He knew exactly what Thom was.

Thom cleared his throat and made himself say, "Wanna play a round of BoB?"

Clay's smile back at him was just a little sad. "Sure, Thom."

★ 29 ★

On the first day the legislature was back in session, a back-bencher senator with ties to Kerry's coalition put a hold on Lennie's student loans bill.

"Kerry Pham," Lennie screamed at Thom, once they were alone in her office. "You were the one who brought Kerry Pham in on this. She was your idea! Your project! And she *fucks* us?"

"Ma'am—" Thom said shakily. The door to her office was closed, but the walls were thin, and he knew the entire staff was listening. "I've been in touch with Kerry—I'm ready to take care of her, I just didn't know she'd—"

"Try to fuck me over?" Lennie asked, her voice now a dangerous purr. "Tell me, Thom. Is that what you want? Are you playing some kind of game?"

"No, ma'am."

"Or maybe you're just distracted," she spat, sinking into her chair. "Playing grab ass with the big ugly giant out there."

Thom stiffened, trying to stave off a wave of unsettling anger. "No, ma'am. I apologize about the delay. I assure you, I will neutralize Kerry, and the bill will be sailing forward by tomorrow morning."

"We'll fucking see, won't we?" Lennie hissed. She put her stilettos up on her desk, the heels like daggers, and glared at him.

He nodded jerkily and left her office.

There were a dozen staffers staring at him in the bullpen, and another half-dozen too smart to look. "Back to work," he snarled, and strode toward his office as quickly as he could.

He hadn't been lying back there. He was going to get this bill passed if it killed him. He knew exactly how to get this dumbass senator to lift his hold, because he knew exactly how to deal with Kerry. He never did business with anyone without making sure he had leverage on them, in case things went sideways. He'd just been stupid enough to think he wouldn't have to use it this time.

Or maybe he'd been stupid enough to *hope* he wouldn't have to.

Maybe Lennie was right—maybe he'd been dangerously distracted. He could usually read people better than this, and he was never caught flat-footed. Then again, he never usually felt this uneasy about the sacrifices it took to get things done. It added to the nausea and shame churning in his gut.

He slammed the door of his office and sat heavily in his chair, feeling sweat cool on his skin. Lennie's bark was often worse than her bite, but Thom had worked in politics for a long time, and he'd learned early that nothing was ever certain. The student loans bill was going to be the centerpiece of the campaign. This fuckup could cost him his job.

Maybe he'd been distracted, but he could see things clearly now. He had to fix this—finish it—decisively.

So he picked up his phone and made a short call that would ruin Kerry's life.

★ ★ ★

Thom went to Clay's apartment straight after work. It was his day off, but when Thom got there the apartment was dark and empty. For a second he thought that Clay wasn't home, and felt a flicker of pure darkness that he didn't want to look at too closely.

Then he saw a line of light under the bedroom door, and heard the tinny sound of music from computer speakers.

He was overwhelmed by a desire to knock on the door. He knew it was a bad idea.

He did it anyway. Clay called out, "Come in."

If Clay's apartment was small, his bedroom was tiny—just a queen-size bed with a narrow strip of floor all around it that was mostly covered with socks. There were a few small knickknacks on the windowsill above the headboard, and a narrow dresser opposite the bed with a TV perched on it. It was even darker and quieter than the living room, still with that cold, rough feeling at bottom, but overflowing with soft colors and the kinds of surfaces that seemed to suck in sound. Thom felt like he had walked into a pocket hidden away from the world.

Clay was lying on the bed, one arm tucked behind his head, reading what looked like a graphic novel. He seemed unsurprised to see Thom. "Hey. What's up?"

"Uh, nothing," Thom said, leaning on the door frame and rubbing a thumb on his forehead. "Wanted to see if you wanted, um. Delivery."

Clay frowned, and let his book fall forward on his chest. "You okay?"

"Yeah. Of course," Thom said, lying as obviously as he could. He had no shame.

And Clay reeled him in easily. "What's wrong?"

Thom put his bag down and crawled onto Clay's bed,

sitting cross-legged. The room seemed bigger from Clay's mattress. He loosened his tie, put his chin in his palm, and sighed. "I just have to have a shitty meeting tomorrow, and I'm not looking forward to it."

"What's shitty about it?"

Thom explained about Kerry and the bill and the senator doing her bidding by putting a hold on it. He explained about Lennie's explosion and the swipe fees, and about the $982 and the drops in the bucket. He explained the call he'd made and what he'd tell Kerry when he met with her tomorrow morning.

Clay didn't say anything when he'd finished. "Well?" Thom asked hoarsely. He felt sick and exhausted. "Aren't you going to tell me I'm a scumbag?"

Clay shook his head. "No."

"Why not?"

"I'm not Felicia, Thom," he said. "I'm not trying to pretend I know what's best for you, or for anyone."

"But I, uh," Thom said. "I thought you didn't want this to be me."

Clay had his arms around his knees, leaning back against the pillows. He shrugged. "Yeah. I get that it *is* you, though."

Thom shivered. He thought of a lot of things to say, and then settled on, "You could never do what I do." It had the cadence of an insult.

Clay smiled and said, "Oh, fuck you."

Thom woke up somewhere he didn't recognize. Slowly, he realized he was in Clay's bedroom. He was fully dressed, as was Clay, and they were lying on the covers, facing each other but not touching. Clay was still asleep, breathing slowly and with a faint snore, hands clasped under his pillow.

The light from the window was weak and pale—it must

have been early. Thom couldn't remember falling asleep the night before. He remembered talking with Clay for hours, about the Kerry thing a little, but also about his stupid comic book, his day off, the way Derek's lawyers had flipped their shit at Thom's article, and a million other unimportant things.

They hadn't fucked. Thom was pretty sure they hadn't even fooled around. And it wasn't like he'd snuggled up to Clay in the night for warmth.

No, it was worse. Thom had apparently broken his No Bedroom rule purely because he'd wanted Clay's company.

He felt stiff from having slept in his clothes. But he didn't change; he just brushed his teeth, splashed water on his face, put on a fresh spritz of cologne, and went to meet Kerry.

He'd chosen an even more out-of-the-way spot this time— a tiny park barely wider than an alleyway, sandwiched between two quiet streets off the busier thoroughfare. The sparse grass was littered with trash, and graffiti covered the walls. It was early, so there weren't many commuters around to listen in. Thom sat on a bench and waited.

Kerry arrived in a thick puffy coat, clutching her bag under one arm. When she saw Thom she smiled slightly— triumphantly. She thought this was the meeting where he would tell her that her plan had worked.

She sat next to him. "So. How's step four going?"

Thom cocked his head. "Which one was that?"

She shrugged. "I forget." Her smile widening, she said, "I decided that instead of going to the press and *trying* to get the bill tanked, I'd just tank it myself. Senator Grijalva actually cares about helping people. Unlike your boss."

He nodded. "It was a smart move."

As the silence stretched on, her smile faded. "Why'd you call me here, Thom?"

"We know about the pills, Kerry."

The last of her smile evaporated.

"A nurse—sorry, physical therapist," he continued, "stealing pills from a hospital? That would've been, what. Intent to distribute?"

She shook her head and closed her eyes.

"That lawyer of yours is impressive, that he got you off with just a warning," Thom said. "Unfortunately, the cops who cut the deal remembered you."

Kerry had gone pale. "How did you—"

"We're in business together," he said. "This is my job."

It took her a moment to speak. "I didn't steal anything," she said finally. Her voice was tight as a piano string. "It was my boyfriend. My *ex*-boyfriend. He was picking me up from work one night, and he stole five oxy—nowhere near enough to make an intent to distribute charge, but the cops didn't care. They didn't care that I had nothing to do with it. They just wanted to charge me, because they knew who I was. They thought I was a troublemaker."

That sounded like the real version of the story Thom had paid some cops for. "Sure," he said.

Kerry sat back against the worn park bench, angry tears hovering in her eyes. "So. You leaked it?"

"No," Thom said. "I didn't have to. I just told Senator Grijalva."

She jolted, a sharp frown tugging at her brow. "You—what?"

"I told him. And he's lifted his hold on the bill."

Kerry swallowed. He could see it dawning on her face—the realization of what he'd done. "I didn't have to destroy your reputation, Kerry," he said. "I just had to let him know that I could if I wanted to. If I had to."

That was all—he'd just cut her legs out from under her. He'd made her politically toxic. She was the one who'd brought student loan reform to their attention in the first place, and now no one would work with her. No one would take her calls, or rely on her political backing to go out on a limb and try to make things better. Not with the knowledge that this oppo research was out there and could be used against her at any time.

She wouldn't have her name dragged through the mud. But he'd silenced her.

Kerry scraped a tear off her cheek. "So," she said, brittle. "The bill will pass—with the fees that'll make Lennie and her friends millions. And take even more away from people who are struggling to get by."

"It's still a step forward," Thom said. "People's lives will get easier. That wouldn't have happened without us."

She looked at him like he was scum. "You actually think you're the good guy," she said breathily. Astounded, and scathing.

He stared at his shoes. "No," he said. "You're the good guy. I just won."

Next to him, Kerry hitched her purse higher up on her shoulder, stood, and wrapped her coat closed tightly.

"This time," she said, and walked away.

It was still barely daybreak when Thom got back to Clay's place. There was no smell to the apartment this time of morning, no delivery food or waffles. There wasn't light or noise from his stupid video game, no dim hum of music.

It reminded him of the early mornings when he'd wake and leave in time to avoid seeing Clay.

He hated those mornings.

He hovered in the doorway to Clay's bedroom. He hadn't closed the door behind him when he'd left, too afraid of the sound waking him, and it remained ajar, inviting him in for a second time.

Clay was lying on his side on the bed, long limbs sprawled everywhere. He wasn't snoring anymore. The light was still pale, the air still. It was like the whole apartment was asleep along with him.

Every part of Thom felt grimy, like he was defiling the soft innocence of this space.

He dropped his bag on the floor and crawled onto the bed. He toed out of his shoes, shrugged off his jacket, and loosened his tie, but the tightness under his skin went nowhere. Somehow all six-foot-plus of Clay seemed smaller when he was asleep, when he smelled like drool and that dust-mote scent of early morning.

Thom had to touch him. As long as he had Clay's warm skin under his, he wouldn't have to think. Have to *be*.

He ran a hand through Clay's hair gently, not wanting to scare him when he was still asleep. But Clay just smiled and rolled onto his back, nodding and rubbing his head against his pillow.

Clay's voice echoed in his head. *I don't want you to be either. I get that it is you, though.*

Thom edged closer to him. He needed Clay to be awake, needed his eyes on him if he wasn't going to be that guy.

His kissed him, soft and lingering, and he could tell the exact moment that Clay shifted from lightly asleep to sleepily awake. His eyes stayed closed, but he snorted and smiled and kissed Thom back, a drowsy, contented sound in the back of his throat.

Thom ached for that easy comfort. He inched closer and kissed Clay again, pressing their lips together more firmly, prompting rumbled, half protesting and half happy noises from Clay. He crawled over him, running his hands over his sleep-warm clothes, kissing him over and over.

Clay sputtered a bit when Thom fondled his morning wood through his pj's. Laughing, he said breathily, "Thom—what—oh, mmm…"

Thom knew Clay didn't share the jittery need that was sparking under his skin, but he was determined to get him there. He ran his palms up his chest and kissed him open-mouthed, tugged on his hair and pressed their bodies together without a hint of subtlety. Eventually Clay started grabbing him back and kissing him lewdly.

He still wasn't as desperate for it as Thom, though. When Thom shoved his hand under the waistband of Clay's pants, he started and pulled back, putting his hands on the sides of Thom's face. "Hey, hey," he said softly. His eyes were still muzzy with sleep. "What happened?"

There was too much air in the room; he felt too loose, too free, like he might break apart at any moment. And he remembered what Clay had said to him, the ridiculous, mis-placed faith he'd shown in him. He wanted to feel it, to make it real. He swallowed. "I want you to fuck me."

Clay just stared at him, and when Thom kissed him again his kisses back were soft and gentle. But then Clay put a wide hand on the back of Thom's neck, and the simple touch was an unbelievable relief. Thom sagged against him, and Clay kissed him with sweet, single-minded focus, his other hand running a soothing track up and down his spine. Then, finally—finally—he rolled them until he was on top.

Thom surged up beneath him, grateful to have Clay's weight crushing him into the mattress, but Clay kept kissing him slowly and nowhere near as urgently as Thom wanted. He struggled out of his shirt, almost ripping the buttons off in his haste, and Clay stripped off his own tee. But Clay grabbed his face when Thom started unbuckling his belt, distracting him with long, drugging kisses when he tried to get naked, his thumbs rubbing down Thom's temples and the hinge of his jaw. He felt like Clay was suffusing him with his own sleepiness, slowing Thom down just as Clay got going. That burning need to get fucked was still there, but Clay was making it a diffuse, heavy need, warming Thom's entire body.

Clay's lips were red and swollen when he finally pulled back, propping himself up on one arm. "Are you sure?" he asked.

His words were solicitous, but his eyes were hungry.

"Yes," Thom said.

Clay stared at him for another moment, then leaned off the bed to rummage around in his bedside table. Usually when they fooled around most of their clothes stayed on, so Thom took the chance to appreciate the wide swath of Clay's skin on display, pale and scattered with moles. He shimmied out of his pants and boxers, watching as Clay put a bottle of lube on the table and pulled one condom off a strip.

Then they stared at each other. It felt like the kind of moment where Thom normally would have made a snide, shitty joke, but there were no words left on his tongue, no breath left in his lungs.

Clay seemed to sense the heaviness of the moment, so he broke it by leaning down and licking a fat stripe up Thom's cock. "Fuck," Thom hissed, sinking back against the pillows and clutching fistfuls of the comforter beneath him. Clay worked him steadily, swallowing him down with one hand braced at the base of his cock and the other holding himself up on the mattress. The hot, wet suction chased most of the thoughts out of Thom's brain, but he still felt like he was vibrating with tension, like he might vanish if he kept his eyes closed for too long. He ran a hand through Clay's hair and tugged on it, and Clay moaned. "C'mon," Thom said on a shuddering breath.

Clay squeezed his hip and reached out blindly for the bedside table. There was some awkward juggling, and soon he felt Clay kneading his thighs, playing with his balls, and nudging a lube-slick finger between his legs. Thom groaned and tried to regulate his shaky breathing as Clay teased him, prodding and massaging, and then pressed inside.

"Fuck," Thom said again, and this time it came out low and slurred. It felt like he was melting into the mattress and tightening into a coil at the same time, burning up and breaking apart. Clay, by contrast, seemed like he'd be content to do this all day—he looked amazing, broad shoulders on display as he crouched over Thom, kissing his ribs and stroking him from inside. When he wasn't holding Thom's eye he was watching what his fingers were doing, and the mental image of it made Thom gasp.

He'd never been this into foreplay. Every touch drove him crazier, pushed him further, pulled him tighter. He felt like he was being stretched so thin that soon he'd vaporize into the air. But that was good, that was what he wanted—to be all sensation, no room left for thought.

"Thom. *Thom*," Clay said. He realized he'd been breathing so hard he was almost wheezing. "Are you okay?"

"Yeah," Thom said raggedly. "Let's do this."

"Okay," Clay breathed, and he grabbed the condom.

When he lined up, bracing himself with his hands on either side of Thom's shoulders, he said quietly, "It's gonna hurt."

Thom spread his legs wider and tossed his chin at Clay. "Fuck you."

Clay grinned, and slowly pressed in.

It did hurt, but not too much. When Clay bottomed out, Thom let out a harsh breath and Clay rested his forehead on his shoulder, clearly struggling not to move. Thom nudged his face back up so he could kiss him, and found his mouth slack with shock and pleasure. It blotted out everything outside Clay's bedroom, beyond the corners of his mattress, the surface of their skin.

It was perfect.

Clay gulped and frantically wiped his hand on a corner of the sheets to get better purchase. Thom watched him and adjusted his hips and laughed when Clay jerked in response.

When Clay started moving again, he went slowly. With each thrust the pain dissipated, while some of it began to turn into a yearning, and then a leisurely gathering pleasure. Thom sighed and mumbled lazy encouragement, "Fuck, that's— yeah. Yeah, Clay, keep going." Clay's breathing was harsh and unsteady, but his movements remained careful and tender.

Eventually Thom had had enough of careful and tender. "Faster," he said, canting his hips.

Clay choked and stabbed sharply forward. It hurt a bit more than it had before, but with the hurt came a bolt of sweet pleasure that made Thom groan. *This* was what he'd wanted—rough, athletic sex that would erase everything else.

And Clay gave it to him rough—he started shoving in harder, jarring thrusts that felt fucking incredible. But he didn't speed up; his mouth dragged up and down Thom's neck, and his fingers fluttered restlessly against Thom's shoulders. It was rough, but it was a measured roughness, a deep, intense fucking that rippled until Thom felt like his entire body was reverberating, one long pleasure hum.

Things went hazy. Thom had broken out in a fine sweat all over, and Clay was shivering and babbling incoherently as Thom grabbed tufts of his sweat-slick hair between his fingers. Their lips jostled and brushed in lieu of kissing, and Thom's voice cracked as he said, "Clay, *Clay...*" It was so fucking *good*, and terrifying, like staring off the edge of a cliff. Clay was worshipping him, owning him, taking him—

Thom was filled with a kind of panic at that thought, realizing that yes, Clay was *taking* him, but it was a white-hot panic that felt more like rolling pleasure, his chest going tight with an all-consuming, piercing ache.

He was almost there when an unmistakable groan erupted from Clay. He grasped Thom's shoulders for leverage, thrusting wildly and moaning something garbled. Then he collapsed on top of him, limp and almost suffocatingly heavy.

Thom sucked in short, frantic breaths. The sudden lack of movement only emphasized how close he'd been, how hard he was, now trapped against Clay's stomach. He shoved a hand between them, working against Clay's deadweight. But even with barely any room to maneuver, just getting his fingertips on his dick had him squirming with razor-sharp need.

Then Clay propped himself up on one elbow, and Thom got a hand around his dick. He jerked himself roughly. Clay glanced down at his hard-on, then up to meet Thom's eyes, and he was so close, so desperate, that he had no wherewithal left to hide from Clay. Clay watched him as he brought himself off, right there with him in his naked, trembling need, braced against him as he finally fell over the edge.

Clay stayed propped up but hung his head, panting like he'd run a marathon. Thom had never felt so boneless in his life.

"Holy fuck," Clay said.

"Mmm," Thom replied.

Clay looked at Thom again. In about a second things were going to get sticky and gross, but just for that moment, everything heavy and sated in Thom felt anchored by the look in Clay's eyes.

A lock of Clay's hair fell forward onto his face. Thom

pushed it back gently, letting his hand linger. Clay smiled at him, and Thom felt himself smiling back.

Then he felt the stickiness starting to set in. He winced and groaned, dreading the clean-up, but Clay just laughed and got up, stumbling over to the bathroom.

Thom stretched a little as he listened to the sound of running water. A few twinges of pain started to seep back in, but he found it hard to care. Clay brought him a towel as the shower heated up. "Thanks," Thom said.

Clay nodded, sitting on the edge of the bed. "Do you want to order breakfast?"

Thom pushed himself up on one elbow. Clay was still naked. There was a line of small bruises on his shoulder, where Thom had dug his nails in. They were both covered in sweat. Clay's lips were red and smudged from Thom's mouth. The room was hot and smelled like sex.

But around him, he could hear the sounds of the rest of the world waking up. Cars passed by outside. The building clicked and hummed. Footsteps crunched over leaves on the sidewalk.

Thom scrubbed a hand over his face, and kept his eyes closed when he said, "Actually, um. I think I should go."

Clay said nothing. Steeling himself, Thom opened his eyes and saw his face. The sight made him hate himself even more than he had this morning. "I mean, I should get home. We both have work," he added. "And I should—change, y'know." He tried to smile. "Don't wanna show up at the office smelling like jizz."

"Right," Clay said quietly.

This was so stupid. Thom had a bad idea, but he did it anyway, leaning forward to tilt Clay's chin up with one finger and kiss his mouth softly.

Clay kissed him back for a moment, then let it break.

Thom sighed. "I'll see you at work."

Clay stood and walked toward the bathroom. "I thought this was work," he said.

Thom would have replied, but Clay closed the bathroom door behind him.

★ 30 ★

Lennie's student loans bill passed. The staff threw a party to celebrate—Clay's first office party since joining the campaign. But it was hard for him to feel festive when Thom was lurking in the corner looking sick to his stomach.

Clay wandered over to him, paper plate in hand. "Hey. Want cake?"

"Hmm?" Thom looked at the sheet cake on Clay's plate and turned an even brighter shade of green. "Ugh, no. What is that, grocery store cake?"

"It's delicious!" Clay said. "Cheap cake is the best, it's all sticky, like eating mud, but it's chocolate."

"I'll pass," he said sullenly.

"Want some champagne?"

"Maybe." He sniffed. "What kind'd we get?"

Clay squinted over at the folding table that had been turned into a bar. "André, I think?"

"Oh, god," Thom muttered, resting his forehead against his phone.

"Hey, c'mon," Clay said, nudging him with his shoulder. "This is good, right? Lennie's happy?"

"Sure," Thom said, sighing. "The bill passed. The press coverage was glowing. Our digital spot about the bill is blowing up online. I can practically hear Warhey's staffers cursing me from Indianapolis."

Clay nodded. "The donors are happy," Thom continued. "And judging by Lennie's mood, I'm guessing her portfolio did well." He looked down at his feet, shuffling in place. "Nothing in the press about the swipe fees."

"Nothing from Kerry?" Clay asked quietly.

Thom shook his head. "This was an even bigger victory for her than for us. But she's probably been turning down interviews, after..."

Clay swallowed a thick mouthful of cake and tossed his plate into a trash can nearby. "Let's get out of here."

Thom scowled. "What? It's two p.m."

"You passed a bill today. Take the afternoon off."

"Clay, c'mon," Thom said, rubbing his temples.

Clay took a step closer to him, leaning forward a bit so that Thom was sheltered in his shadow. "You don't think you deserve a break?" he asked lowly.

Thom glanced up at him, his face drawn and sleepless. He looked utterly plaintive, his eyes full of all the words he wouldn't say.

"Come on," Clay said decisively. "I know someplace we can go where we can waste a whole afternoon, *and* you can lecture me about something I find extremely boring while sounding pompous and douchey."

"You think I *want* to sound douchey?" Thom asked.

"I think it's why you get out of bed in the morning," Clay said.

Thom stared at him, but a smile tugged at the corner of his lips.

Clay took Thom to a music shop by his apartment that he'd walked past dozens of times but had never gone in before. It was a dusty, well-worn kind of place, with fading flyers all over the walls, crates and crates of records in the corner, and an entire wall of guitars on display. When Thom walked in, the sour look on his face melted away and the lines around his eyes softened. Despite the fact that he owned a guitar, Clay couldn't have cared less about the minutiae of music or instruments or any of that crap. Still, when he saw the tension ease out of Thom's shoulders, he smiled and asked Thom to tell him about each of the guitars.

With each speech he rattled off about locking tuners and vibrato systems and amps, Thom's mood seemed to lighten. The happier he was, the more distracted Clay got. A smiling, chatterbox Thom was unbearably sexy, sending Clay's thoughts scattering back to *that morning*.

That morning, and the night before. Because the night before, Thom had *talked* to him. Sure, he'd been evasive and elliptical and glib as usual, but it hadn't been enough to cover up what was really going on: Thom had talked to Clay about something that was actually burdening him. He'd sought Clay out as a shoulder to vent on. He'd opened up. It may have even been sexier than what had happened the next morning.

Okay, no, the morning had been sexier. Yeah, they'd been sleeping together for weeks, but Thom had never been that vulnerable with him before. He'd been frantic, desperate, closed off on some level, refusing to spell out exactly what was going on or why. But his *hands*, his *eyes*, his *arms*—he'd reached for Clay, and let himself be held. He'd been there with Clay. And after that initial wild rush, they'd slowed down together.

Thom had stolen something from him in those breathless, sweaty moments—that's what it was. He'd let Clay in, and made Clay his completely.

Thom with his walls down. Clay would kill to see that again.

He knew he probably wouldn't. He remembered how that morning had ended, and he was quite aware of how fucked he was. He knew this whole thing was going to end badly. Thom would freak out, or shut down, or do something horrible—accidentally, or maybe even on purpose. Thom was very, very good at making sure he ended up on top.

But at this point, Clay had gone through every stage of panic and self-flagellation there was, and had arrived at premature acceptance. He was appreciating things as they came, and not stressing about things he couldn't change. He would enjoy Thom while he had him.

"So," Clay said, when Thom had finished surveying every item for sale in the shop. "You gonna buy anything?"

Thom laughed. "I dunno. I barely have time off to do stuff like this as it is."

Clay shrugged. "That's true."

"Besides," Thom said. "I have your guitar."

"Yeah," Clay said, smiling. "You do."

To his surprise, someone snapped their photo on the way out of the store. Clay frowned. "Did you tweet about us being here?"

"No," Thom said, looking a little disturbed.

"Huh. Guess we're really famous now."

Thom hunched down in his jacket, pulling the collar up around his face. "Let's go back to your place."

"You don't want to parade around in front of the adoring masses?" Clay said, gesturing to the empty sidewalk.

"I overslept this morning. I had to rush getting ready," Thom said. "I don't want to get photographed looking oily."

Clay snorted. "You look fine."

"Exactly."

"Okay, you look amazing," Clay said, laying it on thick. He leaned down to kiss Thom, and instead of giving him shit, Thom kissed him back, smiling against his mouth, a hand on the side of his neck. It was really fucking nice.

When Clay pulled back, the random guy down the street was taking another photo of them on his phone. But when Thom glanced backward and saw him, he turned to Clay and rolled his eyes. "Let's go."

Thom took his hand, and Clay's heart beat a little faster.

Lennie had been busy during the final push to get the student loans bill passed—first glad-handing in the legislature to make sure all the votes stayed in line, then on TV and back-slapping donor calls that went long into the night. So Clay was somewhat surprised, when she was finally back in the office, that she asked to see him.

Felicia and Thom were already in her office when he arrived. "Oh, is this a senior staff thing?" he asked.

"For the last time, Clay, you're not senior staff," Thom said.

"I better be," Clay said, taking a seat. Thom was in the chair next to him, and Felicia was leaning against Lennie's desk, checking her phone. "I thought I got a promotion for putting up with you."

Thom smirked at him, but it was a warm, familiar look. Clay found that he had to physically restrain himself from reaching over and touching him, from feeling the warmth of his skin. His mouth watered at the thought of getting him alone tonight at his place.

Before he could get too carried away with those thoughts, Lennie strode into the room. "Excellent, you're all here," she said. She settled in behind her desk, which was piled high with loot from her pillage—press clippings and binders full of new fundraising leads generated from the success of the bill.

"First of all, well done on student loans, Thomas," Lennie said. "This is actually starting to look like a potentially winning campaign."

"I try, ma'am," Thom said, grinning.

"We have momentum now," Lennie said. "So I want to capitalize on it."

Felicia put her phone away and clasped her hands in front of her.

"On the bill?" Thom asked.

"Yes. We've got a good narrative going," Lennie said. She took a coffee mug off her desk and rolled it between her hands, practically vibrating with excitement.

"Well," Thom said slowly, "the legislative session's almost over, but we can—"

"Oh, Thom," Lennie said. "You're the one who's always telling me to vary my messaging so people don't get sick of the same old shit. We just had a policy win, now we need a personal one. A feel-good story."

"Okay," Thom said blankly. He glanced at Felicia, but she wasn't looking at him or Clay.

"So I had an idea," Lennie continued. She leaned forward, smiling ear to ear, and looked at each of them. "I want you to get married!"

★ 31 ★

Thom heard a high-pitched sound that was probably himself in a parallel universe actually exploding.

Lennie was grinning like a maniac. "A big, beautiful wedding to kick off the campaign," she said. "And I'll officiate!"

The room was very quiet. Clay said nothing, although he looked less stunned and more frozen in a sort of sad pallor.

"Plus, this'll let me outflank Warhey from the left," Lennie crowed, seeming not to notice their reactions. "That fucker. And can you imagine what HRC will do when they find out I'm officiating a gay wedding? Take that, A-no-plus."

Thom licked his lips and tried to speak. "Uh, ma'am," he said. "Are we really sure a—a wedding—" the word felt like it burned his throat on the way out "—is the way to go here?"

"I'm not officiating some bullshit civil union, if that's what you're thinking," Lennie said. "I don't think they even have those anymore, do they, Felicia?"

"They don't have those anymore, ma'am," Felicia said quietly.

"They don't have them," Lennie repeated, looking at Thom.

Thom knew what it meant when she wouldn't break eye contact. The decision had been made.

"Ma'am, I don't, uh…" he said anyway, trying to think of something. But his mind was stunned into stillness. He'd done some wild shit on the job before, told some hair-raising lies. But—

She wanted him to *marry Clay*?

Finally, Clay spoke up. With a strange, calm resignation Thom didn't quite understand, he said, "I'm sorry, but I don't think I can do that. Ma'am."

Lennie squinted at him. "Excuse me?"

Clay looked at Felicia in supplication, and in that moment Thom could see a glimmer of the Clay he'd first met—the nervousness and inexperience underneath the bluster. When Felicia was no help, he turned back to Lennie and said, "It's… personal."

Lennie raised an extremely unimpressed eyebrow. "You can't do your job for *personal reasons*?"

Clay frowned. "You—this—you're asking me to do personal reasons *for* my job!"

Thom was rapidly losing track of the conversation, or perhaps it was the word *married* still pounding away in his head, but Lennie seemed to be following along fine. "Yes, I am," she told Clay. "What is this about? You boys want something more to kick this up a notch? Fine." She sat back in her chair, considering the situation, and then said, "I'll give you each a ten-thousand-dollar raise. And I'll add Senior or Principal or Executive or some shit to your titles."

No one said anything. She eyed them shrewdly, then added, "Any job you want after the campaign. In the White

House, on K Street, CNN, anywhere. I'll personally guarantee it."

Thom looked at Clay, and finally Clay looked back at him. He had the sorrowful, haunted eyes of a kicked puppy. Thom wanted to reach over and run a hand through his hair. He wanted to hold him until he felt his breath even out, until he could sense Clay's calm just from the feeling of their skin pressed together.

He'd never felt this kind of panic before.

"C'mon," Lennie scoffed, seeing their hesitation. "As if either of you were ever gonna get married to anyone else anyway."

Thom said nothing, but Lennie was looking at Clay. He realized that she was taking Thom's acquiescence as a given.

And why wouldn't she? What had he ever done to make anyone think that he wouldn't get married for political gain?

Clay glanced at Thom one more time, then nodded. "Yeah. Sure. Okay."

Thom stood and headed for the door. No one stopped him.

Behind him, he heard Lennie say, "Great! I guess that's settled."

When he reached his office, he shut the door behind him without slamming it. He needed the calm that came with closing it carefully, with choosing not to make any noise.

Clay hadn't made any noise in the meeting. It was very unlike him; Thom wondered if he was getting sick, or if something else was wrong. Then again, now that he was thinking about it, he realized that Clay hadn't blown up at him, or anyone else for that matter, in weeks. And the number of ridiculous things he said on a daily basis was definitely fewer than usual. It was as if his bluster was gone, or at least dialed down. Just now he'd been downright muted.

When had Clay become *tactful*?

Thom sat in his chair and looked at the wall. A long while later, Felicia knocked on his door and let herself in. "You alright?" she asked.

"Sure," Thom said. He was still sitting at his desk, though he couldn't remember what he'd been working on. It was dark outside his window.

Felicia sat down across from him and snapped her fingers a few times in front of his face. "Jesus. Seriously, are you okay? I thought Clay would be the hard sell."

Thom inhaled stiffly, trying to focus. "You're awfully calm about this," he said. "It doesn't offend you? One more fake thing to add to the fake campaign?"

Felicia looked away. "I shouldn't have said that," she said quietly.

"Come on," Thom scoffed.

"I mean it," she said, looking back at him. "I've thought about it, and—" She took a deep breath. "You only get so many chances in life to make a difference. To change things for the better. Lennie is my chance."

"So you're on board for a fake wedding?" he asked.

His treacherous mind said, *A real wedding. You're the fake part.*

Felicia shrugged. "It doesn't affect anyone but you two. If you're okay with it, I'm okay with it."

Thom clenched his fist and said nothing.

Felicia raised an eyebrow. "Really?"

He scowled at her. "Excuse me for taking a second to think before I *marry someone for work.*"

"Yeah, exactly—marry someone!" Felicia said. "It's not like she's asking you to do something really awful, like... endorse a terrible candidate."

There was a moment of total silence, and then they both started laughing. Thom laughed so hard his shoulders shook and he had to hide his face in his hands. When he felt calmer, he wiped his eyes and saw Felicia looking at him with a mix of lingering amusement and worry.

"Or maybe marriage…means more to you than I thought," she said.

"It means fucking nothing, and you know that," he snapped.

"Then what's the problem?" she asked. "Is it Clay? Is it not going well?"

Thom could still feel Clay's palms on his shoulders, his thighs between Thom's, the heat of his skin. He remembered exactly how tired and happy he'd looked afterward, and the warmth in his eyes. The theme song from his stupid video game was perennially stuck in Thom's head. "It's fine," he said, his voice hoarse.

Felicia tilted her head. "Are you guys fucking?"

"Fuck off."

"Wow. Does that make this…worse?"

"Felicia, I swear to god—"

"You're right," she said, raising both hands defensively. "I'm not trying to psychoanalyze you."

"Then why are you fucking here?" Thom asked. He glanced out one of his interior windows to the rest of the floor, but the light was out in Clay's office. He wondered how long he had stayed before going home.

"When Lennie pitched me on this—the wedding thing—I thought it was nuts," she said. "The only reason I told her it'd be okay to even ask you two about it was that I honestly thought you wouldn't mind. I mean, yeah, it's a wedding—it's a big deal. But we're not exactly the marriage generation. And the internet loves you two, your mentions are off the charts—it's really raising your profile. Isn't that all upside?"

"So you think I should do it," he said.

"I'm surprised *you* don't think you should."

Thom was so tired. He propped his forehead up with one hand and said, "Maybe I've been spending too much time with you."

Felicia snorted. "We've basically swapped. Somehow I'm the coldhearted bitch and you've grown a conscience."

Her sheepish little self-hating smile was cute. He *pfft*ed at her. "Your heart's lukewarm at best."

"Aww," she said quietly.

They sat in companionable silence for a moment. Things were always easy with Felicia. Even when they were at each other's throats, there was comfort in the predictability of an opponent with whom you were so well matched.

"So," she said. "Can I tell Lennie she doesn't have to worry?"

Her brisk tone was a step back from the uncomfortable honesty they'd shared a moment ago—she was back to regular Felicia, political Felicia. Political Felicia was too smart to ever out and out flirt with Thom, but she had a way of charming him, of everyone she needed anything from, that was hard to resist. Usually when she worked him, he took just a second to appreciate how fine she was—not just how beautiful, but how skillful she was; the sensuality of her conversational jiujitsu. A negotiation with a woman like Felicia always made him wonder what she'd be like in bed.

He hadn't had that moment yet. He slowly realized that he hadn't thought of Felicia that way in weeks. Now even trying to summon those thoughts made him vaguely ill.

He didn't want her anymore.

The room wasn't cold, but Thom felt a shiver working up his spine. "Thom?" Felicia pressed.

"Yeah," he said. "There's nothing to worry about."

"Great," Felicia said, standing up and folding her hands awkwardly. "I'll tell her."

Thom stayed at his desk, playing with a pen to distract

himself. Felicia took the cue and left, though she turned at the door.

"In the morning," she said, "we'll have to talk about, um. Well—we're gonna have to talk about the proposal."

Thom's heart felt like concrete that was starting to crack. "Sounds great," he said.

She nodded and shut the door behind her.

★ 32 ★

The next morning was the first official staff meeting to plan their—god, their *engagement*. Clay could still barely think about it without feeling dizzy.

He got to the office on time, but he was the first one there. Bex let him wait in Lennie's office.

Thom hadn't come over last night. Clay had given him space at work all day too, but he'd kept an eye on his office. He hadn't missed Felicia going in there toward the end of the day and not leaving for a while. He didn't like the stomach-churning feelings that had stirred up.

He hadn't seen or spoken to Thom at all since that meeting—the one where Lennie had turned the pressure on their relationship up to crushing.

Clay was learning that there were a lot of things in life and in politics that he didn't understand, but one thing he was getting pretty good at was reading Thom. The Clay of a few months ago, the one who'd first become Thom's "boyfriend," might have been skeeved out by Thom's reaction to Lennie's proposal: his passive acquiescence, his near-total silence. But now he knew better—now he recognized that behavior on Thom for what it was: he had probably been panicking.

Instead of making him feel distrustful or cheapened, the whole situation just made him feel sorry for Thom. Clay had tried to fight back against Lennie's proposal, at least a little, but no one in that room had even expected Thom to resist. All they saw was the cold, emotionless Thom that Clay used to see. They had no idea how much more there was underneath.

And he couldn't judge Thom for ultimately giving in, because Clay would probably always have taken that deal. He may not have been in politics very long, but he was a political animal at heart. When you were always looking to get ahead, arrangements like this were part of the bargain. It wasn't so much being asked to get married for the job that offended him—but the idea of having to marry *Thom* as a political stunt made him feel like a part of himself was dying.

Because of course he wanted to marry Thom.

But not like this. Not this soon, and not as a fucking photo op for Lennie. Not when Thom would have never wanted to get married, job or not.

It was a hideous, strange feeling, knowing that he was going to get something that would make him unspeakably happy, for the absolute worst reasons.

He'd been doing that a lot lately. Like that morning with Thom—it had been one of the best moments of Clay's life, but Thom had only come to him because he'd been so torn up about what he'd had to do to get that bill passed. His memories of it, heated and passionate though they were, were tainted with Thom's pain, and the way he had shut down afterward. It was like he couldn't get close to Thom without causing or being a witness to some tragedy.

Was falling in love supposed to be this painful?

Thom walked into the room. He was carrying his suit jacket, his shirtsleeves rolled up to show off his forearms, his brown eyes tired but still as darkly beautiful as ever. He didn't smile when he nodded *good morning* at Clay, but there was a familiarity there, an almost-undetectable loosening of the tightness in his frame.

At least it wasn't all painful.

Lennie and Felicia followed in short order. Lennie was still in an irrepressible mood, beaming as she clapped her hands and asked them, "How are my two lovebirds this fine morning?"

Thom looked like he was about to say something menacing.

"We're—great, ma'am," Clay jumped in. Thom glared at him.

"So," Lennie said, taking her seat. "What've we got? How is this grand romance going to unspool?"

"We should go dark for a while," Thom said, his voice flat. "If we push this thing too far and we're out there all the time, we'll pull a Hiddleswift. People will realize it's fake."

"I don't know what that is, but point taken," Lennie said.

"Okay, so no public events for…a month?" Felicia asked.

"No, no, we can't do that," Lennie said. "I want the wedding to take place before the kickoff announcement."

"Before New Year's?" Felicia asked in disbelief. "I mean, most weddings take—"

"Yeah, yeah, I know," Lennie said, waving a hand. "But look at these two—no one will have a hard time believing they're rushing headlong down the aisle." Her smile as she said this was practically grinch-ian. "Besides, they'd want to get married before the campaign kicks off and they're working for me twenty-four seven."

Felicia glanced at them, trying to gauge their reactions.

"Sure," Thom said tonelessly. "Before the announcement."

"So that means the proposal would need to be...next week?" Felicia said, looking at her phone.

Next week? Clay thought numbly. *They were going to get engaged next week?*

When no one spoke, Felicia said, "Okay. The proposal's next week."

"Who's going to propose?" Lennie asked.

That was an even more depressing thought. Who would propose if it were real? Probably neither of them; he could just see Thom ranting about how a marriage license was nothing but a meaningless piece of paper and how dumb it was for the state to get involved in people's personal lives. Okay, so it would probably be Clay who'd propose, and he'd probably do it just because after a certain amount of Thom living in his apartment and drinking his beer he'd insist on it so they could at least take advantage of the tax break.

Or maybe he just wanted to propose to Thom.

"Clay should do it," Felicia said.

He jumped. "What? Why?" He prayed guilt wasn't coming through in his voice.

But Felicia was looking at Thom. "The internet thinks of you as the cold one, Thom. They'll want to see your reaction face. Y'know, the ladies' man, player, ice-cold political pro forced to show emotion in public? They'll eat that shit up."

Thom was pale. "Fine," he said quietly.

"You are *capable* of showing emotion, aren't you, Thom?" Lennie asked skeptically.

With a murderous look in his eye, Thom gritted out, "I think I can manage."

"Great!" Lennie said. "Somewhere public, then? But nothing tacky, like at a baseball game, or with one of those, whaddya call 'em—flash mob things."

Felicia weighed this, her head cocked as she brainstormed. Clay felt a sudden stab of panic at the sight. He knew that this proposal was fake, that the entire *thing* was fake—but he still felt a wounded sense of ownership, and a frantic desire to wrest at least some control back. If he was going to propose to Thom, even as part of a set piece, he should be the one to decide how it would go down.

"How about Santa Monica Pier?" he blurted out. Felicia blinked at him, looking surprised by his initiative. "The pictures would be great," he explained. "And it's, y'know." He glanced at Thom, and then quickly away. "Romantic."

"That's perfect," Felicia said slowly. "If you propose on the boardwalk, the paparazzi will get photos, but they'll still have to be far enough away that they won't be able to hear you, so you won't have to memorize a speech or anything."

Right—a speech. Because as far as she knew, Clay wouldn't be able to come up with anything to say when proposing to Thom.

He was so fucked.

When all the details had been finalized, Clay bolted out of the meeting like a bat out of hell. To his surprise, Thom caught up with him in the hallway, stopping his attempt at escape with a gentle hand on his wrist. Clay waited, wondering what Thom would say after having avoided him for the past twenty-four hours. But he just nodded, and Clay followed him to an empty, darkened cubicle down the hall.

When they were alone, Thom said, "I, uh, I just wanted to…see how you were doing." He shuffled in place a bit, looking supremely uncomfortable. "Make sure you were okay with all this."

"It wasn't your idea," Clay said. "How are *you* doing with it?"

Thom scoffed. "The next president of the United States—a matchmaking pageant mom."

Clay shrugged. "Yeah." There was a depressed pause, and then he said, "You didn't come over last night."

Thom glanced up at him uneasily. "I didn't want you to feel...pressured."

Clay nodded. "I'm okay, though."

"Good," Thom said, looking queasy. *His groom-to-be.*

"Jeez," Clay said, as something new occurred to him. "I'm gonna have to get a ring."

"God," Thom muttered.

"I think my great-aunt has a family ring she brought over from Poland or whatever."

"A woman's ring isn't gonna fit me, Clay," Thom said. "Plus, I'm not really a diamond guy."

"Oh. Right," Clay said. "Well, what's your, like, ring size?"

"Fuck do I know."

Clay fished around in his pockets. There was nothing there, but he did find a thread poking out of the lining of his jacket, and he tugged on it until it came loose. "C'mere," he told Thom.

Thom looked up at him darkly, but said nothing as he drew closer and let Clay take his hand. He wrapped the thread around Thom's ring finger, leaving enough slack so that it wouldn't pinch, and tied it in a delicate knot.

Their eyes met when he was done. Clay kept a hold on Thom's hand, and found that he couldn't look away. This hurt too, every artifact of this huge, awful lie they were going to tell. But in this moment, with Thom's hand in his and his body just a breath away, all he could think about was getting closer, pulling him in, and tasting him until everything else went away.

Would it make it worse if they fucked again?

He wanted to do it again. He wanted a chance to do it slowly, now that Thom might feel more comfortable. Or hell, Thom could fuck him. He literally didn't care, he just wanted to lock the door and stay in bed with him until there was nothing left between them but shared breath and the sweat on their skin.

"So," Clay said, "are you coming over tonight?"

Thom's eyes were still locked on his. "Isn't that supposed to be bad luck?"

"I think that's, uh. Just the night before the wedding."

The wedding. What a surreal thing to say. And it made him imagine what a real wedding to Thom would be like. Thom would probably insist on the dreariest courthouse wedding imaginable, totally bare-bones, no sentiment. But he could also see them finding someone who'd lend them a car, putting some beers in a cooler, driving out to the middle of nowhere, and sitting on the hood to look up at the stars. Celebrating their first night as a married couple under the open sky.

What was he thinking? Thom hated the outdoors. Come to think of it, so did he. Still, it felt right. Familiar, even though it was just a fantasy.

"Well," Thom was saying, "if we're going dark for a week, we don't need the content."

Clay took a step closer and lowered his voice. "What about the stress relief?"

He was blatantly leaning over Thom at this point. He'd feel bad, but Thom was definitely leaning back.

Felicia appeared around the corner. "Hey, I just wanted to confirm about the timing—"

Thom lurched back from him, shoving him away with one hand. "Confirm with Clay, it's his proposal."

"Thom!" Felicia shouted at his retreating back.

"Sorry," Clay said quickly, and then scurried away from her too, ignoring her theatrical hiss of annoyance.

He slammed his office door shut behind him and sank into his chair, staring down at his fist. When Thom had pushed at him, he hadn't just been creating distance—he'd shoved the circle of thread from around his finger back to Clay.

He opened his hand, staring at the fine black thread in a wobbly circle, and imagined seeing a ring in his palm instead.

What kind of ring would Thom want? He considered asking him, then felt a powerful rush similar to what he'd felt in the meeting, of something like possessiveness. *He* wanted to pick out a ring for Thom. Something he might not anticipate but would like anyway. Something thick and not too much like jewelry—low-profile but masculine. He pictured Thom with a plain silver ring on his finger, and the image made his chest hurt so much that he had to pitch over in his chair, suddenly feeling light-headed.

Maybe the ring being real would make up for the fact that everything else about them was a lie.

★ 33 ★

Thom stayed away from Clay during their "going dark" week. He had a bad feeling that if he kept hanging out at Clay's apartment or fooling around with him, he'd say something he'd regret—that the calm and contentedness he'd felt in Clay's presence lately would spill out into something utterly beyond his control. He saw Clay at the office, and it wasn't intimate or pretend-affectionate; they talked work, and Thom occasionally snapped at him and called him an idiot, as per usual, and sometimes when he was absolutely, positively sure no one was looking, he sat in his office and pretended to work while looking out his window at Clay across the bullpen, watching him fiddle with a pen or get coffee. That alone—just the sight of him, going about his day—it was enough to keep Thom sane.

Felicia kept stopping by to ask them questions about their fake relationship for their very real PR strategy. Thom noted with dull approval that going dark had caused their mentions to spike, full of people asking where all the pics and joint appearances and content had gone. At night he lay in his own, far nicer apartment, on his far more expensive mattress and his far more expensive sheets, and had trouble falling asleep for the first time in his life.

It was going about as well as could be expected.

The hardest moments were at the end of each workday, when Clay was preparing to go home. He'd taken to stopping by Thom's office before he left, always with completely anodyne chitchat, always poorly concealing his desire for it to become something more. But he never outright asked Thom over to his place—he seemed to sense Thom's need to pull back, his guardedness and fear. It was as if he just stopped by every day at six thirty or seven to let Thom know he was there, if he wanted him.

Then, on Thursday, Clay left the office early—around three. Thom lasted thirty-four minutes before texting him.

Playing hooky?

Nah doctor's appointment

Everything ok? He made himself write "ok" instead of "okay," but couldn't bring himself to leave off the question mark.

It took Clay two minutes to respond, in which time Thom got nothing done. Then the three little dots appeared, and what came through was both a text and a picture: Clay on the street, squinting up at the bright sunlight, a thin, colorful tube poking crookedly out of his smile.

Yeah just a checkup

Thom squinted at the picture. Is that...a Pixy Stix? Do you go to a pediatrician?

Nah I always get something sweet after a doc visit though. I deserve it

Fond laughter throbbed through Thom's chest, though none made it past his throat. He stared at the picture of Clay in the sun, having treated himself after his errand, and realized that he could feel the sun on his skin too—the addictive warmth of Clay's absurdity, a joy that seemed to sear him from the inside out.

When he left work that night, he gave his Uber driver Clay's address instead of his.

It was late, and when he got there and Clay answered the door Thom said nothing, just shoved Clay back into his apartment, kicked the door closed, and jumped him.

They stumbled back onto Clay's couch, and landing on it sent up a wave of the scent of Clay's apartment, which made Thom's chest clench with something alarmingly close to homesickness. He straddled Clay's lap, holding his face in both hands, and kissed him so hard it had to hurt them both. Clay's mouth still tasted like sugar.

When they broke apart Clay tried to talk, but Thom just sank to his knees, pulling Clay's jeans off and getting his lips on Clay's skin as quick as he could manage so his objections would die off. The lights were on in the apartment, but Thom felt more akin to the black outside Clay's windows, the sense that this was one tiny, bright haven in a cold, dark night.

Once he'd gotten Clay off, Clay hauled him back up onto his lap and gave him a handjob just as rough and fast as Thom had blown him, kissing him messily the whole time.

He'd dressed as soon as he'd gotten his breathing back

under control. Clay had grabbed his hand and rasped, "Stay," but Thom had just squeezed his fingers and turned away, straightening his clothes as he left the apartment.

They hadn't talked about it the next morning. But on Saturday, Clay texted him a picture of a plain silver ring resting on his open palm.

Thom felt like he couldn't breathe. He texted Clay a thumbs-up, his own thumb shaking against the screen.

When they got back to the office after the proposal, Lennie had champagne waiting.

"I swear," Lennie said, pouring the champagne into Solo cups as they watched coverage of the proposal on TMZ, "I could watch this all day."

Thom focused on the fizzing in his cup and tried to shut out the audio of the television. He wasn't watching, and he hadn't looked at any of the pictures.

They'd done it at the pier, like they'd planned. It was about as California cliché as you could get—the bracing, salty air, the sea-worn wood, the tourist stands and twinkling rides. He hadn't heard much of Clay's "proposal"—the waves had been crashing loudly, and his focus had been split by the paparazzi frantically whipping out their biggest cameras as soon as Clay had gone down on one knee. And there'd been this rushing in Thom's head, a kind of frantic white noise that felt like sweat and hope and dread all scrambled together.

He was pretty sure that Clay's speech had gone something like, *You're the most incredible man I've ever met and I want to spend the rest of my life with you*, and something about being a family.

For one heart-stopping, horrifying moment, Thom had felt like he might cry. Worse, he was pretty sure Clay had noticed.

"Good job, Thom," Felicia was saying now. "Your face in these photos is perfect."

"I knew you could show emotion if the job called for it," Lennie laughed.

Thom downed his champagne and opened his phone. He was getting a blizzard of texts and emails, but he checked the headlines first. So far the proposal was a smash hit—the season finale of everyone's favorite new show. *BuzzFeed* even had an article about them, for fuck's sake ("Literally Just 17 Pictures of Thom Morgan and Clay Parker That Prove That Love Is Real").

He scrolled through the photos, feeling his breath go unsteady. There were pictures there he didn't remember, from events he couldn't cleanly link to the campaign or the job. Some were just shots of him grinning up at Clay, open and unguarded. It wasn't an expression he'd ever seen on his own face before.

"Okay," Lennie said, tapping her Solo cup with one manicured nail. The rest of the staff had filed in to celebrate with them—presumably what they took to be an actual staff engagement. Silence fell, and Lennie raised her cup. "Truly, I never would have predicted this, but—to our most successful campaign initiative. Good job, boys!"

The staff laughed and cheered. Most of them would think she was just giving them shit.

Looking at his phone was making him nauseous, so Thom put it away and glanced at Clay. Back on the pier, when he'd nodded *yes*, Clay had given him this small, private smile, before standing up to slide the ring onto his finger. It was still there now, a dull weight he was trying to ignore. But Thom could remember the feeling of Clay's hand folded over his, and he felt it again now as Clay met his eye across the room with that same small smile. It was half *can you believe this shit* and half something else. Like maybe he thought that this was all worth it.

Thom felt that scramble again, the peace and the fear, the warmth and the cold, unsteady dread. He pushed up from his seat. "We need more champagne," he said to no one in particular.

Clay's smile dissolved into a small frown. Thom turned and walked out of the room.

There was nothing in the kitchen. He wandered the bullpen, then ended up in Fe's doorway, where he spotted an open case of cheap champagne sitting in a dark corner. Of course, Fe had made sure they had what they needed. It was a special day for the campaign.

He ripped the cardboard case open wider and pried another bottle out of its slick plastic packaging. When the sound of the cork popping had faded, he heard a voice behind him. "Are you alright?"

He turned around. Fe was leaning against her door frame, her head tilted as she watched him.

"Yeah," he said. "I'm great. Didn't you hear? It's going really well." He took a long drag off the foaming bottle. Champagne wasn't really his thing, but at least it burned on the way down.

"Careful, Thom," Felicia said. Her tone was teasing in a rote sort of way, like her heart wasn't really in it. "You're starting to seem…"

"What?" he asked.

She didn't answer. As she stared at him, the small traces of good humor slid off her expression entirely, until all that was left was what looked like genuine alarm.

He laughed at her. "Don't worry about it, Fe," he said. He glanced down at the bottle in his hand. "Don't you remember? What you said?"

"What I said?" she asked. "When?"

He took a few steps toward her, until he could look her in the eye properly. "If someone gets hurt, it's going to be Clay."

She blinked at him.

"So I'm fine," he continued. He slapped her on the shoulder. "Let's get back to the party."

She didn't follow him when he walked out.

★ 34 ★

The wedding was set for the very end of December, three weeks away. Everyone had stressed that this was way too soon, but Lennie hadn't wavered in her commitment to keeping up their "momentum." And she wasn't wrong—Clay's proposal had gone mega-viral, boosting the campaign's PR once again. His notifications were full of people eager for details on the engagement and the wedding and his and Thom's happily-ever-after.

There was no turning back now. He and Thom were getting married.

To ease the herculean task of planning a wedding in what was functionally a nanosecond, Lennie had offered to host it herself at her sprawling mansion. It was a helpful reminder for Clay that this wasn't a real wedding—it was a part of the Westwood for America campaign.

That feeling was only reinforced by the process of wedding planning. Clay was shuttled around to fittings, walk-throughs, and interviews, but no one seemed to care about his opinions, even though he had plenty. (He'd always thought it would be cool to wear a top hat to his wedding, but Thom had nixed that idea with nothing more than a chilly glare.) Instead, Felicia and Thom planned the whole thing, designing a wedding that would look stunning on Instagram and as a backdrop for photos of Lennie, and might incidentally leave him and Thom as husband and husband. He wasn't even totally sure about that last part—Lennie was officiating, and he hadn't heard anyone mention her taking that online course or getting certified or doing whatever people needed to do if they weren't ministers or judges or boat captains.

At least the wedding planning gave him a chance to see Thom.

Thom was clearly avoiding him, except for the odd, random times he showed up at Clay's apartment, jumping his bones and then leaving. Their long, lingering weekends of running dumb errands and lounging on the couch together were a thing of the past, and Clay missed them. All he had now was frantic, rushed sex and the pageantry of planning a fake wedding at which he was nothing more than a prop.

And the whole time, he kept thinking *Thom and I are going to be* married, and having panic attacks because no one else except him seemed to be thinking about what would come after the wedding. Every time he tried to talk to Thom about it at the office he would make some cutting joke and then leave, and every time he tried to talk to him about it when they were alone he'd distract Clay with sex and then leave, which was frustratingly effective because the sex was still mind-blowing.

So eventually Clay had no choice but to barge into Thom's

office, slam the door behind him, and demand, "What about our house?"

Thom blinked at him, looking surprised and, just for a moment, vulnerable. Before Clay could react to that, his expression slid back into his pissy default state. "Our *what*," he asked.

Clay sat in a chair in front of Thom's desk. "We've been doing all this wedding planning crap, which I have plenty of ideas about, by the way—"

Thom rolled his eyes. "If this is about the top hat again—"

"No, my point is," Clay said, "we've been spending all this time thinking about the wedding, but what about after? What about where we're going to live?"

"What do you mean *we*?" Thom asked.

Clay frowned. "Aren't we…"

"We're not really getting *married*, Clay. I mean, we are, but it's not—" Thom looked away, straightening some papers on his desk. Without looking at him, he clarified, "We're not actually moving in together."

"But…you're always worrying about people finding out that it's fake," Clay pointed out. "Won't it be a pretty big giveaway if we don't live together?"

Thom opened his mouth, and then closed it.

When he was still stumped after a minute, Clay opened his computer and put it on Thom's desk. His browser was already open to a Zillow listing. "I think we should rent this place."

"Jesus, you already have—" Thom said, looking disturbed, but he broke off as he took in the details of the listing. "Okay, *no*. Are you kidding me? I'm not living there."

"What's wrong with it?" Clay asked, twisting to look at his screen. It was a little house with bright green shutters and a cinnamon-orange door.

"It looks like someplace you'd find grandma's body after

not hearing from her for a few weeks," Thom said. "Besides, *that* neighborhood?"

"It's a little farther out from work—" Clay said defensively.

"A *lot* farther," Thom said. "I'm not signing up for an hour-long commute every day so you can have flower beds."

"I don't care about flower beds," Clay said. "Everything closer to the office is so expensive!"

"We don't need a whole house," Thom said. "Look for something smaller."

"I dunno," Clay said. "This place has a basketball hoop out back. It could be cool to have some outdoor space, y'know, for grilling and stuff, or if we wanted to have people over."

"I've hung out at your apartment almost every day for the last few months," Thom said, "and you've never had people over."

"Maybe I would if I had a basketball hoop."

"Find a nice building close to work that has a pool and one of those, y'know, business center things," Thom said. "Hang out with people there."

"A fancy apartment building in downtown LA?" Clay asked dubiously. "Those places are so expensive we'd only be able to afford a studio, and then we'd kill each other."

Thom cocked his head. "Yeah, that's true. We'd need at least two bathrooms."

"Right, one entire one for your hair products, and another for all your skin creams," Clay said, straight-faced.

"Because you're a fucking slob," Thom returned.

"And I want at least two bedrooms."

"What? Why?"

"So one of them can be an office." Thom nodded like he understood. Then Clay added, "For me."

He stopped nodding. "For *you*?"

"Yeah," Clay shrugged. "I mean, I might not be in politics forever. I might want to start coding again, and if I do, I'll need an office."

The mockery had cleared from Thom's expression. "You might start coding again?" He asked the question in a tone that was, for Thom, almost gentle.

"Yeah. I dunno," Clay said, feeling self-conscious. "That neighborhood relocation idea I had sounded so cool in the *Recode* article."

"It is cool," Thom said, with a small smile. "Have you put any more work into it?"

"Some. I had to move the whole thing off Pinpoint first, so that was annoying." Thom made a grossed-out face at the mention of Derek's company, which made Clay glow inside. "And I was thinking of reaching out to some of my old contacts from the Pinpoint days, people who might…"

"Fund it?" Thom prompted.

Clay shrugged.

"You should," Thom told him, leaning forward over his desk. "I can help you, if you want—go over pitch ideas, and—"

A junior staffer poked her head into the room. "Thom?" she asked. "They need you in this meeting."

"Right. Yeah—I'll be right there," Thom said. He glanced at the papers on his desk, and Clay reached for his computer to move it out of the way.

As soon as his laptop snapped shut, their eyes met. Then Thom looked away and cleared his throat, and it was like all the air in the room shifted with that one broken moment. Just a second ago it had been filled with all these sweet ideas of what it might be like if they actually moved into the little house with green shutters or a fancy high-rise—if they actually made those compromises and found a place they both loved. If Thom helped Clay with his coding, and Clay made waffles when Thom came home late from the office, and they found a way to build a life together.

But those were just daydreams, and as they evaporated, all that was left was the stilted distance between them.

"This is stupid," Thom said, looking down at his lap. "The campaign's going to gear up soon, we'll be on the road. And if Lennie wins we'll all be moving to DC. If she doesn't…" His eyes flicked up to Clay's, and then away. "This whole thing is over anyway."

"Right," Clay said. "Right. Okay, I'll…forget it, then." He tucked his computer under his arm and got up.

"Clay," Thom called out as his hand touched the door, and he turned around.

Thom seemed to fumble with his words for a second, taking a deep breath and then discarding it. "I, uh. I was gonna say you can have that top hat if you really want it, but." He smiled. "You definitely can't."

Clay nodded and laughed a little. "Yeah. I know. It's gotta look good, right? That's the whole point."

A muscle jumped in Thom's jaw. "Yup."

Clay looked at the ground, then opened the door. At his desk, Thom was silent and rigidly still as Clay walked away.

★ 35 ★

In the blink of an eye, it was the night before the wedding.

Online anticipation had reached a fever pitch. They'd done the whole song and dance of *asking for privacy for this special event*, but the campaign had made sure to leak enough details that the entire internet knew the pics would be dropping tomorrow. In fact, Felicia would probably want them to post pictures from the rehearsal dinner too—something that hadn't occurred to Clay until just now.

He was belatedly very glad he'd let Thom pick out all his clothes.

They were dressing for the dinner at Clay's place, changing in his bedroom and helping each other with their cuff links and ties. He had to admit that the suit Thom had chosen for him looked nice—charcoal gray with a skinny black tie. Thom looked drop-dead gorgeous in his suit, which probably meant that Clay wasn't prepared for how much better he'd look in his tux the next morning.

The next morning. Just thinking about it had nerves crawling up his throat.

He was grateful for the distraction when his phone buzzed. He checked it, nodded to himself, and put his phone back in his pocket, but that apparently wasn't smooth enough to keep Thom from noticing. "What was that?" he asked mildly.

"Uh, nothing," Clay said.

Thom merely raised an eyebrow as he did his tie.

Clay sighed. "It was my lawyer."

"Oh?" Thom asked. "News on the lawsuit?"

"Yeah," Clay said, shifting uncomfortably. He waited about as long as he thought he could get away with before he finally said, "I settled."

Thom's arms dropped, leaving his tie dangling around his neck. "*What?* Why didn't you tell me?"

"I'm telling you now," Clay mumbled.

Thom shook his head, sputtering. "But—why now? You just got them on the ropes with the *Recode* story. You could've pressed your advantage."

"Well, my lawyer said the story is why they made such a big offer," Clay said.

"I—" Thom paced back and forth, like he was bursting with questions. "Okay, well how much did you get?"

Clay pouted a little, like *not bad*. "A lot," he said.

"How a lot?" Thom asked.

Clay showed him the text from his lawyer. Thom whistled. "Okay, that's something. But—" He still seemed frustrated, running a hand through his hair. "Did you get anything else? Pinpoint stock? Some kind of—of admission from Derek about everything you contributed?"

Clay put his hands in his pockets and looked away again. "No."

"Then—why did you take the deal?"

Clay shrugged simply. "I wanted to put it behind me. Move forward."

Thom stared at him, a small frown between his brows.

"C'mon," Clay said lightly. "We've gotta leave soon if we're going to get there on time."

Thom went back to work on his tie, still staring at Clay. "We're the guests of honor," he said. "They'll wait for us."

"Pretty sure Lennie's the guest of honor," Clay said.

"True," Thom said, tucking his tie into his jacket once he was done. "Then I guess it doesn't matter either way." He held out his arms. "How do I look?"

Clay shook his head. "Everyone's gonna be jealous of me."

Thom grinned and kissed him slowly. "That's the idea."

Lennie hosted the rehearsal dinner at her cavernous home. The wedding would also take place there, on the lawn out back. The house barely needed to be decorated for either event—it was exactly what Clay had always expected rich people's houses to look like: polished wood, rich red carpets, enormous chandeliers, oil paintings and ambiguous stone sculptures. The air seemed to glitter, and tuxedo-clad waiters flitted between the guests with trays of champagne.

The waiters looked more at home than Clay felt. He may have been dressed well, but he didn't know a single person there aside from Felicia, Lennie, and Thom. The guest list was mostly Lennie's friends and donors, which didn't really bother him, since she was paying for everything. She'd also generously agreed to pick up the tab for Clay's parents to fly in from Massachusetts. They were his only guests, en route right now; he hadn't wanted to invite anyone else to a fake wedding. Plus, the small guest list helped keep up the air of mystery around their "celebrity" relationship.

Thom hadn't invited anyone—family or friends. Clay was pretty sure Theo had called one night after the proposal made the news to ask about the wedding, because he overheard Thom muttering something about not wanting him to have to travel with a young baby.

He hadn't heard anything about Thom's parents reaching out. He was afraid to ask.

He and Thom had been separated by the party's currents minutes after arriving. Thom was busy at the center of the room now, charming the crowd of bigwigs with his usual magnetism. In a dark blue suit, with a hint of black stubble on his jaw, he looked unbelievably handsome in the dim candlelight, like something out of a wedding magazine—the consummate groom. Clay's fingers tingled at the thought of holding Thom's hands in his tomorrow, and letting Thom slide a ring onto his finger.

His phone buzzed in his pocket—a text from his mom, saying that she and his dad had just arrived. He slumped in relief and pushed his way over to the twin grand staircases by the foyer. A few minutes later, he spotted his parents being ushered inside.

"Clay-Clay!" his mom called when she saw him, her face creasing with a thousand-watt smile.

"Mo-om," he muttered in annoyance as he hugged her, even while he was grateful for the soothing familiarity of her perfume. He greeted his dad, then turned and gestured to the room behind him. "So, what do you think?"

"So fancy!" she said, eyes wide as she handed her coat to one of the event staff.

His dad was craning his neck around to take it all in. "Wow. You've really made it, son," he said proudly.

Clay stifled a wince. He hated lying to his parents about the wedding, but there was nothing to be done. "Mom, you want a drink?" he asked. "The booze here is expensive."

She didn't answer him. She'd gone stock-still, her face slowly filling to the brim with piercing excitement. "Phil!" she whispered, grabbing his dad's sleeve and shaking it. "Phil, look! There he is!"

Clay glanced over his shoulder, at where Thom was grinning telegenically at one of the other guests. "Oh, god."

There had been a *lot* of conversations with his parents over the past few months about why they hadn't met Thom yet— and most of those had been before they'd gotten "engaged." His mom's anxiety level had spiked to infinity once she'd learned that her son was going to marry a man she hadn't met yet, and it had taken a lot of sweet-talking to convince her that the rehearsal dinner would be plenty of time to get to know her son's fiancé. All of that was catching up to him now, as his mom dove into the crowd with military efficiency, cutting a straight line toward Thom. Clay had only a second to wave frantically, trying to catch Thom's attention and send some sort of warning.

As it turned out, he hadn't needed to worry. When Clay's mom latched on to him with quaking enthusiasm, Thom looked startled for only a half second before he recovered, clasping her hand in his and introducing himself smoothly. By the time Clay and his dad reached them, they'd blown right past pleasantries, and Thom was saying, "Let's find a quiet corner so we can chat. I want to hear *everything* about Clay."

His mom melted. Clay rolled his eyes.

Thom absolutely crushed it with his parents—he laughed loudly at his mom's jokes, talked bitcoin fluently with his dad, and every time he looked warmly at Clay or laced their fingers together, he could feel Thom's stock rising. It didn't even seem like the standard Thom Morgan charm offensive either—Clay was familiar with the way Thom's eyes tightened at the edges when he was exhausted from performing too long, but tonight he didn't seem strained or artificial at all. His smile was easy, and it made Clay's heart race.

Things only got bad when his mom whipped out the baby pictures. "Mom, what the fuck," Clay shouted, as she showed Thom a picture from when he was three, buck naked and standing arms akimbo in front of a mirror in their house. "Why do you even have that on your phone?!"

"Deirdre showed me how to put things in the cloud!" his mom said happily, swiping at the screen. "Oh, look at this one."

Thom looked like he was biting his lip to keep from howling. "Um, Clay," he said, once he'd cleared his throat. "I'm sensing a theme to these pictures."

"Me naked?" Clay asked darkly.

"Well, that too," Thom said, leaning in close to examine a picture of Clay fuming in front of a toy horse. "But it's also that—you were so freakishly tall, even as a kid, that you never had the right size toys."

"Oh, that's true," his mom said, swiping again. "He shot up like a sprout, this one. We could never keep up."

The picture on her phone now was a five-year-old Clay staring down grumpily at a small toy car. Thom looked at the photo and then at Clay, delight all over his features.

"Yeah, well," Clay grumbled. "Maybe they should make bigger toys."

Thom leaned in and whispered in Clay's ear, "Do you want me to buy you a race car bed?"

Clay shoved him, but he held on to the hot shiver that ran down his spine.

"I'm just so happy for you boys," his mom said, leaning

back into his dad's arm. "And so happy we finally got to meet you, Thom," she added, with a pointed look at Clay.

"Thanks, Leslie," Thom said. He leaned forward. "I have to ask—you weren't...surprised? By how fast this all went down?"

"Well, you two are in love," his dad said indulgently. Thom smiled at him, and now Clay could see that familiar tightness around his eyes. "Besides, folks got married earlier in our day. I'm not sure how you millennials do things now."

"And Clay told us why he needed to keep your relationship secret for so long," his mom said. "It's just a shame everyone sees it as all tied up with your work for the governor."

His dad nodded. "Especially given her shoddy record on LGBT issues."

"Phil!" his mom gasped. "Keep your voice down, we're guests of the governor here."

"I'm a citizen," he retorted stoutly. "I have a right to my opinions."

"You're from Massachusetts. She doesn't care what you think."

Clay rolled his eyes and let his parents argue. Then he realized that Thom was looking pale, and leaned over to him to ask lowly, "Everything okay?"

"Yeah. Excuse me," he said to Clay's parents. "I have to make a few calls. It was great to meet you."

His parents glowed at the niceties, and didn't object when Clay followed Thom.

He found him in a darkened room that might have been a study, though it was curiously void of furniture. Maybe this was how houses looked before weddings? His voice echoed when he asked, "Are we supposed to be here?"

"What are they gonna do," Thom said, looking out a pair

of French doors that opened onto the yard. "Tell us we can't get married tomorrow?"

He opened the door with a soft creak, and Clay followed him out to the stone patio. There were still a few staffers around, setting up for the next day. Lennie's yard sloped gently downward, with tall, well-trimmed hedges all along the sides and back. There were two huge trees on either side of the lawn—big, thick trunks with huge canopies of leaves that probably kept it nice and cool during the day. It felt almost like being under a tent, and the tiny lights strung up between the trees and their branches added to the effect, even though they weren't on. There was some sort of gazebo or arch being set up toward the back, in front of the hedges, and delicate white chairs had been arranged facing away from them. It was exactly what Clay had been expecting.

"Jesus," Thom said, taking it all in, and that was also true.

No one seemed to have noticed they were there. Clay took in the long line of Thom's body in the moonlight, the bob of his throat as he swallowed. "Are you okay?" he asked again.

Thom shook his head. "I—" He turned to Clay, face twisted like something was eating him from inside. "How can you possibly be okay with your family being here for this—for this fake bullshit?"

It was a fair question. Clay felt vaguely sick when he thought about how his parents would deal with whatever inevitably happened when this thing came crashing down. Still, he'd invited them. He shrugged. "Well...it's real to me."

Thom took a step back.

Clay rushed to say, "I mean—look, we're doing this for the job, right? That's real. My parents get that that matters to me." Thom relaxed an inch, though he still looked wary. "And you really do boss me around and tell me where to go and what to wear," Clay pointed out, and Thom smiled slightly.

"Whether that's for a real relationship or a…work project that just looks like one. And I'm doing this for better reasons than a lot of people get married. I could be a gold digger."

Thom huffed out a dry laugh at that.

"I'm not keeping anything important from my family," Clay said. "And… I guess, if anyone has to be my 'fake' fiancé, I'm glad it's you. I'm okay with my family knowing you. That's not fake."

Thom said nothing. It was hard to read his expression in the dark.

"It's getting late," Clay said. "I told my parents I'd share an Uber with them back to the hotel and make sure they get in safe. If—"

He was cut off as Thom surged at him, kissing him with both hands clasped around his face. Clay waited, but Thom didn't deepen the kiss or press their bodies together. They just sort of swayed there together, warm in the cool night.

When Thom broke the kiss, he said softly, "I'll meet you at your place."

"Okay," Clay said dazedly.

When he got home from dropping off his parents, he was sure Thom wouldn't be there. But when he slammed the door of his car behind him and heard it drive away, a shadow moved by his front gate. Thom was there, standing silently, hands in his pockets. Clay felt an almost painful kick of desire at the base of his spine, and he fumbled to get his key in the lock.

Thom didn't even let Clay turn the lights on. They fell back against the kitchen counter, Thom's fingers in his hair and his body pressed against Clay's, kissing him until his lips were sore. It went on and on, until the countertop was digging into Clay's thigh and Thom was rolling his hips against his leg, and Clay had to gasp between kisses, "Thom, should we—do you wanna—"

Without a word, Thom took his hand and dragged him into the bedroom.

He didn't stop kissing him there either. He pressed against Clay like he couldn't get close enough, letting him peel his jacket off his shoulders, hitch his shirt out of his pants and un-button it slowly, his fingers cramping because Thom wouldn't back up enough to give him room to work. Thom's skin felt cold when Clay got his shirt off, so he set about warm-ing him, pressing hot, openmouthed kisses all over his body and running his hands over his back and shoulders. Thom removed Clay's shirt in short, violent motions, the hunger plain on his face.

Clay's breath caught at the sight. There wasn't a lot of light in the room, but there was enough that he could see that the usual Thom facade was gone, leaving nothing to block Clay's view of the thoughts flitting across his face. Thom licked his lips and looked up at Clay, the openness in his eyes pinning him helplessly in place.

"Thom," he whispered.

Thom kissed him again. He scrabbled at Clay's pants as they fell onto the bed, toeing off shoes and socks and grab-bing at each other. Thom tumbled them so he was on top, and loomed over Clay like the picture-perfect hero of a ro-mance novel. He ran a hand over Clay's chest, dipped down to kiss and lick at his nipples, and raked his fingernails across his stomach. He took Clay into his mouth and sucked him, slow and thorough. And all the while, his dark eyes kept darting up to meet Clay's.

"Thom," Clay panted, his head writhing on his pillow. He couldn't stop saying his name.

Once Clay was good and wet, Thom pushed back up and

proceeded to give him the slowest, most torturous handjob ever, tight and twisted and perfect, because he was staring into his eyes the entire time. He occasionally broke the eye contact to kiss Clay's neck or his cheek or, softly, gently, his lips, but every time Clay squeezed his eyes shut, overwhelmed, and then opened them again, Thom was looking right at him. Clay's breathing went harsh as he climbed closer and closer, and he could feel sweat beading on his forehead, could see his fists in the sheets in his peripheral vision, but Thom didn't seem to see anything but Clay, gazing at him so openly that he came with a shaky cry.

Thom breathed against him until Clay stopped shaking. Then his hands moved over Clay again, one behind his shoulder and another around his hip, and he hitched him closer until he could rut against him, panting and nearly growling with need. Clay felt like he'd just run a marathon, but the feel of Thom grinding against his slick thigh sent sparks over his skin anyway. He dug his fingers into Thom's back and ass, kneading and urging him on, and whispered into his ear, sex things but also other stuff he definitely shouldn't have been saying, like, "Come on, do it, fuck, yes, please, Thom, need you, please, need you so much—" He couldn't stop begging, and it was so stupid because he'd already come, but he knew what he was really begging for, could hear it in his voice, feel it in the way his hands curved over Thom and his skin thrilled where Thom's fingers were digging into him: *Please, want me back, please, please love me too.*

Thom came with a guttural noise into Clay's neck, and then went limp.

Clay was exhausted. Every time they'd had sex before, it had been some degree of frenetic—crazed, passionate, and always distracting them from something.

Tonight had been different. Thom had *looked* at him.

Also different this time was the faint sound of snoring that followed. Clay snorted in disbelief, then laughed when he realized that even the great Sex Fantasy Thom Morgan *snored*.

He was sure his laughter would wake Thom from what must have been a sex-induced stupor. But Thom just frowned in a cute sort of way, burrowed slightly away from Clay so that he was on his own pillow, and settled back into sleep.

The snores kept going as Clay lay there and stared at Thom's face, so open in sleep. They kept going while Clay rinsed himself off and pulled pajamas on and climbed back into bed. They kept going as Clay drifted off himself, dreaming of other times he might get to hear Thom snore.

When Clay woke up, Thom's stuff was gone, and the sheets on his side of the bed were cold.

He got dressed in the tux Thom had picked out for him. Once he'd put his wallet, keys, and phone in his pockets, all that was left was the little gray ring box sitting innocuously on his dresser.

The sight of it was so mundane and yet so surreal. He would put that box in his coat pocket, call a ride, go back to Lennie's mansion, and let Thom put the ring inside on his finger.

He loved that thought, and he hated it. He'd hated it since the day Lennie had steered them into it. Nothing could be more wrong than a fake wedding for what was, for him anyway, real love.

It was so stupid, and sad, and pathetic, but all Clay wanted in the world was for Thom to show up today and say, *I can't do this. I'm not marrying you, because this is fake, and I love you for real.*

He took the box off the dresser and popped it open, looking down at the ring Thom had picked out for him. It matched Thom's, a plain, thick silver band. He glanced back at the bed, where the sheets were mussed but otherwise all evidence of the night Thom had spent with him was gone.

For the first time in a while, he allowed himself to indulge in the barest flicker of hope. Maybe Thom would show up to the wedding today and say all the things Clay wanted him to say. Maybe he was ready. Maybe he'd refuse to marry Clay.

He couldn't think of anything more romantic.

He snapped the ring box closed, tucked it in his pocket, and called an Uber.

When he got there, Lennie's driveway was clogged with cars, and there were staffers swarming everywhere to direct early guests and coordinate the vendors. Clay made his way inside.

He spotted Felicia first. She was barking into her phone, hunched over like she didn't want anyone to hear what she was saying, but her face went taut when she saw Clay. She hung up on whoever she'd been talking to and stalked straight toward him. "Something's wrong," she said.

Clay's heart pitter-pattered. Maybe this was it. Maybe this was part of it. Maybe when Thom showed up, he would call the whole thing off.

But he didn't. Because Thom didn't show at all.

★ 36 ★

Thom knew he should go somewhere Clay wouldn't think to look for him, but he couldn't think of a single place that met that description. He wasn't sure if that said something about the dullness of his life or how well Clay knew him. Probably both.

In the end, because he was a predictable workaholic, he chose the office. Clay would definitely think to look for him there, but as the minutes dragged by, the empty office remained silent. No one burst through his door; no one showed up for a dramatic, last-minute confrontation.

He'd turned off his phone. The sight of the flat black screen staring up at him from its perch on his desk was the scariest thing he'd ever experienced. He was completely cut off—from Clay, from his job, from the world at large. Adrift in the open sea.

He remembered yelling at Clay all those months ago about

having cut off his internet. Like an addict raging at someone who'd taken their fix. Except now he was the one who'd gone clean, and it was too little, too late.

Without his phone, he had to use an actual clock on the wall. He watched as it struck 10:00 a.m., and then 10:01. That was it, then—he'd done it. He had officially not shown up for the wedding.

He'd killed his career, and betrayed Clay.

Everything he'd thought he would fuck up, he had.

In the end, it hadn't been anything Clay had done that had broken him. It had been Clay's parents, and what they'd said about Lennie's record on LGBT rights. It had hit Thom like a brick to the chest. Sure, he'd known about Lennie's record—in a distant, professional way. But it wasn't political theater for Clay's parents—they saw a politician's stance on gay rights as critical to the literal physical well-being of their son, who lived all alone across the country. And the people like Lennie, like Thom, who were supposed to be looking out for him—they were using him instead.

That was when he'd known what he had to do. It had just taken him all night to work up the courage to say goodbye to Clay.

He jumped when he heard the elevator doors open. He spun in his chair, hands white-knuckling the edge of his desk. But it was Lennie who walked through his door, dressed to the nines and clutching a shimmery purse. He craned his neck to look around her, confused, but there was no one else there. She came to a stiff halt in his doorway, features tightening and eyes slowly filling with rage.

"Great," she spat. "Just fucking great. The one fucking time I need you to have a personal life, and you're at the goddamn office."

Thom's heart was racing, but he felt oddly numb. Lennie

stalked past him into his office and threw her purse on his desk. He cleared his throat, but she chopped at him with her hand, holding up a finger.

"Don't talk," she snapped. Sitting on the edge of his desk, she took a deep breath and then fixed him with a beady-eyed glare. "Do you know why I never promoted you above Felicia?"

"Uh," Thom said. His voice sounded scratchy, even though he'd been up for hours.

Lennie didn't wait for him to continue. "Because she's smarter than you," she said matter-of-factly. She picked up the television remote on his desk. "Look at how she had me spin this," she said, and turned his TV to CNN.

It was a commercial. "Oh," she said, swiping a strand of hair out of her eyes. "Well, basically, I said something like, *Look, I know the media wants to focus on interpersonal drama between my aides, but I'd much rather focus on my job and doing the work of forty million Californians. All I'll say about Thom and Clay is that they're a wonderful couple and they deserve their privacy as they work to heal.*"

Thom nodded dully. "Yup."

"I looked sympathetic, no-nonsense, and truly gay-friendly," she added. "It actually worked out even better for me than the wedding could have."

She laughed a little. It was chilling.

In the next second, her gaze sharpened back onto Thom, and any trace of amusement melted off her face. "But that's the kind of thing you never would have come up with," she said coldly. "I hope you remember that wherever you end up next."

Thom swallowed. "Where I…"

"Oh, you and Clay are of course fired," she said casually.

"What did you think would happen when you pulled this little stunt?"

Anger burned in his throat—an anger he had no right to, but it hurt anyway. "You fired Clay?"

"Yes," she said. "And?"

He stared at her. Her eyes were incredibly empty—there was fury there, sure, but nothing more complex or nuanced than that. It was like trying to hold eye contact with a marble slab. He shivered and looked away.

"But he—" Thom sighed shortly, and started again. "But I thought you said it worked out better for you."

"Well." Lennie shrugged. "I'm in a better mood than I would have been. But you still fucked everything up. And I'm going to enjoy watching you pack up your things."

There was a long, awkward pause. Thom clenched his jaw. It was just starting to hit him that *he* had been fired. He must have really been dissociating.

At least, he thought that was what it was called when it felt like he was outside himself, looking in. He'd heard that second- and thirdhand from everyone he'd known who'd actually gone to therapy. He really could feel like he could see the whole room—the whole office—and he himself was just a lifeless doll sitting in his chair, like some kind of Politics Barbie. Everything that was happening felt like it was happening to someone else.

Then again, maybe that's what he'd been his whole life—the empty suit. Maybe what was happening now *was* him becoming someone else. He wasn't sure who. The room vibrated and melted a little, and he felt more like himself—enough to stand, at least. Becoming someone new sounded terrible. But it also sounded better than staying the same person he'd been before.

He glanced around the office that was no longer his, and

realized that there was barely even anything to pack up. He took a few notepads and his extra phone charger out of the desk and cradled them awkwardly under one arm. Lennie walked behind his desk and sat in his chair as she watched him.

"That's all you had at the office?" she said, sounding deeply unimpressed. "Jesus. This isn't even entertaining enough to be schadenfreude, it's just schad."

He took his security pass out of his pocket and laid it in front of her. Then he turned to leave.

"Thom, wait," she said.

He faced her again.

She gave him a bright smile and slid his security pass off his desk and into the garbage. "Bye!"

He blinked, and then turned his back on her.

In the doorway, he stopped and asked over his shoulder, "Aren't you worried that we'll go public?"

She leaned back in his chair and assessed him coolly. "Go public with what, Thom?" she asked. "You're sleeping together. You spend all your time together. And you just hurt yourself to try to save him."

Thom said nothing. She smiled again, and he walked out of her office.

★ 37 ★

He went to Clay's apartment.

As usual, the door was unlocked. Clay was sitting on the couch in his sweats, junk food and beer cans everywhere. He was playing BoB, though "playing" may have been an over-statement—his character was dying extravagantly every few seconds, but Clay wasn't really engaging. He didn't look up or say anything when Thom let himself in. Thom's chest felt tight with a horrible, unfamiliar ache.

"Well," he said lightly. "You don't look good."

"Yeah," Clay said flatly, still staring at the TV screen. "I got left at the altar, humiliated in front of the media, and fired—all on the same day."

Thom looked around the apartment, at the pieces of him that were scattered everywhere—his clothes, papers from the office. The waffle iron. "Yeah," he said.

He sat on the couch, careful not to sit too close to Clay but not too far from him either. "I, uh. I couldn't do it," Thom said quietly, looking at his shoes. "I know that makes me a prick. Well, I mean, I've always been a prick, I guess."

There was a long silence. Thom was about to start talking again, but then Clay seemed to snap out of his trance. "Yeah," he said sharply. "You are a prick."

Thom jolted. He'd never heard Clay sound so sure about anything, not even his grudge against Derek. He felt rooted in place by the fury in Clay's voice, but he still managed to lick his lips, saying, "Clay, it—"

But Clay wasn't even close to done. He tossed his controller aside and leaped to his feet, pacing back and forth in front of the couch. "Do you have any idea what that shit was like today?" he said. "You *didn't show.* There was a whole fucking wedding ready to go, minus one groom. Do you know what it's like to be dressed in that stupid tux, with that stupid flower they put in the pocket," he said, jabbing his fingers against his chest, "the most visible person there, and everyone's staring at you because you're the sad sack whose fiancé abandoned him? People taking pictures and tweeting about your fucking train wreck of a life? And once you manage to get away from them, Lennie's screaming at you at the top of her lungs?"

"Clay—"

"You left me there alone," Clay said harshly.

Thom hung his head and swallowed thickly. "I'm sorry," he said, his voice a scrape of sound.

Clay was unimpressed. "Yeah, that's great, Thom." He paced away from him, crossing his arms. "Why the fuck are you here?"

Unbelievably, Clay's whole rant just now had been the easy part. When Thom tried to speak again, his mouth was dry, and it felt like the beating of his heart might just get harder and faster and heavier until his whole body would shake apart into dust.

It took him a few tries to get the words out. "I, uh. I probably should have told you this before, but." He cleared his throat. "I don't want to fake-date anymore."

He'd tried to put the emphasis on the right word. *Please*, Thom thought. *Please get it.*

Clay said nothing.

As the silence stretched on, he tried again. "Clay, do you— do you get what I'm saying here?" He heard the faint desperation in his voice, but he didn't care. He just wanted Clay to look at him.

Clay was stock-still for a moment. Then he walked over to the window and slid it open, which Thom hadn't even realized it could do. He stood and breathed out into the open air for a minute, and when he turned around, Thom realized it must have been drizzling outside, because his white shirt was just a hint grayer, sticking to his pale biceps. He looked cold and fragile, shivering a little, his muscles finely trembling.

Thom tried to analyze the look on his face. His heart sank as Clay clenched his jaw and seemed to consider his words.

Then he paced over to the couch, towering over Thom, and snapped, "Nope. You know what, Thom, I can't do this—this, like, Svengali, don't-say-what-I-mean and definitely don't-let-anyone-see-I-have-feelings crap anymore. I fucking love you, okay?"

Thom's heart jumped.

Clay threw out his hands and yelled, "Yeah, I know, I fucking fell into the trap. But I don't care. I'm tired of feeling shitty because I have emotions and no one else in this business does. I don't think it makes me weak, I think it makes me strong. You might not feel the same, but I'm in fucking love with you and that's that."

Thom tried to talk, once, again, and then again. His mouth flapped uselessly. Finally he said, "...oh."

Clay gaped at him. *"Oh?"*

He tried, he really did. He knew exactly what he was supposed to say, how this was supposed to go. But there was nothing in his life that had ever remotely prepared him for this moment.

Clay was the strong one. Thom was weak.

It felt like there was an engine turning over in his chest that just wouldn't start. "I," he said. "I, uh..."

Clay's face closed off, right after Thom saw a flash of devastation. "Leave me alone, Thom," he said quietly.

Yeah. I deserve this. "Okay." He got up and put his hands in his pockets. The handful of steps it took him to reach the door felt like the longest distance he'd ever crossed in his life.

When he was almost at the door, Clay said, "Wait."

Thom's breath caught. But Clay just walked over to the coat closet by his front door and jerked it open, his face dark. "Take your shit," he said, pulling out one of Thom's coats.

"Oh. Okay," Thom said. Every part of him hurt.

Clay didn't meet his eye as Thom took the coat from his hand. As he turned to shut the closet door, something in the back of it tumbled down with a *thump*.

Clay frowned. He shoved some of the other jackets aside, revealing a small cardboard box. When Thom saw it, he felt like his heart had dropped through his stomach.

"What is this?" Clay asked, reaching for the box.

"I dunno," Thom said quickly. "Okay, well, I'm gonna go."

"Wait," Clay said again, and this time he held Thom in place with a hand around his arm. He was turning the package around in his other hand, looking at the shipping label. "Did you order something?"

Thom had ordered it weeks ago, but when it had arrived

he'd suddenly realized how stupid it was. Clay had been in the next room, so he'd hurriedly shoved it in the back of the closet so he wouldn't see, and then he'd forgotten it was there.

Thom tried to pull away from Clay's grip, but he just held him tighter. His heart was pounding, his whole body hot with panic. "I— It was just gonna be, like, a—"

Clay ripped open the shipping box with one hand, still holding on to Thom's arm with a vise grip, and pulled out the smaller box inside.

It was a set of pancake molds. He'd found them online— silicone molds in the shape of all of Clay's favorite BoB characters.

It was probably the most embarrassed he had ever been in his entire life. Thom could feel all the blood draining out of his face as Clay looked back at him. He stuttered, "Your— the model waffle iron you have, it doesn't let you use custom grills, so I had to—I just thought—I don't know if you like pancakes as much—"

Clay looked at the pictures on the box, then back at Thom. He held up the gift, shook it at him, and said, "This is the shittiest fucking love declaration I've ever heard of."

Something thin and cold cracked in Thom, like frost melting off grass as the sun rose. "Seriously, Thom," Clay was saying, "this is awful. You're so bad at this."

Thom swallowed. "I know," he whispered.

Clay shook his head fondly. "You got me pancake molds," he marveled.

"Yeah," Thom said tightly.

Clay stared down at the colorful box, then back up at Thom. He was still smiling, but it was tempered by uncertainty. Gently, he asked, "You wanna be with me for real?"

Thom took a deep breath. He had already done the impossible last night, when they'd been in bed together. He hadn't held back. He'd let it all show—everything he felt; everything Clay had drawn out of him; the things that had been there before and the things that had grown, slow and stubborn, in the light of Clay's affection. All his terrible weakness, pushed to the surface.

But that had been in the dark. Today, in the daylight, he tried to do that again.

"Yes," he scraped out.

Clay nodded for a second. Then he tilted his head and said simply, "Okay."

Thom blinked at him. "That's it?"

Clay shrugged. "You *are* terrible at this, but." His smile grew as he looked at Thom. "We can work on it."

Thom was shaking when Clay pulled him into a hug. He made fists in Clay's shirt, unwilling to let him go. Clay's cheek pressed into his forehead, his stubble almost hurting as they clung together, but Thom wouldn't let that go either. He breathed in, relishing the way Clay's arms loosened around him and then tightened again, and said, "Clay?"

"Yeah?"

He pulled back so he could look into Clay's eyes, and licked his lips. He wasn't even sure what he wanted to say, but he knew where to start.

"Show me," he said.

Clay smiled, took him by the hand, and led him into their bedroom.

Later, Thom was laid out flat on Clay's bed, wondering if he would ever regain muscle control. Clay was doing better, propped up on both pillows as he scrolled through his phone.

"People are writing articles about what our breakup means about love," he told Thom.

Thom tried to say something—*mmph*, maybe—but his brain still hadn't fully reconnected with his nervous system.

"Teens are sharing memes I…do not fully understand," he added pensively.

Thom managed to turn his head to face Clay. There were hickeys scattered all across his neck and chest, and something that looked like rug burn on his thigh. It was a blessing in disguise that they wouldn't have to look office-presentable on Monday.

"And they're making Spotify playlists. To cope with the pain," Clay continued, grinning.

Thom's stomach growled. Soon, there would need to be food. Waffles, maybe. Or pancakes shaped like donuts.

"Tumblr has lost its damn mind," Clay said, raising his eyebrows.

Thom managed to get a hand on Clay's thigh. Clay smiled and leaned over to kiss his eyebrow, and then the edge of his hairline.

Then he went back to checking his phone. "Oh," he said, sounding startled, and sat up more. He scrolled for a bit longer, then turned to Thom with a widening grin. "I just got a very interesting email from Senator Warhey's chief of staff," he said, excitement thrumming through his voice. He leaned closer to Thom and said, "I think they want to hire us."

On the opposite nightstand, Thom's phone started buzzing. Clay darted up to look at it. "That's probably them."

Thom pushed himself up on one hand and turned to look at his phone rattling away on the nightstand. Then he picked it up and dropped it into the glass of water sitting next to it.

When he turned back to Clay, he found him gaping. Thom crawled onto his lap and slapped Clay's phone out of his hand and onto the ground. Then he kissed him. Thoroughly.

When he was done, he pulled back to find Clay looking

at him, dazed. "We're not done," Thom said, his voice thick like gravel.

"Okay," Clay said dumbly, and kissed him again.

Clay's phone buzzed under the pile of clothes it had slid into, but they both ignored it.

★ 38 ★

Clay came home a week later to find Thom tidying his apartment. He'd told him a million times that he didn't need to do that—especially now that they were both about to move—but he knew Thom found it soothing. He'd clearly never been unemployed before.

More worrying was that he was tidying while watching CNN. Clay shut the door behind him, put down the box he was holding, and said accusingly, "What are you doing?"

Thom startled a little, though he only managed to pull his eyes off the screen for a second. "Uh—what? Nothing."

"And for those who are just tuning in, we're less than thirty minutes from Governor Leonora Westwood's presidential campaign kickoff address," said one of the cable news anchors.

Clay made a face at him. Thom shrugged, unrepentant.

"Why," Clay said. He picked up his box and put it on the

coffee table, then sat down next to Thom. "We talked about this. No good can come of you watching it."

"I just want to see how it goes, y'know. If Fe took any of my ideas," Thom said defensively, gathering Clay's dirty clothes into a hamper without moving his eyes from the screen.

"Uh-huh," Clay said. "Why not turn it off until the speech?"

"And miss the pre-coverage?" Thom scoffed. Clay glanced at the screen, where a panel was filling time blathering about Lennie and the race while a little countdown clock in the corner ticked away.

"Fine," Clay said. "Enjoy your empty rage calories."

"What does that even…" Thom started, but he trailed off when the chyron at the bottom of the screen flashed blindingly and then changed. It now read: Westwood Campaign Responding to Rumors about Sebastian Westwood.

"Huh," Thom said.

The anchor caught up with the chyron, saying, "Terrible timing for the Westwood campaign, we have breaking news now involving Governor Westwood's scandal-prone son, Sebastian Westwood. Online blogs are reporting…"

"Fe was right."

"Right about what?" Clay asked.

Thom blinked and shook his head. "Nothing," he said, then smiled at Clay. "He's someone else's problem now."

Clay took the opening to grab the remote and at least mute the TV. Thom let him, which was a promising sign. The interruption also seemed to finally draw his attention fully to Clay, as he focused on the box Clay had brought home. "You get everything?" he asked.

On TV, when people were fired, the box they carried out always had a plant in it, and usually some picture frames, but Clay's only had some files and a lot of pens and those staple-removing thingies, most of which probably weren't his. "Yup," he said.

"Hmm," Thom said, poking through the box. "Was it rough being back?"

"Nah, not with Lennie and Felicia and basically everyone gone," Clay said. "An intern let me in."

"Sure," Thom said. "You do anything gross to Lennie's office?"

"No," Clay said, though of course the thought had occurred to him. "But I did find this on my desk."

He held up an envelope. Thom frowned. "What's that?"

"It's from Felicia," Clay said. "You wanna know what's inside?"

Thom was beginning to look nervous. His eyes kept narrowing as they moved slowly from the envelope to Clay's face. "Do I?"

Clay took his time removing the sheets of notepad paper that were folded inside. There was also one sheet of computer paper, on which Felicia had jotted a short explanation. "Apparently," Clay said, "a few weeks ago, as part of the wedding planning, you and Felicia decided that we should write our own vows."

Genuine panic flared in Thom's eyes. "Clay—"

"I was very surprised to learn about this," Clay said, unfolding the scribbled-on pages with a flourish. "I guess you scrapped the idea before telling me. Maybe you didn't like any of your drafts?" He glanced down at the first page, took a deep breath, and began to read. "'Clay, you—'"

Thom lunged for him. Clay laughed and leaned back, holding the pages aloft as Thom reached for them. They wrestled, Thom climbing partially onto his lap and digging his nails into Clay's forearm, but he managed to hold him off. "Gimme!" Thom panted, grabbing at him with no semblance of dignity.

"Calm down, you lunatic," Clay laughed. "They were fake vows for a fake wedding."

Thom sat back and ran a hand through his hair. "Right," he said breathlessly. "Mmm-hmm, yes. They were fake."

Clay fought a smile as he watched Thom catch his breath. After a moment, he brought his arm down from its defensive posture so he could look at the pages again. "Although," he said, "they would have been very convincing."

Thom growled at him, and Clay's smile broke free. Thom wavered at the sight, and then his eyes went soft, and he leaned in to kiss him softly. After a moment Clay relaxed and Thom brought his arms around him, holding him gently.

Clay was, however, both totally unsurprised and completely ready for it when Thom lunged for the papers again. "I'll never let you have them," he gritted out, squirming away from Thom's assault. They were on the verge of falling off the couch. "I'm having them framed. Bronzed! I'm dipping them in carbonite!"

A little while later, after the vows had been safely stored away and they'd gotten their clothes straightened out, Thom turned the volume back up on the TV just as one of the cable anchors said, "And we're minutes away from Governor Westwood's announcement."

"So," Clay said. "You ready to watch this and boo?"

Thom glanced from the TV screen to Clay to the laundry hamper and back. "You know what?" he said, and turned off the TV.

Clay shot him a surprised look. "Fuck this," Thom said. "Let's go out."

"Yeah?" Clay asked.

"Yeah," Thom said.

Clay smiled. "Okay."

Thom's whole life had been defined by emptiness. Emptiness as a vacuum that sucked him forward, always propelling him toward *more, better, next*. Emptiness as a tactic, to deceive, outwit, and outmaneuver his enemies. It had just seemed the natural state of things.

So it felt strange to embrace the opposite of emptiness: Rightness. Completeness. Home.

Jesus, he was getting corny.

That's what it was, though. Clay was his home. So maybe that's why it didn't feel too terrible to be moving to Indiana.

He definitely wasn't happy about it, that's for sure, but he and Clay had both taken jobs with the Warhey campaign, and that's where it was based—for now, anyway. In a few months they'd be on the trail, and then they'd be in DC. He could put up with the Midwest for a few months.

And it was totally worth it to have a chance to be personally responsible for crushing Lennie's dreams.

He glanced at Clay, who was on the phone as they walked down the street together. His expression was a little tense, but Thom wasn't worried. Getting fired by Lennie seemed to have lit a fire under him, because he'd been working like crazy over the last week, on his map idea, and on other new coding ideas he kept dreaming up, most of them campaign-related. He'd learned a lot in the last few months, especially given that he was a relative newcomer to politics. Now he was fielding calls from investors and some of his old Pinpoint contacts, interested in how they could help him operationalize his ideas.

Maybe they really wouldn't be in Indiana for long.

He wondered where they'd end up if Clay's new ideas

turned into a full-time thing. Northern Cali? Maybe Austin, or even DC. DC would work best for Thom, but honestly, he could see them living anywhere. His vaunted life plan didn't feel so much like a plan anymore—more like a compass pointing in one general but broad direction. Maybe he'd take a job with the Warhey administration—or maybe he'd do something else. As long as he could kick ass and dominate his rivals—and as long as he had Clay by his side as he was doing it—he'd be happy.

By the time Clay hung up, he was smiling. "Call go well?" Thom asked him.

He nodded vigorously. "They said they could fly out to Indianapolis next week to meet with me."

"Wow," Thom said. "They must really want you."

Clay rolled his eyes at Thom's snobbery. "I think Indy's gonna be cool," he said. "I've been Googling gay bars near our apartment—we've gotta go out clubbing once we get there."

"Clubbing?" Thom asked. "When have you *ever* been clubbing."

"Once," Clay said stoutly. "And it was cool. And I want to go with you."

Thom fought a smile. "I thought we agreed to keep things under wraps."

"Ashamed of me?" Clay asked, clearly teasing.

Thom stopped in front of a mailbox, and Clay stopped next to him. On their job interviews with the Warhey campaign, Thom had gotten Warhey to agree that their relationship was off-limits—not an asset for the campaign to exploit. Some of Warhey's other senior staffers who'd sat in on those interviews had seemed to have other ideas, but Thom was confident that he could handle them. There was no way any of them were savvier than Felicia.

And who knew—maybe someday he and Clay would be a public power couple again. But not now. Their relationship had already been for everyone else. He just wanted Clay to himself for a while.

Thom leaned in and kissed Clay thoroughly, then pulled back. "No," he answered. "Greedy."

Clay grinned slowly. "You are a greedy bastard."

"Hmm," Thom said, and added, "Materialistic."

"Shallow for sure," Clay said, nodding.

"Hedonistic."

"Douchey."

"A liar."

"Oh, a two-faced dick."

"Heartless," Thom said.

Clay looped his arms around Thom's back and gave him a long, considering look. "No," he said finally, with a small smile. "Not heartless."

They kissed again, lingering a while. Then Clay broke off, scrunching up his face in a bratty expression. "C'mon," he said. "I want food."

"One sec," Thom said, and turned toward the mailbox.

Back when they'd been passing the student loan bill, Thom had directed some of Lennie's researchers to brief him on everything he'd needed to know about it, including the buried swipe-fee clause. They'd generated a memo suggesting that the clause might be vulnerable in court, especially if anyone noticed a particular section of the legislative history. Thom had noted it, buried the memo somewhere no one would ever find it, and the bill had passed. Of course, anyone who got their hands on the memo now would stand a good shot of getting the swipe-fee provision struck down in court.

Thom weighed the nondescript accordion folder he was holding. He was wearing a hoodie. He basically had to wear something like it whenever he went outside now—the downside of being a C-bit celebrity who'd had a pretty public relationship flame out. He'd be able to ditch the hoodie when they got to the out-of-the way brunch spot Clay had found. But here, in front of the mailbox, he wasn't taking any chances.

"Thom," Clay whined. "I'm hungry. I want my bottomless mimosas."

The mailing address on the folder was the local chapter of the ACLU, but there was another envelope underneath, addressed to Kerry. Thom looked at them for another moment, then shoved them in the mailbox.

Clay grinned as they turned to walk down the block toward brunch. "Softie," he teased.

Thom rolled his eyes, but he took Clay's hand and laced their fingers together.

And there wasn't even anyone there to see it.

★ ★ ★ ★ ★

ACKNOWLEDGMENTS

Thank you to Chris, who said to me one day, "It kind of seems like you should be a writer."

Thank you to Elyse for beta reading this book. I'll always remember making fun of [Name of Movie Redacted for Legal Reasons] with you in that bar for what felt like hours (what an awful movie); you are my own personal How Did This Get Made costar, and it's excellent.

Thank you to everyone on AO3 who ever left a comment on my fanfic. You made me believe I could do this.

Thank you to Chris, who said it seemed like my fanfic was decent, so I should probably try my hand at writing for money.

Thank you to Laura for being an incredible agent and wonderful career coach. Thank you so much to my editor, Emily, who commiserated with me about parenting during a pandemic, brainstormed titles and taglines with me, and never yelled at me for blowing a deadline.

Thank you to the *Among Us* crew for keeping me sane during the Dark Times and coming up with excellent book titles I will never be able to write a book to match. Joker is good, joker is kind.

Thank you to Chris, who kept me going when there was a pandemic and I'd just had a baby and we were moving and also I had to turn around edits on a book. You come up with excellent book titles too.

Thank you to Phil for being the best grandfather-in-law a girl could wish for. Thank you to Roberta for being the inspiration for a grandmother whose grandson calls her an asshole over the phone. (Lovingly.)

Thank you to Mike for bringing me writer fuel (aka Krispy Kreme). Thank you to April for being the best mother-in-law of all time. Stop smoking. I mean it. It's in the acknowledgments, so you *have to stop.*

Thank you to Sloan and Jagger, because I know you'll complain if I thank Phil and Roberta and Mike and April and not you. Just kidding. I love you.

Thank you to Chris, who makes me laugh endlessly.

Thank you to Mom for being fearless and epic. You taught me I'd never have to choose between being an incredible badass and baking a mean millionaire shortbread. (Although I don't have the patience for caramel—you'll have to keep making those.)

Thank you to Molly for being my nerd twin and introducing me to amazing stuff like *Steins;Gate*. I can't wait for our next TV binge.

Thanks, Dad. I miss you.

Thanks to Johnny and Callie. I will be touched and impressed if you ever read this, because your taste in books really skews more lit fic, and also you are cats.

Thanks to my son, Ollie, the supernova at the center of my universe. I hope to G-d you never read this.

And thanks, of course, to Chris, for being my everything.